NAKED
TRUTHS

Alex Gruenberg

Naked Truths

ISBN 13: 978-1-941700-21-1

Library of Congress Control Number: 2015949247

PUBLISHER'S NOTE

This is a work of fiction. Names, characters, places and incidents
either are the product of the author's imagination or are used
fictitiously, and any resemblance to actual persons, living or dead,
business establishments, events, or locales is entirely coincidental.

Published by Verdant Mountain Press
An imprint of Synclitic Media LLC
1646 White Oak Road
Strasburg, PA 17579

http://verdantmountain.com

For Bonnie, the midwife of my heart.

Prologue

THE GAME was tied at zero near the end of regular play. Charles hoped it wouldn't go into overtime. He was tired of soccer. He wanted to go home and rest. He didn't want to cheer or listen to chatter from the other parents. Then, his son Donald stole the ball from one of the Rangers.

Charles leapt out of his chair as Donald charged forward, dancing toward the lone guard confronting him. Donald darted the ball sideways around the other player, who hesitated a moment, and Donald drove past him, recovering the ball and quickening his stride, dribbling forward faster and faster, closing in on the goalie's box while everyone was still trying to figure out what he had done, and in an instant, he scored. He took another few steps toward the goal before slackening his pace. The goalie turned around, staring at the ball in the net behind him, unbelieving, while Donald, looking aloof and at ease, trotted off in a wide arc back to his teammates.

Mrs. Merriweather was screaming, like always, and Fat Joe screeched his obnoxious laugh, and under it all, Charles heard an odd, grunting sound, *unnh, unnh*. Donald's teammates surrounded him, shouting and cheering, parents poured onto the field, and noise was everywhere, but riveting Charles' attention was that guttural *unnh* sound from somewhere behind him. He turned, and there wasn't much there, empty lawn chairs, a few little kids playing with a worn soccer ball, and one kid on his hands and knees, facing away from him. It looked like Mickey, who wasn't playing because he had hurt his ankle in practice.

"Mickey, what's wrong?"

He ran the few steps over to Mickey and crouched down in front of him. The boy was purple. His face looked like it was going to explode; he was clawing at his neck.

"Mickey, what is it?"

That awful guttural sound again and more frantic clawing. Charles realized he must be choking. God, no, not now, he thought. You know what to do. You know.

"Okay, Mickey, I'm gonna help you. Try to calm down." He positioned himself behind the boy and held both his shoulders.

"I need you to stand up, Mickey," he said, and started to gently but firmly pull the boy up. Mickey struggled, and Charles pulled forcefully. When he had the boy half upright, chest vertical, Charles reached around him, positioning his hands one over the other, thumb crooked to make a point, and felt for the right spot. You know what to do, he kept saying to himself. Mickey squirmed to get away, but Charles held on, found the crest of the boy's abdomen under the ribcage, probed for a moment, and, gritting his teeth, pulled inward.

Mickey jerked upward, but was still clawing, still writhing in Charles' massive bear hug, still making that awful sound. Charles swore at himself briefly, then gritted his teeth again. Come on, they said you had to pull hard. Now pull. Don't worry about hurting him; he's gonna die if you can't do this.

He pulled, and something hurled forward onto the grass. Mickey drew in a huge gulp of air, and they both collapsed onto the ground, Mickey sucking in huge breaths, Charles panting more shallowly, suddenly drained of energy, feeling the fear coursing through his body. He hadn't felt it before, but he knew it had been there the whole time, driving him, focusing his mind, controlling his muscles, and now, released from need, the fear was simply fear. He had just held a boy's life in his hands, could have hurt him, could have failed to save him, could have . . . It was over, though. Nothing was wrong.

2

"How are you, Mickey?"

"I'm . . . I'm okay," Mickey croaked, "I don't even know what happened. I thought I was gonna die." He spoke between gasps, which were shorter and shallower. His color was returning to normal. He was on his knees again, but now he could look up, and he could look like Mickey again. "I was eating a hot dog . . . when Donnie pulled that move, and . . . I wanted to shout, but I was, like, choking, and I couldn't stop. I didn't know what to do."

"Well, one thing to do is to stop scarfing down those hot dogs like that—you almost killed me," Charles said. He could tell the boy was looking for a way out of the moment, a way to stop being afraid. Mickey looked up, angry for a moment, realized it was a joke and took it. They both laughed, and Charles inched forward and started slapping him on the back, for no particular reason except that he needed the touch.

By then, others had noticed and were surrounding them, full of questions for the man and boy kneeling on the ground looking like they'd just run a marathon.

Charles answered them. He told what happened simply, but afterward Mickey told a much better version of the story, full of sound and fury, and Charles let him have the stage. He backed away slowly, accepted a few thanks, got a huge hug from Mickey's mom, which he didn't mind, since he'd always thought she was the most attractive of the team mothers, and he turned away to start his ritual of locating all the team's balls, their cones, their water jugs, and stowing them in the back of his SUV. This was Mickey's moment; he was the one with the brush with death; Charles was doing his job, as always. Taking care of business, supporting those who were in the game.

He loaded up the last gear bag and walked back to the crowd, which had moved beyond Mickey's adventure and was focused again on the last minute win, on the usual game analysis, praise for players, exclamations of joy and surprise, hopes for the next game, and general fun. He even joined in. He was part of the team, after all, even if all he did was carry gear.

****

When they arrived home, Donald ran upstairs to shower up and change. Charles lugged the cooler out back and dumped the water and ice into the yard. He hosed out the cooler and left it upside down on the deck to dry. Charles needed a shower too.

For now, the hammock would do. He wanted to rest. He was tired. He supposed he had saved that kid's life. He supposed he was something of a hero. But he didn't feel proud, didn't feel like celebrating. He wanted to rest. The sun was still high, but not too hot; he felt its contrast with the breeze cooling off his back against the rope mesh of the hammock. He closed his eyes. The feeling of Mickey's back against his chest returned, the clammy skin, the perspiration seeping into his own shirt, the tension of his muscles. He felt the boy's abdomen against the edge of his fist, the sudden give when the hot dog finally popped out. It was all present, still demanding his attention, overriding the sun and the breeze.

The images flooded his mind. In a few minutes, he shook himself back to alertness, rolled out of his cocoon, and went inside.

Ellen was making supper. He smelled fresh basil and followed the scent to the bowl she was working on.

"Pasta salad, with tomatoes and basil. Nothing special, I just wanted a light supper today, figured Donnie wouldn't want to load up too much after a game."

Ellen never faltered as she mixed the basil into the pasta. Charles could see the olive oil glinting in the sunlight. He leaned over and gave her a kiss on top of her head. Her mixing spoon never missed a beat.

"Game go well?" she asked.

"Donnie kicked ass," he said, smiling as she flinched slightly. "He did this amazing switch-up right at the end and shot through the other side like they weren't there. Got the winning goal. It was unbelievable. I'm still not sure of what he did; it was like he could change direction in mid-air. That kid's getting good."

4

Ellen sprinkled in more basil.

"Think they'll make the playoffs?"

"I don't see how they can miss, unless someone gets hurt. They've been unstoppable lately. Eric had some great plays, too, and Matt's like a brick wall at the goal. Nothing gets by him."

No response.

"Mickey damn near choked to death right afterward. Got a piece of hot dog stuck in his throat. Turned ten shades of blue. He's okay, though."

"That's good. Listen, I need to go over to Alice's tonight so we can work on those invitations for the baby shower. You gonna be all right without me? Need anything while I'm out?"

Ellen finished her mixing and turned to face him. Her eyes were a little cold, but the sunlight played through her hair and made it shine around her face like a halo. She was still striking, still the prettiest girl in town, he thought. Despite two children and twenty years, she still had her figure, silhouetted sharply against the counter behind her. He never understood why she'd chosen him of all men, and the sight of her struck him every time.

She stood, unmoving, waiting for his answer.

"Sure, honey, I'll be fine. Have fun."

She pivoted and got a pitcher out of the fridge and headed for the table.

"Tell Donnie we're ready as soon as he is," she said, and started pouring iced tea into their glasses. "I think Laura's downstairs on the phone. See if you can pry her off."

"Sure," Charles headed dutifully upstairs to shout in to Donald that supper was ready and went into his own room to change out of his sweaty game clothes. He felt slighted because she hadn't asked about Mickey and he didn't get to tell his story. But then, she didn't know he had a story. There was no reason for her to ask. She was busy; she's always busy. He should be thankful he had a beautiful wife who still managed to get dinner on the table for the whole family at least a few times a week. That was a rarity these days. Nothing to complain about. He pulled on a polo shirt and trotted downstairs to look for Laura.

****

Laura was curled up in her nest, the huge semi-circular cup of a chair she loved.

"No, like she would even know. Don't listen to her; they're beautiful."

Her back to him, knees almost in her chest, cuddled into herself against the outside world, Laura pinned the phone between her ear and the cushion while she examined her nails. She was such a kid, he thought. So caught up in her world, so oblivious.

"Laura," he called quietly.

"What?" She craned her neck backward till she could see him on the stairs. Her mouth stretched open comically.

"Supper's about ready."

"I'll be there."

"No, I mean it's ready, come on up."

"O . . . K." She stretched out the letters to show how long-suffering and weary she was and retreated back into her phone space, voice hushed so he couldn't make out what she was saying. He waited. She had her mother's hair, radiant and flowing. She lifted her head and caught the phone as it slid down the cushion, and in one incomprehensible, yet graceful movement, unfolded herself, laid the phone on the table, and pounced out of the nest.

"Hi, dad. How was the game?"

"Your brother kicked butt," he said. "Then Mickey almost choked to death on a hot dog. I had to squeeze it out of him. You should have seen it fly!"

She came up and put her arm around him. She was getting tall, he noticed for the hundredth time, too tall to be his little girl.

"You're a hero," she laughed. "Did you do that Himmerbach thing? Did it make a popping noise when it came out? Was he jumping around, gagging?"

As usual, she got in about a dozen words to his every one. They climbed the stairs out of the TV room together, and Charles

6

squeezed her tightly when she made particularly high-pitched squeals.

"Nothing quite so dramatic. He was choking, and I went over and did the *Heim-lich*," he stressed the syllables gently. "No big deal, but I was pretty nervous about it. I've never done that before."

"I bet. They showed us this video about it at school, and it looked like the kid was gonna explode when the stuff popped out of his mouth. I mean, I know it was an actor and all, but it was gross!"

"Yup, it was gross," he said. "I thought about letting Mickey die, saving him being so gross and all, but I figured his mom would have a fit if I did and I'd never get a decent seat at their restaurant again, so I gave in and saved the poor kid. I closed my eyes, though, so I wouldn't have to watch him explode or anything. That'd really be gross."

"Oh, dad!" Her exasperation radiated, along with the enjoyment he knew his kidding gave her. Things were so easy between them. He came alive in her presence and laid it on thick, teasing her and putting on dramatic voices, not like the simple conversations he had with Donald or the focused ones with Ellen.

They entered the kitchen, and Laura bounded off to the fridge. Ellen glared at her for a moment, calmed herself and simply said, "It's all ready. Come on and sit. I have iced tea out for you."

"Yes, mom."

Laura made a show of obediently shutting the fridge door and walking daintily over to the table. She sat down with correct, upright posture and elaborately flicked her paper napkin open and draped it on her lap.

"And on what shall we be dining tonight, madam?" she asked.

"Pasta salad, princess, if that suits you," Ellen answered, and called out to Donald, who was bounding down the stairs, "It's ready, come on in!"

Donald swung around the doorjamb, took a couple of strides into the room, lifted a leg over the back of his chair, and plopped down.

"I'm starving!" he declared, and Charles could see his eagerness dim as he spied the casserole dish of pasta salad.

"Well, there's plenty," Ellen said, and she sat down, immediately busying herself by passing the dish to Donald and taking a slice of seven-grain bread for herself.

Laura was downing iced tea. Donald greedily piled his plate with pasta salad. Ellen spread butter-substitute lightly on her bread. Late afternoon sun painted the room in golden tones, adding dramatic shadows to all of them and to the tall, unlit candlesticks on the table.

And Charles watched it all. Indeed, nothing was wrong. Nothing to complain about

****

The couple was pleased with the house, had the usual questions, made the right noises, said they'd talk it over and promised to call.

Ordinary enough morning. He'd shown this couple three houses already, all in one day, and had recognized the unmistakable signs of a couple in first house purchase syndrome. Usually it took a few weeks at least for these couples to come down to reality. He'd learned not to invest too much time or worry into these preliminary showings. The goal wasn't to sell a house yet; it was to win them over as customers. He needed to convince them he understood what they wanted. As soon as he could see the blinders were off, he could really go to work.

For now, he would go back to the office to check email and phone messages. He still had some paperwork to clear up on yesterday's closing, then he could go to lunch. He had a promising showing that afternoon. Newly married couple in their forties, and they'd each had a couple of houses before, so they were sure of what they wanted. Second marriages were a gold mine. Usually the neighborhood would sell the house, and Charles knew the neighborhoods. He knew which ones exuded calm and which seemed active and fun, which gave a good professional aura and which were wealthy enough to be understated. He'd lived in Westbury all his life, and he knew the neighborhoods well. He was looking forward to the showing. The woman had enticing green eyes, and Charles enjoyed being around her. Some showings were better than others.

This house was in a good spot. Very trendy, very upscale, nice entrance gateway, stone lined driveway, solid, elegant brickwork. Floors to die for, matched by well-joined accent panels on the walls and beautifully rubbed built-in china closets. They'd love it.

Maybe not. Maybe it was too traditional. Maybe they'd think it was stodgy for a couple still in their forties. Who knew?

He decided he was too anxious to go to the office. Maybe a quiet lunch and a beer would calm him down. Step out of the sales world for a moment, read the paper, have a good meal. He was heading up Peach Street, a few blocks from The Station House, a small place with good food that usually wasn't too busy at this time. He pulled into the lot, bought a paper from the machine by the door, and walked in. The dimly lit, wooden interior of the place suited him. He sat down in a booth by a window, opened the paper to the sports pages and looked to see they had any coverage of the high school football game that night.

He enjoyed his meal, washed the flavors down with a local lager, read, and relaxed.

He came to the end of his meal, finished reading the interesting pieces on the op/ed page, leaned back, and there was the worry again. He needed this sale. He wasn't desperate for the money; things were going well, but it had been a dry week and he hated to end it with nothing simmering on the burner.

He straightened his dishes on the table. Tried to take one more swig from his empty beer bottle. Checked his watch. Glanced through the paper again without finding anything worth reading. Checked his watch again. An hour before the appointment. He was stuck. If he went back to the office, he'd barely walk in the door before he'd have to leave; this appointment was on the other side of town, and he wanted to be sure to arrive before the buyers. He looked at the paper again, but nothing seemed interesting. Damn.

Resigned, he got up. He paid his bill, returned to the table to leave a respectable tip, and went out the door. It was a good day for a drive, anyhow. He could go by the lake; the sight of water would relax him. He got in the car, started up the engine, found a quiet station on the radio and pulled out.

Soon, he passed the familiar yellow building. Small, squarish, made of cinderblock, no windows, unadorned with neon, surrounded by a simple parking area. He felt a slight pressure in his gut, but drove on. No time. Not today. He had a showing coming up. He had to stop doing this so often. But at the next red light, the pressure still nagged at him, and he glanced down at the dashboard clock. He had half an hour to fill, and he was only five minutes from the house. He put on his turn signal, doubled back, and pulled in, parking in the back. He got out and walked over the gravel toward the entrance. Damn, hope my shoes don't get dusty from this crap, he thought, and made a mental note to check them when he got to the house. So many reasons to get there first, he thought. So many details to watch. He opened the door and walked in.

Display racks screamed color, mostly pink. Video displays jumped with it, neon signs in the back beckoned customers, and sale signs summoned everywhere. Classic rock filled the room. The counter was off to one side, and the usual guy was talking to a customer.

The place was a visual playground. Video cases were front and center, and there was no doubt about content. Breasts were everywhere; huge, gleaming, bulbous breasts leaned down from every cover. The women all seemed slathered in oil, their tanned, supple bodies always open, legs open, eyes open, mouths open, calling to you.

Other racks were filled with men in similar poses, but Charles never paid them any mind. He didn't dwell on the women either, but it was hard to walk by them without noticing at least a few. They were all the same, yet stunningly varied; it seemed each company had some kind of specialty, some kind of focus: large breasts, women on women, young girls, black women, Asian women, women and men, women alone, groups, it went on and on. He walked by, casually glancing over the covers, feeling himself harden as he walked. He didn't want to spend too much time in the open where he could be seen. The viewing booths were more his speed: private, safe, and more appealing than anything on display up front. No matter how enticing a woman was, photos couldn't come close to what you'd find in the videos themselves.

He chose a booth from the stills displayed outside and went in. Closing the door, he felt safe. The booth was small and shabby. At least it was fairly clean; that was one reason he liked this place; it wasn't grimy like a lot of others. He locked the door and started to feed the machine. Soon, he was lost in his thoughts and his eyes. The plot, such as it was, involved a girl coming home to find her roommate having sex in the kitchen. She hid in the doorway watching, getting turned on. The camera divided its time between the couple and the watching roomie. Charles preferred the roomie shots. Seeing sex on screen didn't turn him on as much as watching a woman get excited.

The woman was fondling her breasts through the incredibly thin top she was wearing. He watched her flesh fill and sway as she pressed against herself, watched her rub her nipples through the shirt, and then the shirt came off as Charles grew more and more excited, trying to make it last. She was working her way downward, caressing her bare belly and sliding her hand down her pants, first behind her, grabbing her undulating bottom, then in front. The camera moved in and she slid down the wall, opening her legs, the camera moving in closer and closer so he could see perfectly.

Shouting.

Voices.

Shouting. Movement. Pounding. Someone was pounding on the door. He struggled to get himself back inside his pants, not understanding. What was going on? He got himself inside and zipped his pants, and then, as if that simple act afforded him some kind of safety, his mind cleared enough to hear a voice shouting for him to open up and get out—now!

He fumbled at the latch, still afraid, not knowing what he'd find on the other side, wondering what kind of crazed pervert was demanding he get out, but knowing the flimsy door would never stop anyone and knowing the anger he heard in the voice wasn't anything he'd ever heard before. Something else was going on, something he couldn't imagine.

Finally, he got the latch undone and was slowly opening the door when it was jolted out of his hands and he saw the policeman, arm locked, holding the door wide open, eyes fixed on his, and behind him, all around, more police, other customers pushed up against walls, and the end of his life as he knew it.

****

It was as bad as it gets. Police everywhere. The salesclerk had handcuffs on and was standing stone-faced beside a rack of dildos. Charles and a few others were cuffed, taken outside, separated, and questioned. Charles felt like he was on display, every question an accusation. Even giving his name, he felt like the officer was examining his words for lies and deceptions. What were you doing here? How often do you come here? What do you buy? Ever see anything unusual? Ever offered anything unusual? Charles struggled with answers. What was going on?

After a few minutes another officer took over and asked all the same questions. Charles asked what was happening and got only another question in return. It went on for half an hour. Cars slowed down as they passed. Drivers gaped. Charles stood on the gravel, sun in his eyes, staring down at his shoes. Dusty. Need to be cleaned. Yes, officer, I've come here for years. No, I never bought anything; I only used the viewing booths. It's hard to remember titles. No, nothing like that.

As it turned out, the police had been working on this raid for months. It was a major bust. The porn shop didn't sell just the usual stuff; if you knew the right people, knew the right questions to ask, they had a special stash in the back, a whole other room Charles had never imagined. They were specialists in child pornography.

There were racks of magazines imported from overseas. Videos. Books. All of it. They did a sizeable web business, too. They had a sham site in Thailand, but the actual business was conducted from this building. A sweaty pedophile in the Rockies could find the site and have his movie in minutes—in regular or high definition format.

The police had been thorough. They had already made a number of buys over the net and in person. They were sure. They'd been watching the place by camera for months, had records of who came and went, checked out every license plate number, every employee's identity. They had the goods on these guys, and, to make sure they got as many fish on their line as possible, they sent officers to the homes of every customer found on the premises. A neutral expression and a simple request to enter the home was often enough for a woman like Ellen to allow them to search. In her case, they found nothing—but they left behind knowledge.

Her husband had been found at an adult book store. He was being questioned. Child pornography was involved. She was stunned into silence and doubt.

Charles, though, had no idea what was happening to Ellen. He also had no inkling of the child pornography. He was so dazed by the questioning and his fear that he didn't notice a reporter from the local paper had arrived and recognized him.

Eventually, the questions stopped and Charles was released. He made his way to his car, struggled to fit his key into the ignition, and sat silently, drained. Where should he go? To the office? Home? What do you do when you've been exposed to the world?

He drove home to a wife who was waiting for him with the memory seared in her brain of walking into her bedroom and finding a police officer kneeling by the bedside table with her vibrator in his hand. The redness of her eyes told Charles she knew. The conversation wasn't easy.

A few hours later, the newspaper arrived, and the kids were home, and Charles was lost.

Chapter 1

THE SUN was already over the broad expanse of the service building when Charles arrived for work. It was May, and every morning the birds were singing even before he woke up. Charles couldn't stand it. Back when he had a good life he was too busy to notice such things. Now, when life was empty, he had nothing to do but notice. Instead of mornings filled with the noise and confusion of a busy household, he faced a bowl of instant oatmeal, instant coffee, and emptiness.

So here, in his new life, he noticed where the sun was rising. He marked its progress against the landscape. Noted who was walking a dog, who was jogging. He noticed traffic patterns, progress on construction sites, daily specials on diner windows, and changes in billboards. He drove past the sign proclaiming "Free Oil and Lube for 24 Months!" and pulled into his usual spot behind the main building.

Charles had been selling cars for almost two years. It wasn't a bad job. At least he worked for a friend who ran his business on a reputable basis. He didn't care much about cars, but that didn't matter. Selling was pretty much selling, and as long as he could be honest about it, he didn't mind.

He said hello to Tricia on the way in. She looked droopy today, her clothing running in the drab range of her outfits. But, she did smile and say, "Good morning, Charles," as he passed her desk. Bill was facing away in the showroom, examining some detail on one of the new brochures, so Charles took the opportunity to walk silently by and pass unnoticed into his own sparse cubicle.

Taking off his shades, Charles settled into his swivel chair and looked over the day's calendar. New car delivery in the afternoon. Couple coming in to look at a minivan later. Finally, that hasty note at the bottom, the woman from the school picking up a donated car. Harry had buzzed him about that right before closing the day before. He was donating a used car to a raffle for a private elementary school. The woman was supposed to come for it Wednesday, but had called to change the time and Harry couldn't make it. He told Charles the car was prepped and Tricia had all the paperwork. All Charles had to do was show it to her, have her sign the papers and be gracious. Nuisance job; he wasn't even sure when she was coming over, morning was all Harry had said. Nice. Well, mornings were usually slow.

He was busy preparing a set of brochures about minivans when the woman arrived. Charles noticed her striding through the door and scanning the room, clearly not pausing at the various cars on display. She stopped suddenly, and began to repeat her scan when their eyes met, and he put his paper down. She focused on him openly and seemed to gather herself for their encounter. He could see her squaring her weight on the balls of her feet, and he thought for a moment she was preparing for a fight. But she was still smiling, and he noticed the dimple in her right cheek. She had warm brown eyes and full lips. Her hair was mid-length, swept back from her face casually, waving around to the back. She was slim and neat, her outfit a touch on the casual side of business casual, but somehow still very tidy, very much in control. This is the woman from the school, he instantly knew.

She started walking toward him. Although slightly too deliberate, her movements suggested a gracefulness of her body, that she was very comfortable with how it worked and how she moved; her legs flowed easily from step to step, and her hips swayed smoothly. He stood up to approach her, and as she neared, he could see more into her eyes and caught a playful glint. She was exactly the type of woman he would have been attracted to before.

Before.

Before what? Before everything. Before he lost it all. Before he crawled in a corner to protect himself and gave up on life. Before everything had been swept away in a tornado whose eye was squarely on him.

****

She was exactly the kind of woman he would have been attracted to in the old days, but now, attraction held in it some kind of negative charge. He felt tension. It was a familiar feeling. It happened whenever he was near an attractive woman and even when he saw one on TV. He had been so devastated by the whole incident back home that he literally couldn't even look at an image of an attractive woman without going on the defensive.

He'd learned to cope, though. Tensing up whenever a female customer walked in was no way to make a living. He had to be warm and friendly. Fortunately, the last thing he wanted to do these days was cross any personal barriers; he didn't want to get close to anyone or flirt with anyone. All he wanted to do was make his sale and retreat back to his cubicle where he was safe and all he had to worry about was the local news, the new traction system on a crossover SUV, and paperwork.

He met her on the sales floor. "Janelle O'Brien?"

"Yes, thank you; I wasn't sure where to go."

"Harry told me you'd be here this morning. You were the first person to come in, actually, and you weren't looking at the cars, so I figured it must be you."

She seemed to relax.

"We're so grateful for this donation. I was surprised when Mr. Fleming said he could help us out, and to be given such a fabulous car . . . I couldn't believe it. We were expecting some old clunker at best, something people would buy chances on for their high school kid, not something a real person would want." She halted, seeming embarrassed about the "real person" comment.

"To tell the truth, I was surprised myself. We got that one on a trade last week, and I thought we'd turn it over in a heartbeat. It's a hot-looking car. I had a few people in mind myself, but Harry said he was donating it and we had to leave it alone. I was a little ticked; I thought I'd lost a sale. But, that's Harry; he's always been unpredictable, and in his way, he's a decent guy. He must believe in what you do."

He gestured toward the hallway that led past the office area to the service lot and started leading her out. He had only taken a step before he realized he was going overboard. He didn't need to demonstrate that much warmth and interest in her before moving in to make the sale. There was no sale to make. But despite the tenseness that still charged his muscles, he liked talking to her. He liked watching the dance of her features as she spoke.

He held the door open for her, and she nodded a thank you; he watched her as she walked through.

"Here it is," he said, gesturing toward a gleaming torch red convertible.

"I still can't believe it he's donating this. It's so wild!"

"See what I mean? I thought it was gonna be an easy sale."

"I'm blown away. Tell Mr. Fleming how thrilled we are. I'm going to call him later, but tell him anyway when you see him. We should sell a million tickets on this!" She ran her hand over a fender and peered inside at the leather upholstery.

"I'm glad you like it." He looked at her, feeling the ease with which he met her eyes, and he was startled. He hadn't been looking anyone in the eye lately, unless he forced himself as part of his friendly salesman act. But he enjoyed looking at her, seeing her energy, enjoying the fluid movement of her lips as she spoke. He wished there was more to do, some details to iron out. Some way to spend more time with her.

"Well, I guess all we need to do is go in and sign the papers. Are you taking it with you?"

"Yes, I can't wait to try it out; it'll be a letdown to go back to my old beater after I drive this to school!"

He wondered what she drove, and felt it should be a sleek, powerful and agile beauty, something exotic. He didn't think anything they had on their lot would suit her. Something fun and earthy, but elegant. Several classic European sports cars ran though his mind.

They walked back in the building, and sure enough, Tricia had all the paperwork ready. For once, Charles was irritated by her efficiency. Rustling through files searching for the forms would have given them more time, but it was all over in a few minutes. Janelle took her file of papers and tucked it under her arm.

"Well, Mr. Stanton, thanks again. I love the car, and thank Mr. Fleming again for me, too. We couldn't be happier."

She flashed one more smile, one last glistening of her teeth and appearance of her dimple, and she walked away.

This time he wasn't watching her body move or noticing her features. He was taking in all of her at once, seeing her presence, feeling the energy she radiated, and lingering on the feeling of life that filled him while she was near. He watched the bounce of her hair as she went out the door and walked out of sight. She was still present in his mind. He didn't want to let go.

His cubicle awaited him. He had coffee. He had the paper. He had his day to get through. He sighed and walked toward it.

****

An hour later, Charles heard Harry bustle through the back door and sweep by Tricia's area, calling out a boisterous "Good morning, doll," and telling her how great she looked. Then he went into his office and slammed the door. Nothing subtle about Harry; he was always the center of a whirlwind of activity, and if nothing was going on, he'd stir something up.

Harry could be overbearing, but Charles couldn't complain. He'd known Harry for almost 25 years, since they roomed on the same floor in college. Harry had given him a job when no one else would. He couldn't forget that.

Days were pretty easy now, anyway. Customers rarely crowded the showroom, so he could take his time with them, and the paperwork involved in selling cars was nothing compared to the details of real estate. Of course, some customers were never satisfied, some deals don't go through; some people were plain obnoxious—but at least it was all easy. Easy was about all he could handle these days.

Back home he had enjoyed his job and his kids, but all that had blown apart.

At soccer practice, a few days after the police raid, no one talked to him. No one. He did his thing, dealt with all the equipment, made the Gatorade, did his cheering act, and it was as if he wasn't even there. The worst part was when Mrs. Leary pulled her kids in close when he walked onto the field. She actually reached out both arms and pulled them a few inches closer, as if he was going to charge the stands, grab her kids, throw them to the ground in front of everybody and rape them. It was a long practice. So was the next one. Then, about an hour after that next one, the coach, Benny called.

"Charlie, glad I caught you. Hey, I gotta talk to you about one thing. It's a little weird, but it's the way it is. Some of the parents, you know, they're . . . Listen, guy, I know you didn't do anything, right? I know that was all a big mistake. But, some of the parents don't want their kids riding to the game with you tomorrow. Weston's mom said she could drive her van, so we got that covered. You can meet us. I don't think this'll last long, but it's the way it is. You know?"

He knew. And over the coming weeks he came to know only too well. Suddenly, he wasn't welcome at school functions. Laura wasn't asking if he'd come to her hockey games. He wasn't even welcome at the supermarket or the mall. He'd see people notice him, cringe, and turn to their friends to talk. People even pointed him out. He didn't go out much after that. When he tried to talk to Ellen, all he got were the right words, the supportive words, but no heart, no sympathy, no understanding of what he was

20

going through. After the first few days, there had been a cold emptiness between them.

When Edwin let him go at the office, it all came apart. Ellen said that was the last straw. She felt betrayed by his use of pornography and didn't see much point in trying to patch up a marriage she felt was based on a lie. She never said so, but he always got the feeling that she didn't quite believe he was innocent. So, she bailed. No, she stayed. She kicked him out instead. He spent a few nights at a motel, exploring daytime TV and depression, then realized he needed to get into action.

His only piece of luck was that Harry was delighted to hear he wanted to come work at the dealership. Harry listened to the whole story on the phone and let Charles talk uninterrupted. When it was over, his answer was simple.

"Charlie, boy, you got handed a pile of shit on a stick. Believe me, I know how hard people can be. It happens around here all the time. One slipup, one rumor, and you get crap for years about it. Just when you think it's blown over, someone says something and you're right back in the shitpile. Don't worry. No one here knows a thing; I hadn't heard a word till you told me. Get your ass down here and let's get to work. I lost a guy a couple weeks ago and I haven't replaced him yet. Didn't have anyone come in I thought could pull his weight. You, I expect you'll pull your weight and pull along the other guys, too. Get your ass down here."

And that was that. Charles talked to the kids, told Ellen, gathered up his clothes and a few books and things, and he was on his way to Hartleton. Telling the kids wasn't fun. They were upset. The worst thing, though, was that among all the other reactions, he saw relief. This had been tough on them. They hated having suspicions about their dad. They hated hearing what other people said. They were glad it was over.

****

It was Tuesday, so after work he had his meeting.

When the marriage counselor had first suggested a Sex Addicts Anonymous meeting, Charles almost thought it was a joke. It was hard to tell, with his low-key manner and voice. But Jim reached over to his desk, picked up a little card, and handed it to Charles. There it was: location and time. Sex Addicts Anonymous. How can you be addicted to sex? Everyone had sex, you were supposed to, for god sake. Hadn't Jim said a dozen times that a lack of interest in it was a sign that something was wrong?

But Jim was insistent. He said if Charles was serious about trying to save his marriage, he needed to confront this issue, and SAA was about the best way to do it. There wasn't a meeting in their town, but there was one about a half hour away. Wasn't his marriage worth half an hour drive once a week?

He started going to meetings. He owed it to Ellen, he thought.

The meeting in Hartleton was held in an uncomfortable church basement. It was about half-way over, and Charles was barely listening. The front of the folding metal chair seat was digging into his thighs, and he was on edge. The room was warm and the air stale. Jimmy was going on and on with a dull story. The coffee was lukewarm. His feet hurt. His gut felt wrong.

Jimmy wound up.

"Thanks for listening, guys."

"Thanks for sharing," they all echoed.

"Hi, my name is Charles, and I'm a pornography addict," he found himself saying.

"Hi, Charles."

"I'm not sure what I wanted to say. I didn't even plan to say anything. Nothing's really going on, days are pretty much okay. I go to work every day, I take care of what comes in the door.

"But something bothered me today, and I didn't even know it bothered me till I got here. It happened when a woman came in this morning to pick up a car.

"The moment she came in the door I noticed her. Man, she was pretty. I kept checking her out the whole time we were talking; I watched her face move, and her eyes. When we went out to look at the car, I held the door open and watched her walk away from me. Nice.

"Best part of my day.

"The problem was, I liked her. I liked talking to her. And the whole time, I kept getting distracted by what she looked like. It's not even that I was getting turned on. It's . . . it's like I was running over some kind of checklist, like we do with the new cars when they come off the truck. Checking out her face, her hair, her chest, her hips, her legs. Everything. The works. I had to check everything out and make sure she measured up. And I didn't like that I was doing that. But there it was."

"Thanks for sharing," everyone chimed in.

"I get what you're saying," Gary said. "I have that trouble with my ex." And he went into some story about his latest confrontation with her about their kids. That's often the way it was. Everyone told their own stories, and half the time it didn't even seem like they had heard what you said. Sometimes they did have good ideas and could help you understand your situation, but other times, it was just people taking turns venting. He was tired of it. If he had anything else to do, he probably wouldn't come any more.

But it helped to tell his story. Telling the story was the only way he could discover what it was that had eaten at him all day. He wanted to talk to her. He wanted to see her again. He liked her, and somehow the fact that she was good-looking got in the way of liking her.

He sat for a while, thinking about comparing women with the checklist in his head. How he made sure he knew what every woman around him looked like and how she stacked up. It wasn't something he thought about doing, but he always did it. Every time a woman walked in the showroom. Every woman he saw on the street, on TV, in ads. At conferences he'd check them all out on entering the room and make sure he would be near, or next to, the most attractive women. He never came on to them, but he always made sure he knew who the best prospects were and positioned himself to take advantage of their presence. It was like a game; he won by being near them, talking to them, having them like him. Where did this need come from? Why did he need to "command" every attractive woman around him?

And then he knew.

It was the porn. He'd always pick the most attractive women. It was always like that. Way back in the garage.

Way back.

****

Fifth grade. That's when it all started. He started being interested in girls. He started noticing who was pretty. He started getting hard-ons. It was a whole new world. Suddenly, the romantic parts of movies made sense. Talk with his best buddy Jerry was more about who was hot than it was about cars or science fiction movies. His days were filled with looking at girls and talking about girls.

They'd find magazines and paw through them in the garage for hours, commenting on the shape of a breast or its size, and how it would feel. They had their favorite magazines, the ones with the prettiest girls and the best photographers. They avoided the trashy ones, where the girls weren't as pretty or as alluring. The sleazy ones. And the ones that wasted too many pages on articles.

So that was the beginning. Charles kept adding to the collection hidden in his closet. He'd pull it out every day and spend hours looking at all of it. So many women! So many. Hundreds of them. He developed favorites, developed his "tastes," such as they were, and in all the hours he spent looking through those magazines, pulling out his favorite shots so he could fit more into his precious secret storage spaces, he was comparing them, judging them, always deciding who was the prettiest, the sexiest. This one had an alluring look, this one's breasts were too small, this one had short legs, this one had great cheekbones, this one had nice nipples.

He even spent time looking at them with their clothes on. Sometimes there were "real life" shots of the models, and he'd look at those photos so he could learn how to translate what he saw on the street into what the women would look like naked. He didn't spend as much time on that, of course; the naked shots were what he wanted, and he always wanted more. But when he was out, he was looking at all the women. He was imagining what they would look like, based on his studies. He noticed the hints of breast exposed by blouses and then imagined the whole breast. He watched legs. He became a connoisseur of women. He had an opinion on all of them. He and Jerry talked a lot about who was prettiest in each class, which teachers were hot, which women on the street were sexy. They were the experts. And, of course, they were also the keeper of the standards; they had them all at home in their stashes.

He'd imagine personalities for them based on the way they looked in the photos. He'd imagine encounters with them. And, of course, they'd always be wildly attracted to him. All he had to do was look a certain way, make a sly comment or two, and they'd be in his arms, and they'd be having sex. Of course, he still didn't know what sex was, really, but they'd be doing it in his dreams. And when they did, they were all so appreciative, because he was such a good lover. That was always part of it—he always saw himself as satisfying them beyond all expectations. It was important that they liked him and appreciated him. That was his own little bit of compensation, because, of course in real life, women didn't have much interest in him at all. He didn't have the chiseled face or strong muscles women would want. He knew somehow he'd have to attract women by satisfying them.

They had to like him. He got them to like him by being good to them. Back in school it was being friendly and helpful. Now, in the adult world, it was being a nice guy, a good guy. Someone they could talk to and feel safe with. That's who he was. Mr. Nice Guy. The one women would talk to and like.

And in return, he got to check them out and rate them, like they did the photos in the magazines.

That's why he was here. That's why it bothered him to talk to Janelle. He was making her one of those magazine photos. He was making her porn and he didn't even realize it.

Nice guy.

****

The meeting was breaking up. Everyone emptied and threw away their cups; a few were talking over in the corner. Charles was cleaning out the coffee maker and putting it away.

Edward came over. He was another older guy, about Charles' age. He didn't say much in meetings either, but he showed up pretty regularly. He tended to wear jeans with a dress shirt and loafers. Too proper for this crowd, but it was who he was. It went with his Rolex.

"Charles," he started. "I heard what you said before."

"Yeah, well, it didn't make a lot of sense," Charles said. He was gathering up the creamer and sugar packets to put in the box with the coffee maker. Somehow he was always cleaning up at the end of meetings.

"It made sense. It always makes sense. You just don't always see it at the time," Edward said.

Charles looked at him.

"You have to let it go," Edward said.

"Let what go?"

"All that judgment stuff. All that looking through the keyhole. That's what you're doing, you know. You're sneaking peeks at them out in public and putting them in your collection. It's the same thing as looking at them in magazines or online."

"Yeah, that's it. I got that tonight. I'm checking them out. I never thought about it before."

26

"You have to let it go. Stop doing it. That's all. You'll be happier for it. You'll get along with them better, too," Edward said.

Then he walked away.

Charles finished packing up the coffee supplies and put them in the cabinet where they belonged. Edward had already left. Charles was alone. Four other guys were still talking, but Charles was alone. He closed the cabinet door and walked out. It was a clear night. Stars were visible overhead away from the street lights. The air was cool and crisp. When he got to his car, he kept walking. He needed that crispness, that clearness. He walked on, aching for it.

****

The next day, Charles worked on not judging women. Even driving to work gave him lots of practice. He saw women in other cars and was amazed, now that he was paying attention, at how quickly and dispassionately he sorted them into categories: too old, too heavy, too plain, nice cheekbones, nice smile, sour look, nice skin. The list was endless, and it all happened so quickly. It seemed like hardly a second passed between first sighting a woman and having her categorized. Once she was in her file, Charles lost interest in looking at her. It became clear to him that he really didn't have any interest in the women at all, but only in judging and categorizing them.

So he practiced not doing it. At first, all he could manage to do was to not look. He kept his eyes riveted on the road ahead of him, noticing nothing but traffic, lights, and signs. That took too much energy, though. It was amazing how hard it was to do nothing but drive.

So, he tried something else.

He tried looking at them, but not judging. The first try was a dismal failure. He saw a very attractive, slender woman driving a German sports car. That was too loaded a sight. His mind went right away to fantasies of what else that car suggested to him, and he had her clearly labeled as attractive, adventurous, sexy, and desirable. So, he deliberately slowed down, forcing a couple of people to pass him.

The next experiment went better. This was also an attractive woman, but she was driving a mid-size sedan, was dressed for the office, and was intently focusing on her driving. He was able to watch her in his mirror for quite a while. At first, the tendency was simply to categorize again, but he kept looking. Who was she? He noticed she was wearing fairly heavy makeup, clearly more than she needed. Was she insecure about her looks? Did she work in a place where the women were very competitive? Was it simply a matter of style for her? After a block or so, her expression didn't seem so intent as it did deliberately focused, as if she were nervous about driving. Maybe she's nervous about something else, he wondered. From time to time she took sips from a stainless steel travel mug, and even her sips seemed very controlled. Control freak, he thought. No, it wasn't control. She was being careful, like she was afraid of spilling on her clothes, or maybe she was careful about everything. Maybe she had to be. Maybe she was trying to work her way up at work and had to watch her step. She seemed subtly filled with tension. Yes, that was it, tension. It was controlled, it was tension she was used to, but it was real. She turned off onto another boulevard, and Charles was left alone with his thoughts.

In his real estate days, when he was driving a female client around, he made studiously sure he only looked in her face when he talked to her. He didn't want to create any impression that he was checking out her legs or body. He was distinctly professional. He had to be, if he wanted to be successful. As soon as that thought crossed his mind, he realized how deceptive he had been. He had learned that in the course of spending time with a woman, eventually he would always see how she looked, so he didn't need to go out of his way. He didn't have to crane his neck or look down at her body. He hadn't been professional, he hadn't been courteous. He'd been sneaky.

That thought brought him up short. Edward was right. He had to let all that go and see the people he was with instead of simply playing his games with them. He wondered how long he had been playing that game and how he had managed to get that good at it.

Charles arrived at the office and got out of his car more slowly than usual. It seemed like he was seeing the details of the building and all the cars lined up more clearly, as if he hadn't really seen them before. The bricks stood out as being more clearly textured, a deeper shade of red. He noticed the curve of car hoods. The sparseness of the gravel in the employee parking area behind the building, the scuffs on the door, the faded chrome of the handle.

When he went inside, he saw Tricia working at her desk. She always arrived early so she could start the coffee and check the calendar to see who needed to be reminded of what. Suddenly, Charles realized how conscientious she was. She was one of the givens of the dealership. She was always pleasant, always said hello, always did what was asked without complaint. Charles had quickly learned to assume that she would do her job well. He rarely spent much time with her or said much to her outside of what was required by the job. Part of that was his own funk, he knew. But part of it was that she was so ordinary looking. He hadn't noticed before, because in his way of dealing with women, being ordinary-looking got her placed in a huge file that didn't deserve any more consideration.

She didn't look up from her desk right away, which was unusual. Most days, she greeted him with a quick hello and a smile. She had a sweater pulled over her shoulders, and she seemed hunched over.

"Good morning, Tricia," he said to her.

She looked up, and he could see the usual sparkle in her eyes was missing. He realized it had been missing for a while.

"Hi, Charles," she said.

"Have a good ride in? It was sure a nice morning today, wasn't it?" he asked.

She looked right at him, and he could see she was only half-forming a smile.

"It was pretty nice. I saw a goldfinch in my yard when I was going out to the car."

He didn't have much idea what a goldfinch was, other than a bird, but he figured it was important to her.

"Great."

He couldn't think of anything else to say.

"Anything happening today?" he asked.

"Not much. Delivery of new cars. Harry is gonna be out for the morning. Not much."

"Okay," he said, and moved on toward his cubicle.

"Hey, Tricia," he called back. "Thanks for making the coffee."

It was the only complimentary thing he could think of to say. But, at least he was being nice to her and seeing her. It was a change, and it felt good.

"Sure thing," she said as he reached his area. He noticed more energy in her voice than when she'd first said hello.

Imagine that, he thought.

Chapter 2

SATURDAYS COULD be difficult for Charles. The best Saturdays were when he worked. Work filled the day with familiar events and filled his mind with simple ideas. The Saturday shift was a prime one, however, and there was a rotation among the sales staff. Most were conflicted about Saturdays; they liked time off with their families but also liked the opportunity for fat commissions. Charles had no conflicts. He liked working Saturday; it was safe. Saturdays off were the problem.

Saturdays home had to be filled. He went to do laundry. He did his grocery shopping. He tackled what few projects or repairs cropped up at the apartment. He went to movies alone. He read. He rented movies. He did whatever he could manage to fill the day, and he waited for it to be Sunday.

Sunday was easier. On Sunday he drove three hours each way to see his kids. They spent the afternoon going to the movies; going out to eat, going to parks to play soccer together, going to fairs, whatever they found to do that would allow them to be together comfortably. Awkwardness still hung over everything they did, but they were getting good at dealing with it.

This Saturday morning, while the wash was sudsing away in two machines, he was reading the paper. Looking for something to do. Soaking up time while water soaked away dirt.

Today was the fair at Janelle's school where they were kicking off the raffle campaign on the convertible. It looked like an all afternoon affair with lots of activities for kids: face painting, games, a magician, music, food. A typical fundraising event, the kind he'd been to a hundred times. Very family-oriented. Not for him. He passed over it.

Not much going on at the movies. Mostly action-adventure stuff. He'd lost interest in all that. The fight scenes had gotten so ridiculously exaggerated and the action sequences so impossible that he couldn't get involved. He didn't get involved in much anymore. Date movies were out. Kid movies were out.

High school musical. Classic car show. That had some possibilities. Church bazaars. Neighborhood yard sales. Usual Saturday stuff. The one washer buzzed, and he went over to unload the wash and start the drying process. While he was unloading, the other machine finished, so he was able to get both loads in the dryers at once. Small victory.

Several hours later, having done his shopping, put away the groceries and the laundry, and polished his shoes, he was on his way to the movies. There wasn't much playing that appealed to him, but it was the best option he'd come up with. Traffic was light. He wasn't observing people today; he didn't feel up to it. At least, though, he wasn't checking out women as he drove by them. He mostly minded his own business and devoted what attention he could muster to a small clicking sound in the car he hadn't noticed before.

He was driving a different route than he ordinarily would have taken. Exploring. No, soaking up time. Not much happening here. Neat houses. Neat yards. Kids riding bikes. A skater from time to time. Nice trees, lots of shade. Then he came across a crowd. Lots of activity, signs, balloons. A banner across the street. It was the school fair, the one that was raffling off the car. Looked like a good turnout, lots of kids running around, laughing. Some light music made its way into the car. He slowed down to watch. A clown was making balloon animals for kids swarming around him. A pair of kids in huge padded Sumo wrestling outfits were bobbing into each other, trying to knock each other down, their arms useless in the bulbous suits. Two kids wearing brightly colored helmets struggled partway up a portable climbing wall. Things had sure changed since the penny-pitching games he was used to as a kid.

Without even thinking about it, when he came to an empty space a half block away, he pulled in, locked the car, and made his way back to the crowd. Kids were everywhere. Half of them had their faces painted as kittens, clowns, devils, the works. Music filled the air; kids were laughing and talking. Parents seemed to be having a good time, too. Most were holding hands of little ones, talking to friends, or getting in on the games themselves. Family clusters lingered at a petting zoo, and a pony was carrying a pirate-hatted girl around a small ring. Some things hadn't changed.

At one end of the field, he saw a large sign advertising the car raffle propped up on the convertible, which had been smartly polished and decorated with bows and ribbons. Nice car, he thought again. He was really surprised Harry had donated such a sweet ride. Several people were filling out slips at the table next to it.

He kept walking around, watching kids playing, hearing voices calling out and laughing. He missed taking his kids to carnivals. They used to have fun. He decided to buy a hot dog and got on line. When he made it to the front, he was surprised to see Janelle busily trying to serve customers while loading up the grill and keeping the hot dogs from burning.

"I didn't expect to see you slinging hash," he said, when she looked at him for his order.

"Pardon?"

"I'm Charles, from Fleming Auto World, remember? I helped you when you came to pick up the car?"

She seemed flustered for a moment, then she recognized him and smiled.

"It sure seems to be a hit. Can I help you?" She was too busy for small talk. She was clearly frazzled, her hair falling into her eyes, her shirt stained and clinging to spots of perspiration.

"Looks like I should help you."

"Yeah, there aren't enough volunteers to go around. I've been working just about every stand all day."

"Really? You should be organizing, not serving up hot dogs."

"No choice; Louise had to get home to take care of her kids when her husband left for work. That's how it goes."

"Well, I don't have to rush off. Need another volunteer?"

"Really? We can use all the help we can get."

"I see that. I put in a lot of hours behind a grill when I was in college. Want me to take over here? Doesn't look like anything I can't handle."

"That's great. I can't tell you how great. Here, come around, I'll show you where everything is. It's pretty basic. Hot dogs, buns, cash. We do have someone running around to replenish supplies for you. If you get low on anything, look for a blonde woman in a red shirt like this. I can't thank you enough."

He took up his position behind the counter. The setup was all too familiar to him from his days at a department store restaurant. Keeping hot dogs on the grill circulating was nothing compared to serving up a full menu. He took the tongs from her, noted the condition of the dogs on the grill, added a dozen more, and turned to face his first customer.

"What would you like, pal?" he asked a boy sporting a bright yellow t-shirt.

Charles was back in business. He was a cook, he was busy, and Saturday was filled.

****

The afternoon moved along nicely. It took him a while to get in the swing of cooking, serving and making change, but not too long. All afternoon he served up hot dogs to a wide range of kids and parents, most of them grinning and laughing. Kids had their faces painted in all manner of animals and characters, many had balloons, some were muddy from playing kickball, and all were having fun.

Sweat poured off his face. He felt pretty damp and wondered how he looked. All around him, most people were in the same boat, but the atmosphere remained upbeat. Once in a while he found himself checking out a woman, but he reminded himself to look more deeply, and almost instantly he would see the mother in her as she looked after her kids, the wife in her as she talked to her husband, the volunteer helping out a school, the friend out for a light afternoon with a buddy. The transformation was remarkable, and Charles wondered that he'd never noticed all these details before. It was like obsessing on women's appearances kept him from seeing them at all.

The kids were the best, though. They entertained Charles all afternoon. How could they be so full of energy? He could see the climbing wall from his booth, and he never got over the looks of determination, fear and triumph he saw on kids in helmets scaling their miniature Mount Everest. One little girl's face went from freckly paleness to an intense red as she made her way up the wall. He could see her trembling the whole way up, and he wondered what inner demons she fought to make her twenty foot climb. She threw one arm high in the air when she reached the top and shouted something Charles couldn't hear. An answering cheer arose from a group of kids and parents at the base of the wall.

From time to time Janelle came by to check on him, face flushed with energy and anxiety, and he kept assuring her he was doing fine. The runners kept him supplied with hot dogs, buns and condiments, and he made his corner of the carnival a successful, smoothly running enterprise.

"You back again?" he asked one kid in line for his third hot dog of the afternoon.

"Yeah man, this rocks!" the boy said, and as soon as Charles handed him his dog, he was slathering it with relish and mustard and jamming it in his mouth, turning to rejoin the activity around him.

Moms and dads seemed relieved when he chatted with their kids, giving them a brief reprieve. Many of them looked more relieved to get some food in their systems. The kids were running the adults into the ground, as usual. But the atmosphere was good, people were enjoying themselves, and all the stands were bustling.

Gradually, things wound down. The crowd thinned, the line disappeared, many booths and activities started shutting down. The climbing wall was closed and the attendants started stowing gear. Charles allowed his supply of dogs on the grill to dwindle, and he started organizing to shut down as well.

Janelle came by and gave him the go ahead to close.

"You know how to clean that thing up?" she asked, motioning to the grill.

"No problem."

She told him where to go in the school to find the kitchen and some buckets. She thanked him again for filling in. In a moment, she was gone, off to take care of yet another detail. She and the other red-shirted volunteers looked beat. He scraped off the grill and poured on some water to work out the grease. It bubbled up satisfyingly, and he went into his old routine of cleaning. He looked around and saw other people struggling with rakes and trash bags, policing the area until it looked good as new. Aside from trampled grass, you couldn't tell the field had been full of people an hour before. About a dozen volunteers remained, and as Charles dragged the grill inside, he was beginning to feel like there was nothing else for him to do. He had nowhere to go, nowhere but home and the TV. Charles was washing his hands when he heard a large group goodbye, and he turned around to see Janelle standing before him, a few hairs straying from beneath her baseball cap, still looking flushed.

"I can't thank you enough," she said. "We were hurting for manpower, and you were a godsend. I was so glad I didn't have to worry about your end of the world; every time I looked over, things were obviously going well. Thanks a million."

"Not a problem," he said. "I've worked enough of these things to know you never have enough people. I didn't have much else to do today, so this was actually a blessing. I liked hanging around with all the kids and seeing them have fun. You put on a great event here."

"It *was* great," she admitted. "The kids were happy. Parents were happy. I noticed a lot of people here that weren't even from the school, so we may have landed some new students, too. The car raffle got off to a fabulous start. We'll be selling tickets till the end of the month, and I think we'll make a lot of money on it."

"You did fine," he said. "I can tell this thing was well organized and the people involved believed in what they're doing. The atmosphere was exciting; everyone was having fun, even the people working. Even you."

She looked startled.

"You know, I did have fun," she said. "I didn't take the time to enjoy it, but I did. Everyone was working hard. Everyone was feeling good, and that made me feel good. I didn't have a spare moment to breathe—but I was having fun. Thank you for making me notice."

He laughed.

"Did you even take a moment to eat?" he asked.

"Eat? No, come to think of it. I made sure everyone else had whatever they needed, but I don't think I stopped moving until right now. I'm starving!" It was her time to laugh.

"Well, how would you feel about a pizza and a couple gallons of something cold to drink?" The invitation was out of his mouth before he even realized it.

"Now? I'm a mess, look at me!"

"No worse than I am. Well, maybe worse. At least I didn't have to run around all afternoon. I had a nice cushy job in one spot. But, who cares, I'm not talking about the country club; let's just get a pizza, put our feet up and relax."

She looked thoughtful for a moment.

"You're on," she said. "Do you know Mannie's, up the road here about half a dozen blocks?"

He didn't.

"You can't miss it. It's on the right, big yellow sign. They have outdoor seating and the best pizza in town."

"I'll find it," he said. "Thanks. This was fun. I liked filling in, and, well, thanks." He halted a moment and looked around. "I'll see you there in a few minutes."

Janelle noticed his uncertainty. What's up with that? Probably tired. It's hot. He was working hard. Seems like a nice guy, though. Has to be to put in a Saturday afternoon working for no reason. She noticed his ambling gait as he walked away, and wondered.

****

The wondering didn't stop with him.

She got into her car and shut the door. She took a moment to settle into the well-worn seat.

She hadn't dated anyone in, how long? Four years. Not that she had ever dated much. Not that this was a date. Was this a date? It seemed natural to say yes; she was starving, she owed him a favor, and he had offered. She'd agreed without thinking. She didn't even know this guy. She didn't know what to say to him. So far, all they'd ever talked about was the car and the fair. Very simple, obvious business stuff. Safe stuff. Stuff she could be on top of, stuff she knew about.

Well, it was only pizza. One hour. What would it hurt to spend an hour with him? The worst that could happen was that she'd be bored. But at least she'd be eating. A beer would be nice, too.

So would some company.

She was approaching Mannie's. Traffic was pretty light for a Saturday evening. Saturday evening. Date night. What was she doing? She flashed back to the few attempts at dating she'd made after the divorce. She always managed a good dinner. She could listen with interest, laugh in all the right places, ask good questions. She gave great dinner.

The problems came later. Sooner or later, the tone would shift from getting to know one another and having a good time. At some point, the guy would want to close the distance between

38

them. It might be some gentle touches at the dinner table or at the movie. He'd lean in so their shoulders touched or he'd take her hand. One way or another, he'd move in on her space. She allowed it, but she always tensed up, like for the first cold shock of a swimming pool. Always. Some would be persistent. Some would give up. Some would simply retreat back into pleasant evening mode. But he'd always make a move, and she always resisted, and they always noticed. Sometimes it took another night or two, sometimes not. But men stopped calling her. And she'd be disappointed, but only for a few days.

So she had given up and filled her life with work, reading, painting, and nice long baths.

And here was Mannie's.

****

"I got such a kick watching those kids on the climbing wall. Some of them were scared to death. I saw the attendant have to go up and help a few down. Then there were the real gung-ho kids who got right up to the top and wanted more. They seemed so comfortable with themselves and what they do. Wouldn't you like to be that comfortable with yourself?"

Charles' eyes were gleaming. His interest in the kids was genuine. It seemed to be a real passion for him. You don't find many men that enjoy kids. Their own kids maybe, but most of them get impatient with other people's kids, and none of them would be entertained like that for an afternoon in the heat selling hot dogs to an endless crowd. Janelle wondered who this man was. He shone with energy and happiness whenever he talked about kids, and he didn't talk about much else. He told her about teasing them because of their face-painting or their appetites and making jokes with them. Consoling them when they dropped their hot dogs.

"I always gave them a new one when that happened, is that okay?" he asked, and she could see he sincerely hoped it was, although he would have done it even if it wasn't. She was able to pretty much sit back and listen to him, and for once, she didn't mind. She enjoyed the cool night air and let her muscles relax, hand nestling her beer mug on the white steel table.

"That one guy must have come back a dozen times. I don't know where he put them all, but we got to be buddies pretty soon. He'd slap the counter and say, 'Gimme another round, partner!' I don't know where he got that, but it killed me."

So, she listened. And she wondered. And when the conversation finally died down, she took a bite of her pizza, savoring the saltiness of the cheese, and asked the question.

"So, what about you? You have any kids of your own?"

And his face fell. Not an out and out crash, no plunging onto jagged rocks at the bottom of a ravine, but it fell nonetheless. He leaned back in his chair and took a long breath. He looked beyond her at some distant point in the sky.

"I do. Two. One of each. Donnie's in 11th grade. Laura's in 12th. She'll be graduating in a month or so."

He paused. His eyes turned inward, and she knew she'd made a mistake.

"What's going on with them," she asked. "What's wrong?"

"They're fine. Nothing wrong with them, I guess. I don't see them much these days. They live in Westbury with their mom. I usually see them on Sundays. They're good kids. Laura's gonna be going to the state university in Rutland next fall, going for a bachelor's degree in psychology, then on to grad school to specialize in something or other. She loves theater, too; she's always in the school plays and musicals, but she knows that's a rough career choice. I expect she'll always be doing something on stage for fun; she loves it. She'll be Dorothy in *The Wiz* in two weeks. I can't wait to see it.

"Donald, he's mostly into soccer. He's a real jock. He does all right in school, pretty well, in fact, but soccer's what he cares about. Plays for the school in the fall, indoor in the winter, league in the spring and summer. He's amazing. I used to help out with his team, and I couldn't believe some of the things he did. I can't

handle a ball with my hands the way he does with his feet. He's a good kid."

He was finished. He picked up his pizza and studied it for a moment, then took a bite. He was chewing slowly, and she could tell he'd come to the end of the story. It was clearly his "my kids are great" story that he told whenever they came up in conversation. It gave information and told you about his kids, but it didn't answer any questions, not any real ones, like why someone who's so into kids wasn't with his own, no matter what happened to his marriage. Why he was here talking to her about someone else's kids with so much energy and joy. Why his face fell the moment his own kids were brought into the picture. He was still chewing. She looked down at his hands, and saw they were trembling. He had a certain delicacy when he held his pizza that she recognized as tentativeness, like if you challenged him for that slice he would hand it over, not because he couldn't claim it, but because he wouldn't.

"I know I should be polite here and ask you about your children," he said. "But, I won't. I'm not sure why, but I won't."

Her eyes raced to his for a moment, held them, and then set them aside.

"Thank you," she said.

That was the question she dreaded. She had heard it a hundred times, working with kids as she did. Parents always asked. Kids asked. Everyone asked. You see a healthy adult woman and you ask about kids, she figured. She had her answer, too. No, I don't have any, she'd say. Didn't work out that way. I have enough kids here to keep me busy. That usually satisfied people. She hadn't told her story in a long time. She'd managed not to think about it much for a long time. She was getting good at that.

She realized she'd been off in her own world for a moment, and she looked over at him. He was watching her quietly and patiently, but he wasn't pushing her.

"Thank you," she said again, and even though she had closed a door, she felt the distance between them lessen.

****

The next few days dragged.

Charles couldn't keep his mind focused on work. Every time he had a woman customer, he found himself comparing her to Janelle. She wouldn't ask a dumb question like that, he'd think, or she's taller. Her smile is broader. She's more animated. Suddenly, instead of lining up every woman he met against his internal standards, they all had to measure up to Janelle. When he tried reading the paper during his down time, he'd have to read an article three or four times to remember what it was about. Talking to men was easier, but still he couldn't pay much attention to them. On the showroom floor he ran on autopilot.

At home, he found he couldn't turn on the TV. Every romantic situation reminded him of her. Even cop shows and action shows were full of love stories. In desperation, he tried focusing on nature and history programs, but found he couldn't concentrate on those very well either.

He replayed every bit of their conversation in his mind, noticing every nuance, every joke, every smile. He thought of her eyes and rediscovered their depth, their warmth, the subtle gradations of color and striations of the iris. He remembered how the laugh lines on her face formed and reformed as she spoke and how clear and fair her complexion was, hardly showing her age.

But it was her energy and her spirit that most interested him. He felt good when he was with her. He felt alive. Maybe he should call her.

For what? For a date? What was he thinking? What would his kids think? How would they react to the idea that he was dating again?

Dating again? No, that was out of the question. He had happened upon the fair and helped out. Nothing was wrong with that. Afterward, two tired, hungry people shared some food and talked. That was all. It was over. He decided. It was over, no more, no more dates, no more pizza. He'd never even drive down that road again if he didn't have to. No reason to.

He sure was spending a lot of time on something that was over, though.

****

Janelle was flustered. Myron was insistent.

"You have to go. We have a great car here; we need to get it out in front of people so they can see it and want it. We already got our usual people to buy tickets, now we gotta get people who never heard of us. You gotta go!"

It was Thursday, and her principal was telling her she needed to take the raffle car out to the spring county fair and drive it around the race track between acts at the concert Saturday. Francine had painted beautiful huge signs to mount on the trunk, and he'd arranged to be able to show it off between the local country singer and the headline act. Thousands upon thousands of people were expected, and he hoped to sell a lot of tickets. That'd be her job, too, sitting at a booth outside the bleachers selling raffle tickets all afternoon in the hot sun.

"Myron, it's gonna be 90 degrees. There's no shade. I'll be alone all day, so I'll feel guilty if I have to close down to go to the bathroom or something. It'll be awful."

"Janelle, girl, don't be defeatist. We can work this out. I'll call around; I'll find an awning we can set up. You can bring a cooler with drinks and food. We can live with a break once in a while; don't worry. We'll sell a million tickets; we can do this."

She cringed inwardly at his use of "we" to describe her sitting alone at the fair.

"You sure no one can go? You ask Kelli?"

"Yes, and I asked Cory and Mary and every parent I've seen for the past few days. Everyone's either already got family plans to be at the fair or they're busy. Hey, maybe if someone's gonna be at the fair anyway, they can take an hour off to relieve you."

"You forget what having kids is like, Myron. You don't take them to the fair and leave them. It takes two to make sure kids don't disappear and get lost."

"Single parents do it."

"Not by choice, they don't, and you'll usually see them teamed up to improve their odds, too, if you look."

"Well, Janelle, I know you'll find someone. We can do this. Don't let a little thing like this stop you. A journey of a thousand miles . . ."

"Begins with one small step. I know."

"So you're already one step on the way. Stick to it girl!" he turned and made his way quickly back to his office. Janelle was left standing in the hallway feeling abandoned and abused.

He was right; they would sell a lot more tickets this way, and someone should go. As fundraising chair, she was the one who was nominated, unless she could find someone else to do it. She'd endure. Too bad Charles couldn't help out; he'd be fun. He could get pizza. She imagined him fishing around in a cooler and handing her a drink, and before she got the imaginary top open, she caught herself. What was she thinking? Why was she even thinking of asking a man she'd just met, who had no involvement with the school at all? How could she call him, anyway? It was too soon, and she shouldn't be the one to call.

She realized she was back in dating mode. She was back to wondering if a guy was going to call her again after a date, figuring it would be at least two days because he wouldn't want to look too anxious, but hoping he would anyway. But why was she even thinking about that? They hadn't had a date. They'd gone out to eat after a long, tiring afternoon to unwind, chat and relax. Besides, she didn't call guys. She simply didn't.

Janelle sighed and walked back into her classroom. The school always seemed extra empty when the kids were gone. It felt eerie, in a way, like the familiar halls were someplace else, someplace she didn't belong. She slunk into the hard wooden chair and stared at the calendar. Two days. Two days till Saturday. She'd called everyone she knew who had the slightest connection with the school and a few friends who were helpful and loyal. She was out of options. In a moment, she was rummaging through the drawer for Charles' business card. She picked up her phone and dialed.

****

"So, how did your first race go?" Charles grinned.

"I felt like such an idiot," she said. "The emcee told me to take two laps and drive slowly so people could get a good look at the car. You ever drive five miles an hour? With the top down, I was right out in the open! I never want to drive a convertible again!"

"Sorry, I couldn't see a thing from out here, but at least I didn't hear the crowd laughing," Charles said, "so you must have done okay."

They had taken turns wandering around the fair to get some exercise and ease their tired behinds, but most of the day they had been together chatting. Both focused mostly on kids, and kids were an endless source of amusement. They were doing fine together. Weirdest date I ever had, Janelle thought. If this is a date. She still wasn't sure. Charles had sounded glad to hear from her when she called, and he only hesitated a moment before agreeing to work the fair with her. She had worn a comfortable sun dress that was loose and airy for the heat, but still showed off her figure, which was pretty good for a woman of thirty-six, she thought. She liked the way her leather strap sandals looked against her skin, and she'd added, at the last moment, a simple turquoise beaded necklace. She looked good, but still casual and appropriate. Charles was wearing khaki shorts and a polo shirt. Nice, she thought. Ordinary, but nice.

The day went well, and they took in almost five thousand dollars. She was very pleased with the take and kept telling Charles to thank his boss for donating such a good-looking car. When the various booths in their area started shutting down, they decided to wait another half hour before leaving. The crowds had thinned considerably once the concert started, and the guy in the booth next to them said that once it was over, people would pretty much go home. They took down their table and stashed it in the back seat.

"Want to take one more walk around?" Charles asked.

"No, I've been ready to go for a while," she answered, and they climbed in the convertible. Janelle drove. She navigated confidently in the general direction of the main street through town, and once they reached it, she turned toward Hartleton.

"Long day," she said. "How'd you hold up?"

"Not so bad," he answered. "I thought it would drag more than it did. We had a pretty steady flow of people, and," he paused, "I liked talking with you."

She stared ahead at the road, her confidence shaken. Was this happening?

"Would you like to stop for a drink?" he asked.

Janelle hesitated. "I don't drink much."

"Coffee's a drink," Charles said, sounding a little uncertain himself.

"Sure," she answered, and in a few minutes she turned into a cafe on the edge of town. They ordered a couple of decaf cappuccinos and found a pair of soft upholstered chairs in the corner.

They settled in, luxuriating in the deep padding, such a relief after a day in folding steel cafeteria chairs. The room was dimly lit, with soothing soft music in the background. It felt like relaxing in a familiar living room after a hard day.

"What are we doing?" Charles asked suddenly.

"Drinking coffee?" She focused on the few swirls of dark in the foam on her cappuccino.

"Besides drinking coffee. What are we doing? Are we dating?"

She felt his eyes on her and continued examining the dark swirls. She was trying to see exactly where they ended, but couldn't. They seemed to dissipate into the soft foam without clear boundaries.

She started to say, 'Do you want it to be dating?' but stopped herself. She didn't want to be too flip. She didn't know what she wanted herself.

"I'm not sure," she said. "That's not what I had in mind."

Her answer swirled around with the foam for a moment.

"But this is nice," she said finally. "I like spending time with you." She paused. That much was true.

"So, if you'd like," she said. "I guess this can be a date." She kept staring at her swirl. It seemed safe. It seemed like a problem she could handle.

He didn't know what to say. He watched the curves of her cheekbones.

"Well, I guess I should ask you out sometime," he said. "I can't expect you to keep finding jobs for me to do."

She glanced at him and smiled.

"I guess this isn't exactly how it usually starts," she said. "Hey, you're cute, wanna sell hot dogs? How about working a county fair for eight hours?"

"I could find some excuses of my own," he said. "Wanna come wash cars for a day?"

They laughed, and each felt a layer of tension release, and they resettled themselves in their chairs.

"I'm rusty at this," he said. "I haven't dated in a long time."

"Me either," she said. "I used to, but it wasn't going so well, so I sort of gave up on it."

"How about if we do this real slowly, then? Let's not rush anything."

"Slow is good," she said. "I like slow. And gentle. Don't push me."

"I won't. Let me know if I do."

"All right."

Charles was softened by the look of vulnerability in her eyes. She was staring down at her coffee cup again, cradling it in both hands as if it were a crystal ball. He wished he had a way to tell the future—or even the present.

"How about this," she finally said. "How about if we figure it out together. What I mean is, let's not play the game. I'm sick of the rules, I'm sick of the whole thing. Let's do what we decide to do, and if it seems wrong to either of us, if we don't feel comfortable with something, we'll say so and drop back and figure out where to go."

The rush of words surprised him.

"All right," he said. "That sounds good to me. I don't even know what the rules are these days, anyhow. If I tried to follow them, I'd be following twenty-year-old rules that probably don't mean a thing anymore. You're on."

"Good," she said, and she faced him squarely. He looked open, and sincere. Can I really trust him? Can I really believe him? She saw the same kinds of questions playing in his eyes, and she felt the muscles in her neck relax.

"So," he said, "to start things off . . . Janelle?"

"Yes?"

"Would you like to go out with me tomorrow night?"

She giggled.

"Charles, I thought you'd never ask. Certainly."

"A nice, traditional date? Dinner and a movie?"

"Sounds delightfully traditional."

He hesitated.

"This is where I'm supposed to be suave and thrill you by mentioning a lovely place to go, but the truth is, I have no idea where to go. I don't know the night spots in this town at all."

"Well, leave that to me. Pick me up at seven?"

"Seven it is."

The ride back to his place took only a few minutes. She pulled up in front, parked easily, and turned to him.

"Thank you again for helping me out today, Charles."

"My pleasure. I can honestly say I haven't had a better day in ages."

He saw she'd half turned toward him and was looking at him with a mixture of expectancy and hesitation. Easy, he thought. Slow is good.

"Thank you, Janelle, for asking me, and for being so easy and fun to be with."

She smiled. He unfastened his seat belt and turned toward her.

"Since this isn't our first real date, let's skip this moment of uncertainty. I'll just say goodnight, and we can look forward to tomorrow."

She nodded, and he saw her relax. He'd made a good call.

"Thank you, Janelle. Good night."

"Good night, Charles."

He got out of the car and shut the door slowly, but firmly. As her tail lights eased up the street and finally turned off, he looked up at the stars. They were there. He smiled.

****

The next evening, Charles picked up Janelle and she directed him to The Olive Branch, a small, cozy restaurant run by a Greek woman who plainly took great pride in her food and service. She advised them energetically on their choices, and every selection was a treat. The crust on the spanakopita was flaky and dissolved instantly, leaving a gateway for the delicately spiced filling. They had a lentil soup flavored with fresh thyme, and a lamb main course she said was marinated with rosemary. They finished up with baklava and a cup of authentic cappuccino.

The movie was good, a light romantic comedy that entertained and surprised. Halfway through, Charles reached over to take Janelle's hand, and he marveled at the touch; he had not had any kind of intimate contact with anyone in so many years.

After the movie, they stopped in a quiet café and had a glass of wine. Janelle chose a cabernet, and Charles, not having been much of a wine drinker, had one as well. He was surprised at how good it tasted, the initial tangy impact, followed by a mellowing and a slow cascade of flavors. He couldn't remember having had such a complex response to a drink before.

Their conversation flowed. They joked, they talked about the movie, they reminisced about some of the fairgoers of the day before, and at times they were content to allow a few moments of silence between them to taste the wine and look at one another. Janelle wore a simple black print dress that shimmered slightly as she moved, drawing his attention over and over again. Her hair was brought up in a casual, almost careless way that made her look even more alluring. He had chosen a striped dress shirt and solid sport coat without a tie. He hadn't been sure about that. He was pretty sure people weren't too formal these days, but he didn't want to look too casual, either. This was a special night, and he wanted it to go right. So far, it had. He was floored. He hadn't even thought about dating the whole time he was in Hartleton, and here he was with a beautiful, tantalizing woman. How could this be happening?

When they were finished, he drove her home. She lived on the northern end of town, in a small brick building designed with small lawns and staggered fronts so each unit gave an impression of being a separate house. Small maple trees lined the street. The night air was clear and cool, but not cold. He got out of the car and came around to open her door. He was pleased that she allowed him that bit of graciousness.

He walked her to her door, and she turned to face him. Her eyes were bright, and he was sure she had enjoyed herself. He felt a huge weight in his chest, but he breathed through it, then bent down to kiss her. She raised her mouth to him, and when her lips met his, his heart swelled. He held the touch of her lips for a moment, and drew back. He took her hands, squeezed them gently, said good night, and returned to his car.

The night was perfect. She was perfect. The weight in his chest was gone, and he could scarcely force his attention from the memory of her kiss to the road ahead of him.

****

Two weeks later, Janelle was doing battle with her dreams.

Light filled the sky; the whole world was filled with light, and she floated along aimlessly in it, as if she were a dandelion puff in the breeze. She rode undulating currents, carefree and easy. Then, darkness intruded ahead and she feared she'd be thrown into a terrible storm. She cringed and drew herself in. Soon, the darkness somehow transmuted into a cave and she was trapped within it. She was human-shaped again, trying to squeeze through narrow, twisting passages, wincing as the rock cut into her. Sharp, overhanging jagged edges forced her to squeeze and contort as she desperately tried to discover a route through the rock, and soon she became aware she was being chased by something. She was quite sure it wasn't a person, but she couldn't tell what it was. It could move easily through the cave, and her only advantage was that it didn't know exactly where she was. She tried to be evasive, changing her direction over and over. Gradually, her limbs grew sluggish and stiff. She had more and more trouble contorting to fit through the crevices, and her progress slowed. Her fear grew, and she was sure the menace would find her at any moment. She longed to give up and simply lay down to be devoured, but some spark of hope pushed her forward.

She awoke from the dream tense and frightened. It took her a few seconds to assure herself she was indeed in her bedroom by looking around and taking inventory of familiar objects. Once she felt safe, she burrowed deeper under the covers. Her sleep had been troubled for several days, and she was getting frustrated.

Janelle knew the dream had to do with Charles, but she wasn't sure how. She was puzzled by her response to him. She definitely liked him, but his polite, almost deliberate gentleness confused her. He was clearly going out of his way to fit into her life, but he also made his opinions and preferences clear. He was always willing to help her, but usually waited to be asked, and he seemed to enjoy the fact that she would take charge of the situation from time to time. He was an old-fashioned gentleman in that he'd hold doors for her and would pour her wine first, but yet with him she felt more like she was being respected than pampered. He never pushed himself on her in any way, yet he was neither passive nor pandering.

Something else bothered her, too. Whenever she looked into his eyes, she saw nothing but enjoyment and adoration for her. But, on that first real date, when he held her car door as she got out, she noticed that he had looked away from her. She had actually had a moment's anticipation of enticing him with her legs as she pivoted out of her seat, but he wasn't even looking. Wasn't he interested? He often complimented her on her appearance, but she never caught the admiring gazes at her legs or chest she expected from men. He seemed to studiously avoid looking at her body, and she wasn't sure why. In some slight way, she was relieved; it took some pressure off her, but she was puzzled. Was he gay? She didn't think so, but she was confused. Likewise, he had never tried to do any more than kiss her goodnight. Granted, they'd only had three dates, but most men pushed harder. And, weren't people a lot more forward now? She wasn't at all ready to sleep with him; that wasn't it, she was just surprised she didn't have to fend him off. Besides, she wouldn't mind a few more and longer kisses and the occasional more intimate touch. She would turn him down if he asked to sleep with her, but it might be nice to be asked—and, somehow, she knew he would ask. He wouldn't plow in like so many other men. And, when she said no, he'd stop. She knew it.

On the whole, life was good. Janelle was having more fun than ever with her kids at school. She was winding down the last few obligations as fundraising chair and looking forward to having her time to herself again, well, to herself and Charles. Even simple phone calls and grading of homework went more quickly as she was filled with the first flush of happiness over a new honey. Her days were cheerful and bright. Her time with Charles was fascinating. Her time alone was filled with musings.

And her nights were just as full, incomprehensibly, with fear.

Chapter 3

"GOOD MORNING, Tricia," Charles smiled broadly.

"Morning, Charles," she returned. "Not much going on today, I'm afraid."

"Didn't think so. We'll make it happen." He had paused briefly on his way to his office, as usual, and was about to resume his pace, but stopped.

"How are things with you, Tricia? Life treating you good?"

She looked up at him, surprised. He wasn't one for small talk.

"Oh, pretty good I guess. You know."

Actually, she looked worn out, odd for her. Especially in the morning. She'd always been pretty chipper in the morning. It had usually irritated him. Her eyes looked a little hollow, shrunk back in their sockets, and her skin seemed to be drooping.

"Don't I know. We working you too hard these days?"

She turned away slightly.

"No, no, life here is pretty much the same one day to the next. I've been at it long enough I've seen about everything. It's, well, never mind."

She fiddled with her pencil.

"Well, I asked because you've been looking down lately. Nothing wrong, I hope."

Charles continued on to his area. He sat down behind his desk, put down his coffee and stretched back to begin reading the paper.

He first took a small sip of his cappuccino and paused to savor it. For a couple of days, he'd been picking up a cappuccino on the way to work instead of relying on the in-house coffee. It brightened his morning by reminding him of Janelle. He couldn't believe his good fortune in stumbling upon her. He might have finished out his life with his senses and desires stuffed in a small closet out of sight. For two long years he'd crept along without a whisper of love.

He stopped.

It had been a lot more than two years. He'd been alone for two years, but what he lost when he lost his family wasn't love. Not by a long shot. He and Ellen had always gotten along, but it had been a long time since they'd felt much for each other. Most of the time they went through their days easily, without fighting or tension. Like an ideal couple, he had thought. Whenever anyone asked him, when he ran into an old school buddy, for instance, he always said marriage was fine, he was happy. Always. Whenever he thought about it on his own, he came to the same conclusion. But now he was remembering that every day when he came home from work, or every time he entered a room where Ellen was, he felt a moment of trepidation when she looked at him, a dread that she was going to be disappointed in him. Whatever it was, she'd bring it up pleasantly, without open hostility, but he could always read the message loud and clear; he'd let her down. That seemed to be the crux of it; he'd let her down. He hadn't given her the life she wanted, and she resented it.

Their conversation had devolved to the mundane.

"Charles," she'd say, "the car did that thing again today, you know, the thing where you step on the pedal and it doesn't want to go, it sort of gasps and hesitates, then finally catches and goes ahead. It worries me."

Charles remembered that one well. Her sedan had been acting up occasionally for weeks. He'd taken it in to the shop several times, and they could never find anything wrong with it. They said it was almost impossible to find an intermittent problem until it acted up while it was in the shop. He'd explained that to Ellen, but she didn't buy it.

"They have to find it. I can't have it give up in the middle of some intersection or something. I'm scared! They have to fix it!"

He offered to drive her car whenever he could, but between soccer practices and showing houses to clients too old or too heavy to fit in the Toyota easily, he couldn't take it very often. She kept saying they should get a new car, but he couldn't see replacing a two-year-old car because of a minor issue. He was also irritated that somehow the problem was his. Because he was the man, she thought he should take care of the cars. The truth was, he didn't know much more about them than she did. It was the same thing when they found that Laura was smoking. For some reason, that was his fault, too. It was because his father smoked, or because he was too easy on her, or because he didn't show enough interest in her acting. He never understood, but he got loud and clear that it was his fault.

It hadn't always been that way, of course. In the beginning, it was exciting. Ellen was darn attractive. Downright sexy. She had a way of dressing that showed off her body even though she never revealed too much. It drove him wild. He always looked forward to seeing what she was going to wear. It could be a simple sweatshirt, but somehow she'd manage to make it alluring. She had a great smile, long bouncing hair, and a stunning body. Her legs were long and lean; she had nice hips and a large chest. She was about perfect. He was starting to think long term about his life, about developing some kind of career instead of simply getting through school, and he was becoming aware that he'd like to be married and have a family. Ellen seemed perfect. She was the kind of woman you admired from afar and wished you had, and she was in love with him. He pursued her, and by the end of the summer between junior and senior years in college, a summer they spent bouncing back and forth between their homes on weekends, he proposed to her.

Senior year was a dream. They got a small off-campus apartment together and set up house. He liked coming home to her every day, and they had a number of dinner parties for their closest friends, which made them feel all grown up now that they were hosting real parties instead of just getting together to drink and carry on. What Charles enjoyed most, of course, was the free, unrestricted access to sex. Every time he took off her sweatshirt or unbuttoned her blouse, he was astonished at the round fullness of her breasts. He loved to feel them pressed against him, and he got lost in the heat of his desire. They made love often and freely, and he reveled in actually living with a woman beautiful enough to be a centerfold. He was in heaven.

How did they lose that joy? Would he lose it with Janelle? That was an odd thought. They were carefree and had fun, too, but it was different. With Ellen, he had always felt like he was on a cloud, in a dream. With Janelle, he was grounded. And, of course, they hadn't made love yet. In fact, they hadn't done much more than kiss and hold hands. He didn't know if they ever would, if he ever could be with someone other than Ellen. The pain of losing his family still drove his daily life, and for two years even the thought of looking at a naked woman had filled him with guilt because of the raid and the aftermath. He had been scrupulously careful to stay out of trouble ever since, avoiding any reminder of what had ruined his life.

But that wasn't all of it. He was getting to know Janelle as he had known no other woman. He knew before she started a meal how she would begin. For some reason, she always delayed the main item till last. She'd try the garlic mashed potatoes first, then the vegetables. Finally, she'd cut off a small piece of steak and chew it tentatively. Every time. She really enjoyed desserts, though she wouldn't finish them. Often, they'd split one to avoid any waste. She took small bites, and he could see her face light up at the combination of flavors in the parfait or the cheesecake. He could tell as each flavor became dominant and melted away. He loved watching her. On some level, he couldn't imagine how you could have sex with someone who enjoyed food so much. It seemed wrong, like he'd be crushing her spirit by making her go along with his desire. Her pleasures seemed too delicate to bear his weight. Her body too . . . genuine.

From her intensity when she talked about her kids at school, from her delicate enjoyment of a fine pastry, to the way she sipped her cappuccino, to the direct, earnest look in her eyes when she listened to him speak, she was genuine. He realized that authenticity was what he valued most in her. She was real. No pretense. No manipulation. He knew he didn't know her completely yet, but he knew what he did know of her was true. He also knew she would insist on the same from him, and that he wanted to give it. He hadn't been genuine with anyone for a very long time, but he knew she would accept nothing less, and she was such a gem, such a light in his suffering life that he could not risk losing her. And that, he finally realized, was why he was avoiding getting physical with her.

How could he tell her?

****

"Charlie, boy, come here."

Harry barely paused in his march past Charles' cubicle. Charles got up and followed him into his office. Harry's office, unlike every other area in the building, was well-furnished. He had a large cherry topped desk fronted by three nicely upholstered wing chairs, a small bar, cherry bookshelves housing a large flat-screen TV, and deep, cushiony carpeting. Heavy, damasked curtains covered the windows, which was just as well, since the view of the neighboring fast food restaurant was not appealing. Still, he could have sunlight if he wanted it, unlike Charles.

"Sit down."

Charles dutifully sat down in one of the wing chairs. Harry settled into his luxurious leather desk chair. The mass of the desk between them was imposing. Charles waited for the bomb to drop. This kind of summons always meant more work for him.

"I gotta go away for a few days, Charlie. Not sure how long it'll take, maybe a week, maybe more, so you'll be in charge. Putting you up front is gonna ruffle Steve's feathers, I know. He's been here longer, but frankly, the guy doesn't see all the details. When I leave him in charge I always have a mess to clean up when I get back. Don't worry, I'll deal with him. He's easy to handle; you tell him what's what, and he sulks, but in the end he gives in. He's got a good thing here; he's not going anywhere.

"So, anyway, I gotta go away. Last minute. You know; things happen. That means you're in the driver's seat for the pre-summer clearance sale next week. That sucks, I know, but it won't be so bad. The advertising's all lined up, the banners and such are ordered, and I sat down with Tricia this morning and we kinda sketched it all out the way I want it, so you don't have to do any planning. Keep on top of things, keep the guys psyched up, and make sure we're well-staffed every day. That means you might have to pull some extra shifts, but I'll take care of you, don't worry. You'll be fine. The way you been waltzing through here the past few days I know you got the energy for it. What happened, you finally get laid, or what? Anyhow, it's all in your lap, and don't think I don't appreciate it. Now, I gotta get ready, I got a shitload of stuff to do.

Charles said he'd handle it and left the sumptuous office. This was a load of shit, as Harry would put it. He knew it was going to mean long hours for him; he'd have to stand by the whole time to swoop in and close deals when the guys couldn't quite pull them off. That was Harry's big role these days. If Steve or one of the other guys had someone inched right up to the line but couldn't nudge him over, he'd buzz Harry and the grand old showman would swing by, as if he was just passing through, and start laying down a barrage of words so innocent and yet so overwhelming that few people could resist. He could sell condoms to nuns, he always said. He had the gift, and he knew it.

The storeroom door opened and closed immediately. Charles heard the lock fasten. He never understood why the storeroom had to be so secure, but that was Harry. You never understood half of what he did, but you had to admit it worked.

Charles wondered what all this was going to mean for him and Janelle. He wouldn't have any free nights from Tuesday through Saturday. Damn. He'd have to make sure this weekend was good to make it up to her. The school was announcing the winner of the car raffle at the opening of the area's amusement park, a fairly small old-fashioned, family-run place. Janelle said the park was like walking into the past and it wasn't so large that you got overrun by crowds and concrete. It was nicely shaded and low-key. So, they were going to make a day of it. The giveaway would be at one, and they'd stay the afternoon till they were ready to leave. Janelle had warned him she wasn't into big, scary rides, but he'd cooled on those rides himself since his kids were small and he used to take them.

How long ago was that? He used to like taking Donnie and Laura to amusement parks; they were both crazy about speed. The three of them would ride roller coasters, water slides, the Himalaya, the Tea Cups, anything that moved fast and swooped around. He loved their gales of laughter, and he encouraged them when they were little and sat up front in the roller coaster for the first time. He remembered them working up the courage to ride with their hands in the air and looking up fearfully at their first loop-the-loop coaster, getting in the car grimly and putting on a tough game face until they finally got lost in thrills as they went upside down and were pressed into their seats. Charles became a child again on those rides, and he was never sure who enjoyed them more, the thirty-year-old or the kids. Both of them loved him for it, too, and they ganged up to tease Ellen because she didn't like the fast rides. It was always good natured teasing, but still, on those outings, a line was drawn, and Charles was glad to be inside it. Those were some of the best times he had ever had with his family, and they convinced him that a child's spirit was precious and never to be lost. He swore he'd keep that closeness with his kids forever. He saw no reason it had to end.

But it did. They started growing distant, first Laura, then Donnie. Being with dad wasn't quite so much fun anymore. They started insisting on bringing friends everywhere, and soon family outings became expeditions, and although the kids were open and happy, they were clearly more bonded with their friends than with him, and soon he found himself on the other side of the line. Once, he insisted on a "family only" trip to Ohio to a huge park and aquarium. He wanted to recapture the old spirit, and he figured if they got away from town so the kids wouldn't worry about being seen with their parents, and if it was a new environment, all would be well. But the trip was a disaster. The kids were sullen in the back seat on the long car ride, and although they had fun at the park and rode the big rides with Charles, the glow was gone, and he noted painfully that instead of jostling to see who would sit next to him this time, the commotion was about who was going to be polite and ride with him. He lost a piece of his heart that day. The kids retreated to their room as soon as they could after dinner, and it was plain that his days of being their favorite person in the world were over.

That led to the other realization. Left to themselves at the park much of the day, left to themselves on Saturday afternoons and even on weeknights as the kids got more independent, Charles and Ellen discovered they didn't have much to talk about any more. As they had raised the kids past the point where they needed constant care, as they had set up a household in a good neighborhood with good schools, as they had made stability and wholesomeness the cornerstone of their home, they had become adults. But they had become different adults. Charles had his work. After a few years of various low-level management jobs, he had discovered his talent for selling and began his real estate career, devoting many hours to polishing his skills. Ellen had her volunteer work at the kids' schools, then started working part time at her friend's fitness club. They shared many social connections, didn't share others, went to the usual parties, ferried their kids around to practices and games, took care of the house, and became parents. They were no longer young lovers thrilling to the idea of constant companionship and exploring their emotional and sexual connection; in fact, their connection had faded.

With babies and infants in the house, they were often too tired to make love. And when their sleep deprivation ended, they discovered their sexual interest had waned as well. Charles still found Ellen attractive, but she was no longer a sexual dream come true for him, and she seemed to sense the difference. Their lovemaking was less frequent, less intense, and certainly less mutual. Every time, Charles felt as if Ellen was simply doing him a favor, and sometimes, especially when they were making love after a week or more, he found himself just "taking care of her," as he put it to himself, and he wondered that he could be so perfunctory.

Soon, he rekindled his interest in magazines. At first, it was only once in a while. He'd pick up a magazine at the convenience store and leaf through it in his car waiting for appointments. He'd bring it home in his briefcase, and sometimes masturbate late at night when no one else was awake. Nothing wrong with that, he thought. Everybody does it. It was a release, some enjoyment squeezed in when he could. Didn't hurt anyone.

After a couple close calls, he decided he'd better not have any magazines in the house. It wouldn't do for an inquisitive Laura to find them while playing in his office, and Ellen would flip out if she knew. He could imagine her reaction: wasn't she enough for him? Did he need other women to excite him? So, he stopped buying magazines, and as adult bookstores started cropping up around the area, he started visiting them and soon got hooked on the video booths. They were perfect: brief, exciting, exotic, and safe. He had developed and refined his habit. He knew which stores had the best material, when to go to each to avoid seeing too many other customers, where to park, and how to look nonchalant as he entered and made his way to his favorite booth. No harm done; just killing time, just taking the edge off the anxiety that preceded all sales appointments. No problem. Nothing to worry about.

****

The next Saturday was the day Janelle chose a winner of the convertible, and Charles had been looking forward to the event. The presentation went well: a fair-sized crowd gathered, the president of the school association made a speech, the amusement park owner made a speech, and Janelle got to fish around in a large barrel of tickets to choose the winner. A woman in the crowd exploded with joy when she heard her name called. She threw her popcorn in the air, hugged her friend, then turned around and started hugging everyone within reach. When she got to the stage, she hugged Janelle, then the president and the owner, and then Janelle again. She explained she'd been nursing along an old station wagon and worried every time she drove it that it was going to die on her, and she was so grateful to finally have a decent car. Charles was glad it was going to someone who needed it, and he was filled with a glow as well.

After the ceremony, he and Janelle had a leisurely afternoon. They rode the Ferris wheel and pretended to be a pair of teenagers all awkward and unsure as they sat down together and made flirty small talk while the seats were slowly loaded. On their first trip around, Charles made a big show of "sneaking" a kiss as they approached the top, and Janelle giggled and snuggled into him. The day passed with conversation ranging from work concerns to old memories, to comments on passersby and simply enjoying the warm sunshine and light breezes. They ate corn dogs and funnel cakes and joked about how much they'd weigh when they got home. They spent some time sitting on benches watching people going by and holding hands silently. The old-fashioned park even had an ancient Tunnel of Love ride, and once again they pretended to be teenage lovers as they rode through the darkness. Charles was surprised when Janelle pulled him to her more forcefully than usual and kissed him openly. Her lips were a sea of softness, and the touch of her tongue on his tantalized him.

They stayed till the sun was about to disappear behind the hills to the west, then headed home. They skipped dinner since they had been nibbling all day. The radio seemed to know what they wanted and played a host of favorite songs for them to sing along with. Charles drove to her place, and they went inside to settle down for the evening. They were cuddling on the sofa with an old movie playing, and again, Charles felt that Janelle was closer than usual. She seemed to melt into him as she lay with his arm wrapped around her. From time to time, she turned upward to kiss him, and finally, she scooched up to his ear and whispered, "Would you like to go in the bedroom?"

Charles was caught off guard. He released her from his arm, and she quickly got up and took him by the hand. She held him close for a moment, and he felt her warmth up and down his body. Then she led him to the bedroom and turned to kiss him again. He felt her body pressing against his. She rotated him around and gently pushed him onto the bed. She dropped to his side and started undoing his shirt, kissing the skin as it was exposed. Between kisses she gently murmured how much she wanted him, and she moved downward with each button. The touch of her lips on his flesh melted him, and he lifted his chest, then belly to meet her. Finally, she laid her cheek against his penis, and his desire became unbearable. She paused for a few breaths, undid his pants and slid them down. When she took him in her mouth, he almost exploded with excitement. He writhed under her, trying to reach out for her but failing as she wrapped her legs around his. She looked up at him with a mixture of passion and curiosity, and his heart once again melted at the look in her eyes, and he finally did explode in a sudden and intense orgasm. He collapsed, and she crawled up to lay beside him and stroke his chest.

"Was that good?" she murmured, a wry smile on her lips.

He couldn't answer. He was still catching his breath, allowing his heart rate to return to normal.

"I'll take that for a yes," she said, and snuggled in closer. He managed to wrap an arm around her.

"I wasn't expecting that," he finally said. "It was amazing. I still can't breathe."

"I figured it was time," she said. "I didn't want you wondering too much."

"There's nothing to wonder about now," he said. "I can barely find words."

"You don't have to say anything," she said. And they lay together in silence. He felt her head against his shoulder and the warmth of her chest rising and falling. Soon, he drifted off to sleep.

Janelle was pleased it had gone well. She had debated long and hard for almost a week and hadn't made up her mind till that moment, laying on the couch with her back up against his side. It felt right, it felt cozy, and she didn't want to lose that feeling. Sooner or later, she thought, sooner or later he's going to make his move, and I won't know what to do. I don't want to ruin it. I don't want to disappoint him. If I do it now, it'll all be over, the tension will be over, the wondering. So, she turned to him and invited him to the bedroom to do the one thing she knew he'd love. She was surprised by the intensity of his response and at how quickly he came. Well, it's been a long time for him, she thought, a long time. I'm glad that's over. He wants me. He likes me.

****

Janelle made a simple breakfast of French toast and bacon, with a very strong dark roast coffee. They took their time eating, washed up and went into the living room. Soon, once again they were cuddled up on the couch, radio playing dimly in the background as they luxuriated in their senses.

After a long silence, Charles spoke up.

"Janelle," he said, hesitantly, "Why?"

"Why what?"

"Why did you do that last night?"

"Don't tell me you didn't like it," she smiled, and snuggled closer.

"Oh no, you were incredible. It's not that I didn't want you, but I didn't know what to do. I had the impression that you weren't, well, weren't. . ." he was having trouble finding words.

"Easy?" she suggested.

"No, not easy, not that. Well, it seemed you weren't all that comfortable with our touching yet. I always got the feeling that I'd better wait for you to invite me to go any further. I was afraid I'd scare you off if I pushed too hard."

Janelle was silent. Charles grew nervous.

"Well," she began. "I'm not sure why I did it either. I hadn't planned on it. At first, I only wanted to cuddle. But, then, the idea came over me. I guess it bothered me that you weren't trying anything else. I was starting to wonder if you wanted me."

She had turned away slightly as she spoke.

"Did you want to wait?" she asked.

"I guess I thought it would be best."

"Would it have been? Do you regret it?"

"No, not at all. In fact," he said, "it's a whole new day." He straightened himself up, and she pulled her back away from him to give him some room to move. He stood up and reached out his hand.

"Now it's my turn," he said. "Madam, would you like to accompany me to the boudoir?"

In answer, she arose and went to him. Her body, clad only in a light nightgown, pressed against him softly. He felt her chest against him, took her hand and led her to the bedroom. He lay her down on the bed and began kissing her. After a few moments of gentle caressing, he moved over on top of her, and as he took himself in his hand to guide himself in, he went soft.

"Oh," he murmured.

"What?"

"Um, I have a problem," he said, and he moved off her. She propped herself up on her elbow and saw.

"Oh," she repeated. "Don't worry," and she gently reached out to stroke him. In a moment, she pushed him onto his back and kissed him. She continued to stroke him with her hand and kiss him delicately.

After a few minutes, he said, "Well, I think it's not going to happen. I don't know why. It's not that I don't want you; you're incredibly beautiful. I don't know. I haven't been with anyone but Ellen for so long, maybe I don't know how to respond to anyone else. Maybe it's too soon after last night. I am getting older, after all, I don't know."

"Don't worry," she said. "Don't worry."

"Last night I think you took me by surprise; there was no time to think, no time for anything but to react. This is different. This time we're thinking about it."

"It happens," she said. "Don't worry about it. Here, come here," and she pulled him toward her, this time putting her arm around him. He lay with his head against her chest, her arm around him, and he could feel her breathing. He was embarrassed. He was frustrated. He was even angry at his body for betraying him. But, in a few minutes, feeling her comforting presence, he placed his hand on her belly, and he was shocked at how good the soft smoothness of her skin felt against his hand. In only a few minutes, he was no longer embarrassed or frustrated. He was happy laying beside her. The peacefulness of the sensation confused him at first, but he stayed with it, and eventually felt nothing but contentment.

****

He awoke slowly, taking a few minutes to orient himself to where he was. Janelle's bedroom, Janelle's apartment. Janelle, right beside him. He lay quietly, taking in the feel of her thigh against his. Gradually, his mind came to life.

How could this be? How could he be laying her with her, close and warm, and, yes, happy? The worst had happened, and it didn't seem to matter to either of them. He pulled back and rose on one elbow to look at her. He noticed the subtle shift in contours as she breathed, her skin golden in the morning light. He saw its texture and shape and noticed how shallow her belly button was. He looked at the peacefulness of her face, and he felt even more in love with her than ever.

In love?

Yes. He hadn't yet allowed himself to put it in words, but there it was. He loved her. He wanted to be with her, he wanted to know her, all of her, and to be known by her. He wanted to see her every day, to hold her and feel her against him. More than anything, he wanted her to love him. To be cherished and known and valued and cared for was everything. As he watched her sleep in the morning light, he decided he would do whatever it took to make her love him, and, almost as soon as the thought was formed, he recoiled against it. Some deep part of himself told him it was a mistake.

He had never been at ease with women. Once he started going out with girls back in high school, he always felt a little nervous around them. He wasn't sure how to act. He did the best he could. He tried to be nice to them, always, polite and friendly. He hated seeing guys leaning girls up against their lockers as if trapping them, and he resolved early on never to be like that. So, he was nice to girls, and enough of them liked him that he rarely went without a date when he wanted one. They seemed to like him as a boyfriend because he wasn't jealous or controlling. He wouldn't ignore them when his friends were around or act as if he didn't care about their feelings. He was a good boyfriend.

He wasn't sexually aggressive, either. He remembered his first kiss, in the dark, walking home from a party with a girl he had been seeing for a couple weeks; he pulled on her hand and bent over to kiss her. There was a mass of hair, and he wasn't sure he'd actually found her lips, but she didn't resist, and after they pulled apart, she shook the hair out of her face and he tried again. This time, he found her mouth without question, and the sensation thrilled him. He had done it. He had kissed Rachel, and she seemed to like it. That hurdle over, they quickly fell into a pattern of a lot of holding and kissing, and Charles was in heaven.

Soon, she seemed to lose interest in him, and almost as quickly as they had gotten together, she was gone, wrapped up in an exchange student from Austria, and he was alone again. Soon after, he found another girlfriend, and this time the transition was easier, and the next time easier yet. It took him a while to become bold enough to start fondling a girl's breasts through her shirt, and then under her shirt. It was the same deal, the same process. He didn't know how to make the hurdle at first. Once done, however, the uncertainty was past and he learned how to pace things, how long to wait, how to recognize the signs that she was ready. He tried never to force himself on a girl; he was always willing to wait, and once he learned how to read the signs, he was amazed at how many were ready very quickly.

The girls floated in his memory. Jessica loved reading, so he read right alongside her, literally, sometimes. Some of their dates involved laying in the hammock head to foot, reading side by side. That is, Charles made reading *The Sea Wolf* part of his courtship. Marie, on the other hand, was more of a jock, and while that presented some problems for him, as he wasn't very athletic, he could be supportive of her soccer and basketball success, and he went to every game she played, and often to practices. Alexis loved romance, so flowers and small gifts and notes made her swoon right into his arms.

Whatever it was a girl wanted, Charles learned how to supply it with genuine enthusiasm. He loved having a girl, and he figured all this activity was simply how you got one. His romances didn't last terribly long, six months, at most, but he wasn't bothered by the brevity. Around that time, someone else would be catching his eye, and his eye went everywhere. He was already expert at sizing up girls the moment he saw them. He was developing his tastes, deciding what face shapes and body contours he liked.

It was almost a cliché when he had sex for the first time. Senior year. Prom. The classic setting. He had started going out with Jenn shortly after Christmas when she had caught her boyfriend making out with another girl. Charles was very sympathetic. He was good at sympathetic. Jenn was actually pretty easy to hook; she was a romantic type, and he knew how to swoop in with a single rose, a card slipped into her locker, other touches. Soon, they were together, making out at the movies and going on ski trips that had more to do with kissing and fondling than actual skiing. It didn't hurt that it was their senior year and prom was approaching. He knew she was interested in making sure she wouldn't be scrambling for a date at the last minute.

He planned a grand evening for them. He picked her up in a white limousine, gave her an orchid and took her to an elegant restaurant for dinner. Charles kept complimenting how her dress enhanced her figure and brought out the color of her eyes. Finally, they were off to the prom where she was radiant and beautiful, and Charles couldn't stop staring at her. More than a few guys leaned in to tell Charles how hot she looked, and he could only grin and say, "Damn straight!" When the queen and king were crowned, he told her she was his personal queen, and her face flushed. During the last dance, a nice, slow one, she murmured that the night was all she had hoped for. He smiled and held her closer. Then she pulled back enough to whisper in his ear, "What next, lover?" And he told her he had reserved a room at a hotel. "I was hoping you'd say that," she whispered, and pressed in close.

They arrived, dismissed the limo, and went to their room. Jenn told him to look away while she undressed, and he did. He heard the bathroom door close, and when he turned around, he saw her shimmering blue gown folded neatly over a chair. He took off his tie and removed the decorative pillows from the bed. He closed the curtains and turned off all but a single lamp. He wanted romantic lighting, but he wanted to be able to see her. He turned away from the bathroom door and waited. He heard it open, and then Jenn said, "All right, lover boy."

He turned to face her and gasped. She'd put on a short, clinging, sheer gown that made her body a showpiece. Her legs were displayed in black lace stockings that made his heart pound. Her breasts seemed about to pour out of the gown as she stood, one foot advanced slightly, and Charles thought he was staring at one of his centerfold models. She said simply, "Come here," and he was there. He wrapped her up in his arms and felt her flesh press against him. He started wildly kissing her and reaching down to hold her bottom in his hands, pulling her closer. He could feel her pressing against his erection, and he kissed his way down her neck to her chest and her breasts, burying his face against their softness. He started frantically shedding his clothes. The cuff links enraged him with their complexity. He managed to pull his shirt over his head, then his pants were open and he stumbled as he tried to get them off. Finally, he was naked, and he reached for Jenn and almost fell onto the bed with her. He was wildly kissing her and fondling her, running his hands over her breasts, over her bottom, and, after a moment's hesitation, between her legs to feel the incredible softness, and soon he was on top of her, holding his penis in his hand, fumbling blindly to get it into her, missing, and fumbling, and missing, and finally, he was inside her and he almost collapsed from the unbelievable sensation of actually being in her at last, being in anyone at last, and he started pushing in and out, and in a moment, it was over. He collapsed beside her on the bed, panting. Spent. Thrilled. Disappointed it was over so quickly. Wanting it to last longer, but too drained to even think of how it could.

Jenn lay next to him, a smug smile on her face.

"You liked that, didn't you?"

All he could do was gasp.

"Yeah, I thought you'd like the lingerie. I was hoping you'd want this tonight. I was getting kinda impatient, in fact, but I didn't want to push you too hard and ruin it for prom."

He was still panting, but was beginning to come back to his senses.

"Oh my god," he said. "Oh, my, god."

"Good," she said. "I aim to please. This was a great night; you made it everything I wanted for my prom—the dinner, the limo, the clothes, dancing. It was great. Thank you."

"No problem," he sputtered, thinking to himself it was definitely worth it. This was turning out even better than he had hoped for.

"Now, when you catch your breath, let's see about finishing it up right."

He wasn't sure of what she meant. This had all been too easy; she had been too easy. She didn't want to push him too hard, she'd said. She was so ready for sex tonight, so ready. And it finally dawned on him. This wasn't new to her. This wasn't her first time; she had been playing him! The whole time! For months! What the hell, he thought. At least I'm here.

They lay quietly for a while, Charles recovering his breath and his senses. What the hell. She was gorgeous, and this was great. I'm here, right where I want to be. And with that, he rose up again, leaned over her and started kissing her again, more slowly, more carefully. He took his time. And this time, when he entered her, he didn't fumble, and he lasted longer, and he enjoyed it even more. This is the life, he thought.

He had to take her home later that night. She said her mom was willing to let her stay out as late as she wanted, but she had to come home. So, a little after three, after they both had napped and cleaned themselves up, he called a cab. He decided to walk home from her house to clear his head. He paid the cabbie and walked her to the door. He gave her a long goodnight kiss, filled with meaning and depth, he thought. Now they were really together. Now he was a man. He walked home slowly, allowing the night to play through his mind. Mostly the last part. He played over and over the moment when he turned around and saw her in the lingerie, that gasp of disbelief in his mind at having a thousand photographs finally coming to life. She was everything he'd always wanted. And to be inside her! That was the best part. Better than he had imagined; he'd had no idea what to imagine.

****

All that seemed so distant. Jenn had dropped him as soon as school was over. She had kept him around for the final few weeks of graduation parties, ceremonies and dinners. He guessed she didn't want to have to go to any of those alone, so she kept him on board, but as soon as summer came along, she was off to visit a cousin in California, and the day before she left she told him there wasn't much point in his waiting around for her. She was nice about it, but she was also very clear, and he was totally certain he wasn't much more than a convenience for her, a guaranteed ticket out of being alone for the last few months of high school.

So he moved on. There was a whole world of women available, and he wanted them. He had a summer romance that didn't go anywhere. Every time he tried to nudge Penny into sex, she resisted, but he only needed her to fill the summer, so he didn't mind. He worked days and hung out with her at night. She was pretty, and she didn't mind his fondling her as much as he wanted, but she had a boundary, and he didn't cross it.

College was different. College was like the whole world opened up to him. He was astonished at how many women were as actively looking for sex as he was. He was still a nice guy, and he treated them well. He never became the kind who would pick up a girl at a party, sleep with her and brush her off the next day or even the same night, like a lot of his friends did. He only slept with women he was dating, and he found that if he let a relationship run its course, he would meet a girl, get to know her, start sleeping with her, and grow apart, usually in a few months, occasionally longer, sometimes less. Though the breakup would never be fun, it would be more or less mutual, so he never got the reputation of being someone who was out for what he could get. But still, he was getting about all he could handle. So, college was a dream. He did reasonably well in his classes, made some good friends, including Harry, who'd rescued him from unemployment when things went bad in Westbury, and saw more women, clothed and unclothed than he'd ever dreamed he'd see. Then, when he'd matured and started feeling a yearning for something more permanent, more real, Ellen came along, a drop-dead gorgeous woman who found him funny and interesting. He got serious about her, they fell in love, and he began his adult life.

He realized his story was pretty common. At the time, he thought he was living the life, that he had the world by the balls, but now, he could see he was muddling his way through like most other guys, letting his hormones do most of his thinking. It seemed a hundred years away.

Now, he had Janelle. He was still watching her face, watching how innocent and peaceful it looked. And, after replaying all that history in his mind of how he used to chase after women because of how beautiful they were, how large their breasts, how long their legs, here he was, noticing the pattern of crow's feet around her eyes, the faint wrinkles beginning to form at the edges of her mouth, the pattern of pores in her skin, and he was completely entranced. He wasn't seeing her only as a beautiful, sexy woman; he was intrigued by his awareness of her as a complete woman. Complete. Whole. She seemed willing to give him all she had, and everything he wanted lay within her. He leaned over and kissed her cheek lightly. She stirred, shifted her weight, and fell back to sleep. He wasn't sure why, or how, but he was sure she was a miracle in his life, and even if he could never have sex again, he wanted to be with her always.

He got up, careful not to disturb her, and went in the kitchen to do the dishes. He could hardly believe his good fortune.

****

John was at it again. He, Bill and Eddie were off in a corner of the sales floor, drinking coffee and telling tales while they kept an eye on the world through the plate glass.

"No, really, guys, I mean it. She was all over me. I could barely breathe! When she goes down on me, god, I can't even keep track of what she's doing; I'm practically falling out of bed she has me going so hard."

He looked triumphant. John had been dating a new woman for the past couple of months, and he loved coming in to work the next morning and regaling the others with her sexual performances. Bill and Eddie lapped it up. They were both married and seemed jealous of John's freedom and adventure.

"Honest to god, guys, that woman has a tongue that'd make a screwdriver come."

John was using a loud whisper, like he was trying to keep their conversation private, but he actually wanted to make sure everyone in the place heard. Charles wondered what Tricia made of these stories. Himself, he just stayed away. Even before he started seeing Janelle he'd had no interest; John was swaggering way too much. Charles didn't believe even half of what he said was true.

Now that he was seeing Janelle, the stories disgusted him. As John worked his way through the latest tale, Charles would flash back to images of Janelle's face and how earnest and loving she seemed whenever they touched. He couldn't imagine her as the focus of stories like these, couldn't imagine how anyone would want to talk about a woman he cared about like John was. Even back in his carefree college days, Charles never used women to impress his friends. He didn't like this.

He couldn't shut out the sound, however. He tried diverting himself with the newspaper, but John's theatrical whisper kept intruding.

Men, he muttered to himself. Why are we like this? Why are they listening? Don't they realize it's all a farce?

"Honest to god, guys, I thought my prick was about to explode!"

We can only hope, Charles thought.

****

Janelle rolled over in bed, annoyed by the constant sound of her refrigerator through the open door. It had a slight rattle whenever it ran, and tonight for some reason it was keeping her awake. She felt the pressure of the mattress on her shoulder and fidgeted to find a comfortable position. The sheet felt strange against her skin, her toes cold, the slight sunburn on the back of her neck biting.

She wasn't going to be getting much sleep tonight. She knew this restlessness, knew it very well. Every time she resettled and told herself it was time to sleep, her mind would go blank for a few minutes, enjoying the luxury of soft sheets, fluffy, lightweight blanket, and deep pillow. She'd take a few breaths, and she'd be right back to wondering how long it was going to last and when Charles was going to leave her.

She'd made it through the first test, the first time she'd be able to disappoint him. Well, not the first. She could have disappointed him right at the beginning, bored him with all her school talk and kid stories. She had lost a lot of men in that phase over the years. Losing out in that phase wasn't so bad. Getting through the first date wasn't so bad either. After a few years, she more or less saw it as a screening device. It let the good ones through and filtered out the jerks and bores. That was fine, too. But damn, she liked Charles. Against all odds. Against her instincts. And he had come from out of nowhere; she hadn't even been looking.

How long would it last? Did he really like her? She cringed every time that thought crossed her mind; she felt like she was in middle school again, wondering if a cute boy liked her. Why didn't it ever change, she wondered. Did he love her? Had she pushed too hard? He was surprised by the oral sex; she knew that. Was it too much? But men like that, they always liked that. Unless he thought it was slutty. Did he think she was a slut? He said he didn't, but that was before she practically dragged him to bed and forced herself on him. What did he think now?

Her one glimmer of hope, when he had gone soft, was the look of, what, tenderness? Concern? She had been surprised by his reaction. When it happened, it was the most natural thing in the world to reach out and hold him. She kept going back to that time, sensing again in her skin how he felt, feeling the connection between them. He had settled in to her and she had held him and the contact was heavenly. They had made love right then without any sexual contact. She was puzzled by the notion, but knew it was true. Whatever it meant to make love, they had surely done it. Or, at least, he had. She had been holding back, not being completely honest with him. There was no future in that. But there wasn't much of a future in honesty, either; she knew that from experience. Men just didn't want to know certain things. She couldn't tell him. He'd hate her. He would definitely think she was a slut. But all that was for later. For now, she wondered how she could ever tell him that when he had held his soft penis in his hand, feeling embarrassed that he couldn't satisfy her, all that was running through her mind was relief.

Chapter 4

"THANKS, DAD, that was great," Donald said as they walked toward the car.

"Yeah, I haven't seen so many dead bodies in at least a week," Laura said. She wasn't a big fan of action/adventure movies, but it had been Donnie's turn to choose.

"At least it wasn't too gory," Charles said. "No actual spewing guts or anything. It wasn't so bad."

She smirked as she perused the parking lot for people she knew. Charles never knew if she was hoping to see someone or dreading it.

"Well, what do you want for dinner?" he asked.

"Pizza," Donald said instantly.

"Chinese," Laura cut in.

As usual, all decisions were squabbles. Charles was used to it. They rarely fazed him much anymore.

"How about Rocco's?" he asked, and they both turned toward him.

"Really?" Donald said. His eyes widened out of their customary cool aloofness. "What's up?"

"Nothing's up. I just want a safe way out of this argument."

Rocco's was an exceptional Italian restaurant they all loved, but it was a little pricey, so they didn't go often. The food was stunning, and Charles was pretty sure it'd be a hit with both of them.

"Sounds great," Laura said. "I love the eggplant!"

The two of them kept up their bickering all the way to the restaurant, and for a while inside. Once they could focus on food, life got easier for Charles. Donald started gorging himself on Italian bread, peppers and parmesan cheese as soon as it was brought, and he and Laura could talk.

"Getting everything ready for the big move?" he asked. She would be going off to college in a little over a month.

"I have no idea how I'm going to fit everything into that tiny room," she said. "I'm gonna have to rotate my clothes for the seasons. You or mom will have to run out my new stuff every few months. We found a cute TV with a DVD player built right in, so that saves some space. I think I can even plug the laptop into it so we can play music right through the speakers. My roommate's bringing a refrigerator. I can't believe they won't let us cook. It's not like we're going to burn the place down making ramen noodles or anything."

"You'll do fine, Laura. As soon as you move in you'll be so busy, you won't care about any of this, I promise. You just have too much time to worry about it right now."

"Kelly says she wants to pool money for buying snacks and stuff, but I think we should get our own. I can't believe we'll actually use everything equally. That's bound to lead to arguments. I don't want to be arguing about who drank how much soda." Kelly was going to be her roommate. They hadn't met yet, but they texted about a hundred times a day, Charles estimated. They had the closest relationship of two people who'd never met he'd ever seen.

"I think you're right. Get your own stuff. Keep it simple. That's the key to nearly everything: keep it simple." He knew she wasn't listening, was asking him to be polite, but he played the game. He'd played the teenager game for a long time, but he wasn't quite ready to believe they'd hit this stage.

"You'll be fine, Laura."

She went on with all her worries and the thousand arrangements she had to make in a month's time. Charles listened and smiled. All this seemed so daunting, so important to her, and it was, he knew, but he also knew in six months it would all be behind her and she'd barely even remember this anxiety. Donald joined in with some barbs about all her preparations, focusing mostly on how Kelly would probably turn out to be an alcoholic lady Sumo wrestler for all Laura knew, but mostly he concentrated on his lasagna. The afternoon went pretty well, pretty much like all the others, and when it was time to go, Charles took them home. He let them out of the car in the driveway, said his goodbyes and watched them bounce on up into the house.

Charles turned onto the main road out of town and began the long ride home. His regular Sunday trip had limited his morning with Janelle, and the drive back to Westbury was mostly filled with thoughts of the kids and if he should mention her to them. At first, there wasn't anything to tell; he had met a woman at work. That happened nearly every day. Then he'd helped out at her carnival. That at least would have been a good story; he might have mentioned that. Then, they went out for pizza. That was starting to be real. Then, he went to her county fair gig. And dinner. And that was getting real. Now, they were sleeping together, sort of, and that was definitely real. He was holding back from them, and it felt wrong.

What business was it of theirs, anyhow? He was grown up, he was single. He could do what he wanted to, couldn't he?

He knew better. It would matter to them. It would be a big deal. To Laura, anyway, it would be. How would she take it? How would he tell them? Why would he tell them? He came back to that one. It would be so much easier not to tell them. They were three hours away. They would never see him and Janelle together. It would be so easy. Why bother? They didn't seem all that interested in his life, anyway.

He knew the answer, though. He had to tell them. He'd kept too much from them over the years. That much he'd learned from SAA meetings. Keeping secrets was always a bad sign.

He'd always tried to live his life with some degree of integrity. It was one of his professional hallmarks. He figured if he couldn't tell his kids about what he did and how he did it, he was doing something wrong. So he steered clear of the shady deals, the sellers who wanted to hide defects in a property, the buyers who wanted to cheat sellers. He always managed to talk them out of whatever they had in mind. It would be better in the long run, he'd tell them, and he meant it. He always wanted to be able to be proud of whatever deal he was working on. To be able to tell his kids about it. Always. Well, almost always. There had been the one big secret, and he couldn't deny where that secret had landed him. No, he had to tell them. They might not like it, but the longer he waited, the worse it would be. Every week he delayed was another week of secrecy they'd resent added to whatever reaction they'd have to Janelle herself.

That train of thought was easy enough. The next one was harder. When was he going to tell Janelle about his past? How would she react to knowing she was dating someone who'd been swept up in a raid on a child pornographer? Would she be horrified? She seemed so decent—not innocent, not that at all, but simply so pure and straightforward. She didn't keep secrets. She didn't hide anything from him. How would he tell her? Should he?

As soon as he started down that path, he knew his answer. It was the same as for the kids. He had to tell her, and it had to be soon. The longer he waited, the worse it would be. How would he bring it up? How would she react? How could he tell that sweet, loving woman what he had done?

****

Monday night Janelle had a parent group meeting. Tuesday was his SAA meeting. Wednesday night they were getting together for dinner. They had a few good phone calls, mostly just checking in and saying sweet things. Charles felt like a teenager in love, anxious about his big date and badly wanting to see her again, to see the smile he knew would fill her face when she opened the door to him.

When Wednesday arrived, his anxiety sharpened. He went through twice his usual number of cups of coffee. He ate four doughnuts. He actually cut off Harry in the middle of a joke, and he barely muttered a greeting to Tricia as he went by. He spent most of his day in his cubicle. He let two prospective buyers go by, and he broke his mechanical pencil while fiddling around with the lead mechanism. He was wired.

When he got to her place, Janelle greeted him with the smile and hug he'd expected. The feel of her hair against his cheek and its delicate scent nearly changed his mind. How could he risk this? How would he ever find it again if he lost it now? How could she see him as a good man once she knew?

"Wow, you must have missed me!" Janelle grinned when he let her go. "Maybe we should always space things a few days apart!"

"I missed you," he said. "I did. I couldn't believe how much."

"Me too. I had trouble playing with the kids today. All I could think of was you and seeing you tonight. Where do you want to go?"

Charles took her hand and led her inside. She followed easily. He marveled at her touch. How could he do this? He took a deep, slow breath, grateful for the brief reprieve walking into the living room had given him. He closed his eyes and exhaled. He led her to the sofa and they sat down.

"Actually, I thought we should do something else first."

The tone in his voice told her they weren't on the couch to kiss. Her inner alarms went off. This is it, she thought. This is it. He's leaving. What did I do? Why? Why now? Already?

"Janelle," he paused. "There are some things I think you should know before we go any further."

He's still married, she thought. He has an illegitimate kid. He has AIDS. He's gay. He's impotent. He's celibate. The list ran through her mind in an instant.

"I never told you why my marriage ended, and I think you need to know." He took another deep breath, held her hand with both of his, as if he could hold her to him, and began.

He told her the whole story, how he and Ellen had grown distant, how he started with the magazines, how he switched to going to book stores, the raid, the scandal, how mortified his family was, counseling, losing his job, coming to Hartleton to get away from it all. She listened patiently. After a few minutes, she took her hand back and settled deeper into her cushions, moving away from him slightly, but still listening, always listening. He plowed on. His fear grew at first, but slowly abated as he wound his way through his past. When he was finished, he felt like he had expelled a huge, dense mass from his body. He felt lighter, like a space in him that had been filled with lead was now open to be filled with life.

Or not.

He waited. He looked at Janelle's face and saw how passive it had become, how she had withdrawn to take it all in. She was looking downward, hair cascading around her face so he couldn't see her clearly.

She didn't speak for a long time.

"Do you have any idea what it was like for those women?" she asked. Her voice was gentle, soft, quiet. It sounded calm, but very, very serious.

"What do you mean?"

"I mean being in those pictures. Did you ever wonder about them?" She looked up at him, her eyes fastening on his, her gaze intense and probing.

"I don't think so. I don't get what you mean."

She resettled herself on the sofa, drawing herself up to sit cross-legged against the armrest. Her head tilted to one side and her gaze softened, as if she were looking inside at some notes.

"My parents didn't help me pay for college. They wanted me to go to a local school so I'd be closer. I wanted to get away. I needed to get away. I got all the scholarships and grants I could.

I worked all through my junior and senior years of high school. I saved everything I made. I worked all the way through college. At first I had a work study job in the library, but it wasn't much money. I had a waitress job, too. You know, the usual thing for an eighteen-year-old girl. But I was always looking for something that would bring in more money. I needed the money.

"One day, I saw a notice that a local modeling agency was having an open call, so anyone could try out. You didn't have to be a professional. I was pretty back then, so I thought I'd give it a try. I figured it would be easy work. The audition wasn't bad. They took a lot of shots from different angles. They said they were testing to see how you looked to the camera.

"I didn't think too much of it. A lot of girls showed up. I figured if I got it, great, and if I didn't, well, nothing lost. Sure enough, in a few days, I got a call. They wanted me to come in again. So I did, and this time they had a makeup person and a hair stylist, and they took a lot of dramatic shots. I got to wear a lot of spiffy clothes, and it was kinda fun. I did what they told me and I went home.

"About a week later they called again, and I was in. It was a local agency that did a lot of work for department stores and such. The kinds of ads you'd find in the local paper and in catalogs. They did a lot of catalog work. They weren't an agency big enough to be doing national ads. You wouldn't have seen anything I did, I don't think. This was back in Huntington, you see.

"My first few shoots were for things like earrings and eye shadow. Lots of closeup work. That got frightfully dull. They spent hours getting the lighting right to show off the jewelry or the makeup or whatever they were selling.

"One day, they called me and asked if I'd mind doing an ad for some panties. They said it wasn't for anything sleazy. It was about a new line of panties a local department store was getting, and the photographer thought I'd be perfect for what he had in mind. Well, I needed the money, and I figured I'd seen those ads my whole life in mom's catalogs and even in the Sunday paper, so I decided what the heck, how bad can it be?

"So, that's how I became a lingerie model. They really liked me, and I got a lot of work after that. The money was even better, and I was able to quit my library and waitressing jobs. I had more time for myself, I was less tired. It was great. Except, it wasn't.

"Suddenly, it was like I was in a whole different world. Doing lipstick ads, I was more or less part of the scenery. They treated me pretty much like any of the props. They weren't mean to me or anything; they were just busy. Now, with the lingerie stuff, all I heard were complaints. I had to shift myself this way or that to get rid of a crease they didn't want or to improve a 'line" or sharpen up a curve. The makeup people were never satisfied; the hair person would scream if I moved too quickly or angled my head wrong.

"Sure enough, when I saw the finished products, they looked good. Those guys knew what they were doing. I couldn't believe it was me in those photos. And, to be honest, I'm not sure it was. Once, on a multi-day shoot, while he was showing me proofs, one of the photographers explained how he was going to retouch a photo. That's when I discovered how good those guys were and why only basic bone shape mattered; pretty much whatever else they didn't like they could fix, either right on the spot with makeup, or later on with the computer. I found that photo once it was finally published, and the difference was astonishing. That's why I looked so good and why I had trouble believing it was me in those shots; a lot of it wasn't me. Or, maybe a lot of me wasn't there; they did a lot of slimming down. I don't know. It was pretty incredible, though.

"Anyway, that was my life for a while. Wasn't too many hours, wasn't too physically demanding. Pay was good. The down side was it made me feel like shit."

Charles didn't think he'd ever heard her swear before. The word almost shocked him.

"What do you mean?" he asked.

Janelle was fiddling with one of her toes, her legs drawn up in front of her. She looked intent, almost fixated.

"Well, I told you how critical they all were. Nothing was ever good enough, my skin, my hair, my eye color, my mouth shape, my belly button, nothing. It seemed like they spent more time criticizing me and fixing me than they did actually shooting. Sometimes it was a whole crew: photographer, makeup, hair, wardrobe, someone from the ad agency, someone from the magazine, all kinds of people. Sometimes I had no idea who they were, all staring at me and criticizing me.

"And then, there was always some Casanova. Usually the photographer. They were always guys. Most of them were decent at first, but sooner or later it would start. 'Hey, doll, you know you don't have to go home when we finish up. You can come over to my place.' 'You wanna get a lot of work? I can make that happen.'

"The weird part was half the time they didn't even seem all that interested, you know? Like they weren't even trying. It sounded like they'd say that stuff to everyone hoping to score once in a while. I guess they did, too, or they wouldn't be doing it.

"And even if they weren't asking, they were pushing." Janelle stopped. She was still fiddling with her toe, but her face was even more intent, and more distant. She was barely in the room with him. She was clearly somewhere inside, reliving scenes she'd tried to forget.

"It would usually start small. He'd be working on getting the pose right, telling me over and over what he wanted, then he'd get exasperated and come over and move my leg or arm and go back to the camera. Pretty soon, he'd be doing that all the time, and his hands would get higher and higher on my leg. He'd be brushing against my breasts. I'd be crouching on a carpet or laying on some settee or something, and he'd be leaning all over me, like he could drop right down on top of me. It was like he was showing me how much power he had. He'd be holding my face, moving it this way or that, repositioning my shoulders and arms, and his forearm would be pressing against my breasts, or the back of his hand would be touching them. I always had something on, of course, remember, these were lingerie shots, but it wasn't much, I always felt pretty much naked. But I would have hated it even if I'd had a winter coat on.

"Some of them didn't bother to hide it. They'd cop a feel now and then. Right in front of everyone. Like they didn't care. All I could do was take it; I needed the money. Once in a while, if someone went too far, I'd call him on it.

"And sometimes, while they were in close with me, they'd be talking dirty. They'd tell me how sexy I was, how nice my breasts were, how long and inviting my legs were, how they could see a hint of pink through the panties and it was turning them on. That was always up close, quiet so no one heard. But I heard. And these were gross guys, guys I wouldn't date in a million years. Old guys.

"And sometimes, once in a while, they made other offers. 'I do some other work, too, you know. More exciting stuff. More interesting stuff. Without the clothes. You could be good, baby. You'd look fabulous. I could make you a star. Interested? What do you say? Wanna be a star, baby? Let's show everyone how sexy you are.'"

She was still fiddling.

Then she looked up at him, with a searing, focused intensity he hadn't seen in her before.

"So now do you know what I mean? Do you have any idea what it was like for them? Can you imagine how they'd be touching me if I was posing nude?

"Did you ever think about who those women are? Why they're doing it? Do you know who the other models were I worked with? Some of them get involved because they think it'll be cool to be able to say they're a model or that it'll attract guys. They don't last long. The ones who last need the money. For college, or because they have kids, or some loser of a boyfriend who drinks up all their money, or because they were thrown out of their house and can't find any other way to support themselves. Models are not happy people, Charles. I did hear about some of the nude models, and the way it sounded, they had it even worse. One girl claimed to like it. She modeled nude, and she worked at a strip club, and she always talked about how great a life she had making a living off sex—but the story was also that she was drunk most of the time and lonely and clung to whoever she was with at the moment.

"That's who your models were, Charles. They weren't sexy women trying to turn you on. They didn't even know you or care about you. They weren't feeling sexy at all, I promise. They were feeling stiff and sore and resentful and insulted. Those were your women. I can't even begin to imagine what it was like to shoot a porno video with a crowd of people telling you how to do it, how to look, how to sound, and all trying to make it good for the audience. For you."

She finished. Her eyes were solid, clear and focused.

While she had been talking, a million questions had come up in his mind, a million answers, a million defenses. He had nothing to do with how models were treated. He didn't ask anyone to be cruel to them. He wasn't cruel to them. He never met them. But, as soon as each defense popped into his mind, he knew it was hollow.

"I had no idea," he finally said. "It never occurred to me to think about that."

"I know you didn't," she said. "If you knew, you wouldn't have done it. That's not the way you are.

"No one ever told you. The way that stuff is presented, it seems like the models are having a great time. That's what those people did. They were good at it. They could take a tired, hungry, resentful 19-year-old and make her appear to be bursting with passion. But it wasn't true. None of it was true, not ever."

"That's it," he said. "Every one of those pictures would make me feel like I was there with the woman. They're always looking right at you, like they want you. That's what that stuff is all about, I guess, making guys feel wanted." Charles was staring off into space. It was his turn to examine memories he'd rather forget.

"I remember when I first started seeing porn. Back then, it was pretty innocent, compared to what they make now. We were poring over magazines, and the women in them were so happy, so on top of things. The captions always talked about how much the women liked being photographed and how it made them feel proud and how they liked the thought of men wanting them. We didn't spend much time on captions, I guess, but the message sank in. I always assumed the women liked it. Pretty stupid, I suppose."

"You weren't stupid. They're good at it. They know how to create the illusion men want to have. Men never think about it because they like the illusion.

"I knew a girl in college who worked at a strip club. She'd gotten married right out of high school and had kids, and then the guy ran off on her. She was trying to work her way through school so she could give her kids a good life. She hated it. She absolutely hated it. But check the help wanted ads sometime and see how many part time jobs a woman can get that'll pay her way through college. This culture will pay a woman big bucks to take her clothes off, but they won't pay her squat to actually do something productive. Seven or eight bucks an hour to work in an office. Three hundred bucks for a good night at the club. Pretty basic math. She went for the money. She was afraid all the time, though. Afraid of the drunk customers and especially afraid to leave at night. The guy she worked for was a real creep, too. He kept hinting she'd better not quit, or he'd come after her. So, when her senior year came along and she was ready to graduate, do you think she was happy, she was looking forward to graduation? No, she was scared. She told him she still had a year to go because she'd failed some classes. And when the time came, when she finished her last class and took her last final, she cleared out. Just up and left town. She didn't even tell me where she was going. She just left, and she didn't go to graduation. She wanted to make sure he could never find her.

"You don't see that when the girl is on stage. They don't talk about it in the magazines or on the talk shows. When you hear an interview with a nude model or a porn star they make out like it's a great life, like they're the luckiest people in the world, but that's all marketing, too. It's part of the illusion.

"And don't forget the ones who didn't choose in the first place. I believe you when you say you didn't have anything to do with the child porn, I really do, but the porn was real. Do you suppose any of those kids went into it willingly? Do you suppose any seven-year-old wants to be a porn star? What do you think that whole experience does to them? What would have happened to your daughter if she'd been taken in by one of those creeps when she was little?"

Janelle's eyes were still riveted on him, and he had no answers. He couldn't begin to imagine Laura being treated like that. He had a hard enough time thinking of her dating and living a normal teenage life. The thought of someone poking and prodding her into poses and making suggestive comments turned his stomach. He struggled for what to say.

Nothing came.

He closed his mouth awkwardly. He had many good excuses, but they all seemed hollow. How could he defend himself?

Then, he realized, she wasn't attacking.

The thought stunned him. He was so used to disapproving glares and people avoiding him. Everything he was afraid would happen if he were caught masturbating as a boy had happened in real life, his adult life. He had come to expect the reactions, but never gotten used to them. It still bothered him. No one had ever talked to him like Janelle, though, and she wasn't attacking or criticizing. It was more like she was teaching him, patiently explaining fractions to a confused student. He was trying to understand. He didn't want to disappoint her. He didn't want to lose her.

"It hurt you, didn't it?" he said with a quiet voice. He was having trouble meeting her eyes.

"Yes, it hurt me, dammit! What do you think I was saying?"

"No, no, I mean, I got that, I was trying to tell you I heard you, I can see how hard it was for you."

"No, you can't. You see the grown-up me, the me who's spent years putting all this behind her. Let me tell you, I wasn't so calm about it at the time. I was seething. I dumped more than one guy because of it.

"Now I can see it as something that happened a long time ago, and I can see what losers most of those guys were. They were pathetic, lonely men. I feel sorry for them. But I don't accept what they did, and I don't accept anyone or anything that supports what they do."

She was still staring right at him. That last statement was absolute. Charles knew it. He knew he was on shaky ground here. He knew that he'd better say the right thing, right now, or he'd lose her.

But he didn't know what to say.

He had to be honest. If he tried to handle her, to wriggle out of this, he'd lose her. He allowed the room to go silent. He took a deep breath and paid attention to what he was physically feeling. Deep down, deep inside his gut, something was growing, something small. He focused on it, clearing his mind so he could recognize it. He waited until he was sure.

"I don't know how to say this, other than, I'm sorry," Charles finally said, quietly. "I think of the strong, capable woman you are, and I can't stand the thought of your having to put up with people treating you like that, and I'm—I'm ashamed to be a man. I'm ashamed that we did that to you. I'm ashamed that was the only way you could get enough money to get by. I'm ashamed men treated you like some kind of toy.

"I wish I could do something to help ease that pain, to erase it all. I feel helpless. I can't take on your pain, and I want to so badly."

Charles searched her expression.

She was looking right back at him.

"You can't do anything," she said. "This is mine. I have to deal with it."

"You have to do it, I know. I wish I could help, but all I can do is be here and love you and be with you while you do."

The words were out of his mouth before he was aware of them. He certainly hadn't planned on this being the time and place he told her he loved her. But he did. It was true.

"It's enough that you understand. I can handle this. I've done it for fifteen years; I don't need your help to handle it. But," her eyes opened a shade, "it would sure feel good to have someone hold me while I do."

He slid over on the couch, and she unfolded her legs to allow him to get closer. He took her hands in his.

"Thank you, Janelle. Thank you for not hating me."

"I don't hate you at all. I'm glad you could listen. I needed to say it. I couldn't let it go."

"Thank you for letting me be honest."

In answer, she reached out for him, and they held each other quietly and gently for a long time. They had no words; they simply held each other and felt each other's presence.

****

After a while, as the sunlight streaming in through the window softened, Janelle finally spoke.

"So, where are you?" Her voice was shaky.

"What do you mean?"

"Where are you now with all that stuff? Are you still using porn?" Her voice flattened, like she didn't want to ask.

"Oh, no. No. I don't. Ever."

"Not ever? How do you manage that?"

"It hasn't been that hard. I was pretty shook up when it all happened. Ever since, I get sickened when I even get near anything like that. Watching TV can be hard. I have to be careful about movies. Nudity is pretty much everywhere."

"Female nudity," Janelle said quietly.

"Yes, of course. What do you . . ." he paused. "You're right. In the movies, TV, it's all about female nudity. I hadn't thought about that."

"No, you wouldn't."

"When it first happened, we went to a marriage counselor. Obviously, that didn't work out so well. It was pretty clear the marriage was over. It was pretty rough on Ellen. She had to watch police search her house. All the neighbors knew. All her friends knew. I think she wanted it all to be over.

"We went to a counselor for a while. I tried to do whatever it took, but nothing helped. About the only good thing to come out of it was that I started going to meetings."

"Meetings?"

"Sex Addicts Anonymous. It's for people with sexual addictions. There are separate groups for people who use porn, but not in my town, not here, either. So, I went to the big group, the grand circus tent of sexual addictions. Porn was about the least of them. Some guys couldn't stop picking up strange women every night. Some slept with their nieces or sisters or whoever. Child molesters. Rapists. You name it. I didn't feel like I fit in, but I stuck it out."

"Stuck it out?" she asked.

"It scared me. It still does. I go to keep myself straight. I don't want to make those mistakes again."

He stopped. Again, he wasn't sure how Janelle would react to any of this.

"It scares you," Janelle said.

"Yes."

"You feel like you don't fit in."

"Right."

"Charles, that doesn't sound like an addict working a program," Janelle's face took on a harsher note.

"I've known alcoholics, drug addicts, smokers, people with food problems," she went on. "I lost a couple friends to that sort of thing. I knew one guy, my father's age, who was an alcoholic. Once he had some kind of huge health scare, and his doctor told him point blank he had to stop drinking or he'd die. Not sometime, but right away. So he holed up in a cabin in the woods for a week to dry out, then checked into a rehab. He did it, he got clean, but he said it was a struggle. He had to completely reorganize his understanding of life and of people. And he never described meetings as a place to be scared. Meetings saved his life."

Charles stared at her.

"Well, yes," he said. The guys are fighting for their lives; I know that. I see that."

"Yes, but are you? You don't sound like you're fighting. You sound more like you're whining."

"Whining!" Charles stiffened. "This is how I stay straight, Janelle. I'm not complaining about it. I'm being honest."

"Yes, and I appreciate that, but you talk like you're a spectator. Do you share at the meetings? Are you working a program? Do you have a sponsor?"

"Well, no. I mean, I did, in Westbury. Here, I never got around to it. I told everyone I was keeping my old one."

"No sponsor? Keeping a secret from the others? That doesn't sound good."

"It's working fine, Janelle. I told you I'm not using. I'm not even thinking about using."

"Right, because you stay away from it. Like you stay away from people. Staying away doesn't solve the problem."

Charles sat up straighter, gathering his strength.

"I don't stay away from people. I talk to people all day. When I get home, I'm tired," he said, each word ratcheting up his frustration.

"Charles, you never talk about anyone but your kids and work. It's pretty plain. You're hiding."

"It's working."

"Is it? Are you happy? Do you feel like your life is going anywhere? Do you have plans?"

He hadn't had plans in a long time. He let out a long breath.

"I don't know what else to do. Going to meetings feels like I'm being productive. I help out. I make the coffee and clean up. The other guys have bigger problems than I do. I'm helping them by listening."

"Helping them," Janelle's voice was gentle.

"Yes! Is that so bad? I listen, and it helps them and it keeps me straight. It gives me someplace where I'm doing something more important than selling cars! It's all I have. What do you expect me to do?"

"What I expect doesn't matter. What do you expect?"

"I expect to get by."

"With me? Is that what I'm for? To help you get by?"

"This isn't about you, Janelle!" Charles prepared himself to lay into her, but stopped.

"Janelle, I don't want to fight with you. Fighting never got me anywhere."

"Me either. But hiding never got me anywhere either. I thought we were going to be open with each other. I was saying what I saw. You're a good man, Charles, but you always seemed like you were afraid. I never knew of what."

"I suppose I am. I don't like admitting it. I think that's why I started to get angry. You're right. I kind of hide out at meetings. I hide out a lot at work."

"So, what can you do about it?"

"I don't know. I guess I thought seeing you was going to make it all better. I'm happy when I'm with you. At first I couldn't believe I asked you out, but I'm so glad I did. I followed my instinct. I got out of my rut."

He saw the softness return to her face.

"I guess that's what I need. To get out of my rut. To get in the game. No more hiding."

Charles thought a moment. He struggled with what came up.

"Maybe I should stop going to the meeting. You're right, I never felt like I belonged. Maybe it's because I don't. I think I went because I felt guilty."

"Are you sure?"

Charles allowed his weight to settle, squaring himself on the sofa, feeling his breath.

"No, but I think it's right."

He felt relief as he spoke. That's something, he thought. That's important. Maybe he did know what was right. Feeding his guilt kept him tense and bound up. Every time he was honest with Janelle, he felt more at ease. She was so good for him. She'd taken this so well.

She had, hadn't she?

Had she?

"Janelle," he felt his voice waver. "Are you still with me? I haven't scared you off with all this?"

"You mean are we still dating?"

"Yes."

"I think we are. This changes things, but yes, we are. Besides," she grinned. "a while back, when you were all worried about me, didn't you say you loved me?"

At the time he wasn't sure she'd noticed.

"I did. I mean, I do. I know this is very early, and this isn't at all the way I'd want to tell you, but yes, I do."

"Well, I guess we'd better keep seeing each other. Wouldn't want all that romantic sophistication to go to waste. We better not have any kids, though; I wouldn't want to have to explain to them when we first knew we were in love." She was smiling openly.

Charles felt his chest rise. He felt it lift, and marveled at the sudden expansion of his chest, of his breath, of his soul.

And then he kissed her.

****

They didn't make love that night.

They didn't discuss it or openly decide; it was in the air. Something had shifted. The path they were on had changed with the evening's revelation, and Charles felt like they needed to step back and find their way. Janelle didn't seem to mind. They had eventually gone to dinner as planned, and had a good time. Janelle told a story about a kid at school who insisted on being called "Super Ben" all day. He wouldn't answer to any other name, and he made a big deal about being able to become a superhero whenever he wanted to.

Near the end of the day, when his teacher again called him by his usual name, he stood up on his desk, pulled off his shirt and pants, revealing a full length red, white and blue outfit and said, "See, I told you I was a superhero!"

"Funny kid," she said. "I love the way they can get into things. I don't know what I'd do without them."

When he took her home, Charles came in for a few minutes, then said he figured he'd better get home early and get to bed. He felt drained.

"Are we all right?" he asked. He was holding Janelle lightly.

"We're more than all right," she said. "I'm not sure what we are, but we're more than all right."

She burrowed into him more fully.

"We weren't sure how to do this when we started," he said. "But it seems to be working out. On the one hand, I feel like the ground was ripped out beneath me tonight, but on the other hand, I feel like we're even more solidly on the ground than ever before. I know that doesn't make too much sense, but that's how it feels. Let's keep on doing this. Let's face whatever comes up. Saying that scares me, but I don't know what else to do. I ruined one life already; I don't want to ruin this one."

Janelle could feel his sincerity; she could feel it in the way he trembled slightly as he spoke. He meant it. And, indeed, they had gotten through a night that would have shaken a lot of couples. Maybe he was right. Maybe they could do this. Maybe they would last.

She held on to him. She pulled back slightly and raised her mouth. He leaned down and met her lips lightly, tentatively. She was surprised at first, but, after all, they'd been through a lot tonight. He probably wasn't sure how welcome he'd be, even after what he'd just said. She felt his lips against hers, felt the length of his body, the tenderness with which he held her, and, strangely, she thought of hair, the light, soft hair of a newborn baby, warm, downy, inviting. This was new, and she lingered and cherished every tender puff of sensation she felt. Something taut in her belly let go, and she lost herself in his lips.

Chapter 5

TUESDAY CAME and went, and Charles didn't go to his meeting.

He was apprehensive about not going. Meetings had been an anchor for him; meetings and work and Sunday visits with his kids were all he had to count on. He wasn't sure he was ready to take away one of the legs of his secure tripod. But he had Janelle, and he had reason to move on.

He kept returning to Janelle's story. He hadn't realized he'd been so suckered by the media message. He couldn't imagine treating a woman the way she'd been treated.

But he could remember thinking about women that way. He was suddenly back in the garage with Jerry, pouring over their latest acquisitions, rating the women, talking about how sexy they were, how much they'd like to sleep with them, and, sometimes, they'd fantasize: "Man, wouldn't you like to be the one who took those pictures! Imagine being with her naked all day!" "Naw, man, I'd want to be the guy who posed her." "Posed her! I wanna be the makeup guy! I'd get to touch her all over, feel her up and get paid for it!"

He was only a kid. He was fantasizing, the same way they fantasized about getting a hot sports car or being a secret agent. It didn't mean anything. All kids do it. You grow out of it.

Sort of. He did grow out of those conversations. But as he got older, and he did finally get to touch women and even sleep with them, he had similar thoughts. He clearly remembered the high school comments, always made when the girls couldn't hear:

"Man, I'd like to put it to her!" "Check out the legs on that one!" The same thing. More fantasy. In college he was able to act on his fantasies more often. But it was still mostly fantasy. He'd see a woman and pursue her. The attraction wasn't based on anything more than what she looked like and what he imagined was under her clothes. That's all it was. He wanted to sleep with them. He wanted to see them naked. He kept searching for the perfect body. It was his own personal quest.

Once he overheard a couple arguing at a party. The girl was obviously upset, and the guy didn't seem to care. Finally he heard the guy say, "Laura, I don't give a damn about your feelings. I only want your body." He remembered being shocked. You didn't talk that way to a woman. But now he realized he hadn't given much of a damn about them either. He'd just never admitted it. Basically, his relationships with women boiled down to sex; that's about all.

He realized that not caring was also part of his plan. How could he have fooled himself? It was so clear. By not caring, he'd eventually frustrate the woman and she'd want to leave. By that time, the novelty would be wearing off for him and he'd be ready to move on anyway, more or less. And, if she was the one who left, he wasn't the bad guy. He wasn't a user.

He made it through the night without going to his meeting. Janelle had some work at school, so they couldn't get together. Charles had gone home, made a simple supper, and sat down to watch a couple of action-adventure movies. He figured he'd need something fast-moving to keep his mind occupied. He made some nachos at one point, and he stared at the TV, but he kept flashing to memories of meetings. After a while, he turned off the screen and simply stared out the window. A light rain was moistening the ground and gently tapping on the windowpanes. His right leg started shimmying up and down uncontrollably, then slowed down to the rhythm of the rain, then stopped.

The world hadn't ended. Once the meeting time had come and gone, it wasn't so hard at all. Meetings, it seemed to him, were one more habit. He'd substituted that habit for the other one. Maybe Janelle was right; maybe he wasn't a real addict. Maybe, and this thought choked him for a second, he was a little kid who never got over ogling the girls in his magazines. It was time to take women seriously. It was time to grow up and be a man.

****

"Timmy, watch, he's going to have that big bird swoop down and attack. It'll be cool," Janelle whispered.

She was trying to keep order in her band of forest revelers. Timmy didn't seem convinced; he was still fidgeting on the bench, looking everywhere but at the man talking about falcons. They'd spent all day at a nature preserve taking hikes and getting talks from the various staffers. The kids were wearing Robin Hood hats they'd made in art class the week before and were getting a taste of what it was like to live in the forest. Right now they were learning how people used birds for hunting, but so far, the bird trainer hadn't done anything exciting. He was showing them birds with their leather hoods and leashes. He was dressed as an authentic old-style woodsman and was pretty good, Janelle thought. Just not good enough for Timmy half an hour before lunch.

"Oh, man! Cool!" Timmy burst out as a peregrine falcon swooped down, missing them by only a couple feet. The assault had come from out of the blue, and the kids were surprised; a few even seemed scared. Now Timmy was riveted. The falcon had gone right over their heads, and Janelle could feel the rush of wind from its wings as it passed over them.

Finally, Timmy was engaged, and Janelle could relax. She loved these outings. It often seemed like nature couldn't possibly compete with what kids saw on TV, and she tried hard to show them life could be a wonder. Sometimes it worked. Sometimes not. This morning, they'd seen some brand new baby robins, hatched only a few hours earlier. The kids were fascinated. A few were grossed out by their rubbery skin and outlandish proportions, but they understood. They saw that even birds have lives and get born and grow up.

Robin Hood's Merry Band gasped as a red-tailed hawk plummeted out of the sky to attack a decoy swung from a cord. Janelle could see its talons reach out for the bit of leather as it silently found its prey. Timmy was wide-eyed.

Janelle was fascinated, too. The adaptations animals made, she thought. Amazing. How did some landbound creature eons ago make that first flight? How did its very bones become light enough to fly? How did it develop the vision needed to spot a mouse in a field hundreds of feet below? It was a miracle. How could living creatures change that much?

Why not, she thought. She had. Charles had. Here she was, a second mother for a band of green-capped kids, showing them the wonders of nature, doing all she could to be a good influence on them. She was respected by their parents. Envied. How many times had mothers told her they wished they could hold a boy's attention the way she did? The kids admired her, too. Many of them asked if she could come home with them. More than one boy said he was going to marry her when he grew up. They were so innocent. How would they feel if they knew what a slut she had been?

And how was she going to tell Charles?

It hadn't been too difficult to get analytical and talk about his pornography problem that night. Not hard at all. Like putting a Band-Aid on a scraped knee and ignoring the broken arm you didn't know how to treat. She felt like the insects they'd seen this morning that disguised themselves as plants to fool birds. She'd displayed her own adaptation, her own protective device. She'd deflected attention onto him. She'd made him the bad guy so she could be the good one, the one who cared and was willing to work through problems. Any problem, so long as it was his.

Timmy was grabbing her now.

"That was so cool! Did you see the way he attacked that leather thing? He flew right down, like he was gonna crash into the ground and he got it!" He swooped away, raptor style, to join

102

a bunch of other boys. A couple of the girls turned to her, their faces ashen. They didn't think it was quite so cool, she guessed. Oh well. Back to work.

"Come on, Katie, Monica, let's go get some lunch. This afternoon we'll see some butterflies. That'll be more fun."

She put her arms around the two little girls and they headed toward the picnic pavilion. Kids were so easy, she thought. You always knew what they needed, and they were so willing to take it.

****

"You look beat, Tricia. You gotta stop running around at night!" Charles grinned as he teased her.

"Yeah, right. Like I can run at my age."

"Never too old," he said, but he noticed she didn't have her usual sparkle. She hadn't had it for quite some time.

"Tell you what," he continued. "Let me take you to lunch today and I'll see what I can do to perk you up. It's that or we go out to the shop and let Mike hook you up to the battery charger."

The words were out of his mouth before he knew it. He was surprised. He hadn't done anything social with Tricia at all.

Tricia turned to face him.

"Why, Charles, I never knew you had it in you. You mean you can actually do something besides work?"

"I'll try," he said. "You might have to coach me, though."

She grinned.

"You're on," she said. "But I warn you, I can eat a lot."

"I'll stop at the ATM on the way," he said. "See you then."

He walked on to his cubicle. Where did that come from? It wasn't like he had any sudden urge to make friends. Figuring out what to do with Janelle and coping with Laura's imminent departure for college pretty much filled up the spare room in his head. Well, Tricia could use it. She'd been frazzled for a long time. Maybe he could use it, too. He'd actually like a chance to talk about Janelle with someone. He wasn't ready to face his kids yet, and he didn't often talk to anyone else. This was starting to feel like a real life again. He had news, and he had someone to share it with.

The morning flew by. He still didn't know what was going to happen with Janelle, but he was elated that he'd made it past this hurdle. She hadn't rejected him. From here on, they could manage anything.

Harry popped in for a while and bent his ear about the ball game he'd been to the night before. Their town had a minor league team and they were doing pretty well. Harry went on and on about the one batter.

"He's got what it takes, Charlie boy. You shoulda seen him! That pitcher had some speed on him, but Evans took everything he could throw. He's smooth as butter; you can see the power in his swing. I betcha he's gone next season. I betcha. They can use him in the majors. They'll move him up sure as I'm standin' here."

Charles listened to it all and even managed to bait Harry a few times about his team's prospects. Harry enjoyed the banter and walked back to his office hurling friendly barbs back at Charles. It was a good morning.

Lunch with Tricia went pretty well. She gave him a lot of office gossip about the other salesmen and a couple guys in the shop. She complained about Harry's odd work habits, coming in late in the day then staying after hours doing who knows what. He asked about her family and found out she had two kids, too. The younger one was a boy who sounded a lot like Donald, busy all the time with sports. Her daughter, Darla, was a sophomore in high school and apparently a handful. Charles knew too well the worries of getting a girl through those years, and he commiserated with her and assured her it was possible. Tricia seemed to lighten during the meal. Charles remembered what it was like to spend time talking with someone.

When Tricia asked about his life, he first went into the standard report. Donnie was kicking butt on the soccer field, doing all right in school and starting to think about college. He described feeling left out as Laura prepared to leave for school, making a thousand preparations and buying a million supplies, mostly with her mother. He'd hear about it after the fact, or when the requests for money came. He supposed it was natural for her to be more involved with her mom, but still, it felt weird to be missing most of this huge transition.

At last, he told her about Janelle. He was hesitant. He felt like he was back in high school telling his friends about a new girl he was seeing and hoping they'd approve of her. He was glad when Tricia said she was happy for him, that she'd wondered when he was finally going to get his life in order. She said he was a good man and he should have a good woman in his life. Hearing that was gratifying. Ever since the raid, he'd walked around assuming people wouldn't like him or approve of him.

They agreed to be sinful and get dessert, and as he attacked his sundae, Charles described Janelle's work with the kids at school, and he found himself getting carried away. He admired her, and he felt proud that a woman like her had chosen a man like him. As he felt the ice cream melting in his mouth, he enjoyed the taste of life going well.

****

Telling the kids didn't go so well.

Charles decided it would be better to do it sooner than later, buoyed by the warm reception to the news he got from Tricia. So, he deviated from his usual pattern and showed up at the house with tickets to an area amusement park.

"Let's get wacky!" he said, as he flashed them the tickets.

Donnie grabbed them out of his hand.

"They have this new roller coaster that corkscrews you upside down four times!" he said. "Let's go!"

Laura rolled her eyes in the way Charles had grown accustomed to once she had hit that pinnacle of sophistication, tenth grade. Now that she was about to go to college, she was expert at it.

"Dad," she said. "Really. I have a lot I need to do. I don't need to spend an afternoon with a bunch of kids." Her one hip protruded to balance the sudden tilt of her head as she struck a classic exasperated teenager pose.

"Come on, Laura, it'll be fun. We haven't done anything like this in ages. You'll see."

Indeed, after a car ride filled with sports talk with Donnie while Laura lounged in the back seat, lost somewhere in ear bud land, they arrived, and it only took half an hour before Laura was riding her old favorites.

"Dad, come on, we have to do this one! Remember?" She ran toward the metal cage swings. There was no name on the ride, and it was horribly old fashioned. He was surprised it was still standing. Metal cages large enough to fit four people were mounted on steel arms. A bar was mounted at waist height across the cage at the each end. The attendant gave you a push, and by shifting your weight and rushing back and forth, you could work it like a playground swing, except in these you actually could go all the way over the top, over and over. Laura had been proud of herself the first time she and Charles made it work, and it remained her favorite ride ever since. Charles was surprised she wanted to try it one more time.

He was stiffer than he'd been the last time, five, six years ago? But he managed, and he had fun.

Donnie, of course, was addicted to speed and thrills. He rode all the roller coasters, and the new one four times. He had a few other favorites, and he tried them all. After a few hours, Charles herded them toward the picnic area. They picked up some snacks on the way and headed for a far corner. It was late in the afternoon, and few people were eating. The sun shone brightly, and they were glad for the shade of the old-fashioned wooden roof. Laura sat cross-legged on top of one of the tables. Donnie propped himself against the end of another. Charles perched between them, one leg on either side of the wooden bench.

"I've got something I need to tell you two," he began, and told his story quickly. Meeting Janelle at the dealership, the carnival, the fair, going out, deciding they were getting pretty serious. It didn't take more than a few minutes.

"Cool, dad," Donald said. "Is she pretty?"

"Yes, very," Charles said. "But that's not the point."

"Well, hey, it's your life," Donald said. "I figured you'd start seeing someone sooner or later. It's cool."

Laura had been silent so far.

"How old is she?" she finally asked.

"What?"

"How old is she?"

"I actually don't know," Charles said. "You don't usually ask women that right away."

"Well, about. I mean, is she twenty?"

"Laura!"

"No, I mean it, dad. That's what men do. I don't know how many kids at school come in one day to say their dad ran off with his secretary or some other woman from work, and they're usually half his age."

"No, Laura, it's nothing like that," he said. "If I had to guess, I'd say she's about four or five years younger than I am. That might sound like a lot to you, but it's not such a big deal when you're over forty. She doesn't seem any younger than I am. She's very intelligent and she's been around. She's no innocent, helpless kid."

"She have any kids? Am I gonna suddenly have a little sister?"

"No, no kids."

Laura unfolded herself and paced the row between tables. "You know, dad," she finally said. "You could have picked a better time for this. I mean, I'm getting ready to go to college, and that's a big deal. It's about all I can think about, and to suddenly have to deal with you going out and getting a girlfriend, it's not right. I suppose I'm gonna have to meet her, and that's gonna soak up time, and she'll wanna be friends or something, and how am I supposed to get to know some thirty-seven year old woman who's trying to be like a teenager so I'll like her? This sucks, dad. I hope you know that."

"So, are you getting married?" Donald asked.

"Oh, no, god no, it's nowhere near that serious," Charles said. "I haven't even figured out if I'll ever get married again. No, nothing like that." He paused.

"I'm not alone all the time now," he finally said. "That's all. I found someone I like, and who likes me. We enjoy being together, and it's been a long time. It hasn't been easy being away from you two. I haven't made any friends. I go to work and go home and that's about it. But she's good for me, and I wanted you two to know. I didn't want to have to surprise you with her in six months and have you asking why I didn't tell you about her sooner. I wanted to do this right."

"Yeah, dad. This is the right way to date someone besides mom. You got it just right."

"Laura!"

"No, dad, no. This isn't right. You expect us to cheer for you? You ripped our lives apart and left mom alone and you want us to be happy because you are? I don't think so. It doesn't work like that."

"Laura, I can't help what's already happened. All I can do is try to live as well as I can. I promised myself when your mom and I split up that if I couldn't show you what a good marriage and a happy home was, at least I'd show you what a good divorce was and what a good, loving father was, even if I had to do it from a distance. I'm doing the best I can, and believe it or not, telling you this was the right thing to do. It'll be better that you know. If I'd kept this a secret, you'd end up resenting me even more when you found out, and if I'd kept myself buried in the hole I was in, you'd have to deal with seeing me turn into a bitter old man, and you wouldn't like that either."

Charles finished. Laura was still pacing. He wasn't sure if she'd heard him. Then she stopped.

"Well, dad, don't expect any medals from me." She was standing defiantly, like she was taking over a meeting or stonewalling a deal. "Can we go home?"

He took them home. Laura retreated again to her earbuds and music. Donnie wasn't quite his cheery old self after witnessing the argument, but he tried.

"Don't worry, dad. She's been crabby about everything lately. She thinks the whole world should stop and help her pack for college, like she's the queen or something. Don't worry. She'll get over it. I'm cool. Mom's doing pretty well these days, and we are too, no matter what the snot-queen says."

Charles thanked him, and let them out when they got to the house. He had time to think about what Laura said on the way home, and he understood her rage. It had been hard on her, very hard. But Donnie was right, she'd been self-fixated for a while, and she was always moody and volatile. She'll be all right, he decided. He was glad he'd told them. The air was clear, the path open. But for what?

****

It was end of summer clearance time, and Charles was working extra hours, so he wasn't seeing Janelle as much as he'd like. The staff was making a game of trying to sell one particular color every day to add some challenge to the routine. One day, they decided to push turbos to everyone, with a prize for the one with the most sales. Charles participated, but he couldn't quite work up enthusiasm for selling turbocharged monsters to retired women and men who looked like a strong cup of coffee was about all the excitement they could manage. The games helped, though. The August sale was always rough, with the heat and relentless sun, so anything that would lighten it up was welcome.

Janelle was done with the school's summer program and was preparing for the regular year. She was pretty busy, too, so they didn't have much time to brood.

The next Saturday, they went to an outdoor concert. The band played covers of a wide range of pop hits from their youth, and it was fun to remember the songs and sing along. The amphitheater was located in a lushly grass-covered hollow with gently rolling hills arising around it. They brought a picnic dinner and sat closely, enjoying each other's touch as they'd hug occasionally or lean against one another to join in on a chorus. They nibbled at the chicken salad Janelle made and ate pieces of cut-up fruit. Charles had brought a light Riesling that balanced the sweetness of the fruit.

The sun slowly set over the park, lengthening shadows and cooling the air. Lights came on around them, and with the nearby audience grayed out and the colored lights on stage more dramatically offset, the evening took on an aura of magic. Charles enjoyed some delicate kisses and kept glancing into Janelle's eyes to catch the gleam of life balanced in them. He rarely let go of her, enjoying even the touch of her knee against his, and he felt his spirit soaring to the emerging stars.

On the way back to the car, they walked slowly, hand in hand. They took a roundabout route, enjoying the feel of the summer night and the seclusion of darkness. Gravel crunched under their feet, and they occasionally brushed against an overhanging branch, tickled by the smooth leaves. As they passed a small gazebo, Charles pulled her inside. He lifted her onto the bench and stood looking up at her. Her face seemed to be glowing in the moonlight.

"I can't tell you how happy I am," he said. "You've made such a difference in my life."

He lingered over the gentle shadows on her face, her eyes, her lips. He held her loosely at the waist and his hands seemed energized by her warmth.

He took her home in a ride made magic by the night. They silently enjoyed one another's presence, occasionally holding hands.

She invited him in. She turned on a small lamp by the sofa, bathing the room in a soft glow, and turned to him. They shared a kiss full of the promise of passion, and she led him quietly to the bedroom. She lit a few small candles on the bureau, and turned to face him. They kissed again, this time fulfilling the promise. The softness of her flesh thrilled him, and in a moment, she was pulling off her blouse and shorts and tumbling into bed. He struggled out of his clothes and was soon embracing her, feeling the delight of her skin up and down his body. When Charles could stand it no longer, he entered her and began a slow dance that gradually increased in tempo and passion until he was spent, and he collapsed beside her.

"Was that good?" she asked, suddenly propped on one elbow.

"Oh, was it ever," he panted.

She reached out and began to caress his chest. She ran a finger down his sternum and traced the pattern of his abdomen. "Good," she finally said. "I want to keep you happy."

He reached over and pulled her on top of him.

"You won't ever have to worry about that," he said. "You're an incredible lover."

She smiled smugly and lowered her head to his chest. They lay silently for a while, then she rolled off him and they snuggled next to each other. Soon, Charles was asleep.

****

As Charles dozed off, Janelle lay on her side, enjoying the sensation of his body pressed against hers.

Good, she thought. He liked it. He's happy. Maybe this will work out after all.

She was glad they had made love by candlelight. The romance was important, but even more important was that it helped hide the signs of aging she had noticed more and more often once she had started seeing Charles. She wasn't twenty-two anymore. She had crow's feet. Her skin wasn't as resilient or unblemished as it had been. She was in pretty good shape, but her belly sagged, her thighs and bottom weren't as firm as she'd like, and she didn't have a perfect tan.

In her modeling days, she had to make sure she was evenly tanned. Part of her earnings went regularly to the tanning salons. She didn't go now, and it made no difference to her, but what

111

would Charles think? He knew what she should look like; he'd seen thousands of those perfect, young bodies in his lifetime, thousands of carefully made up, coiffed, posed, coached, and retouched women. Her mind replayed dozens of criticisms she'd heard in various shoots: why couldn't her legs be longer? Had she been eating too many donuts? Had she ever thought about working out—this when she spent an hour in the exercise room every day. Could her eyelashes be any thinner? Too bad her breasts were so small, so uneven, so droopy.

And, she realized. She hadn't been shaping her pubic hair! What would he think? What could she do now? He'd already seen it, an unmanaged, wild jungle of hair. The first time she'd been told to trim herself, she'd been shocked and offended, but she dutifully made an appointment for waxing.

But that meant nothing; this mattered. Charles seemed happy, but then, he'd been without a woman for a long time. Once he'd had enough, he might lose interest. She couldn't reverse her aging. She'd just have to hope. She still was pretty, for her age. And he was older, and he was saggy, too. Not that it mattered. She didn't care, but he was a man, and he'd have a man's tastes.

She'd enjoyed their lovemaking. He had a very delicate touch. No, delicate wasn't the word. He seemed to be more aware of her than her previous lovers. He wasn't touching her because he wanted to get his hands on a woman's body; he was celebrating her. His hands on her, his whole body on hers was genuine contact; they were communicating together. He seemed to want to know how she felt; he was exploring; he was gentle. He responded to her response and learned from it. He made her feel safe and alive. He had a loving touch.

She reached out and lightly stroked his chest. He was strong, and he was real. He was guarded, not very spontaneous, very cautious, but he was real. She felt she could trust what he said and what he did. The hairs on his chest tickled, and she enjoyed the sensation. His breath was a little labored, but he was sound asleep, and he seemed happy, and Janelle began to believe she might be, too.

Chapter 6

THE NEWS was bad that day. It had begun like any other day for Charles. Shower. Breakfast. Coffee. Drive. Office.

There, the routine shattered. Tricia was crying.

She was holding back the tears, but her eyes and nose were red, and tissues filled her wastebasket.

Charles dropped to one knee and asked what was wrong.

She handed him the morning paper, open to a full page story about a woman who had been arrested for killing her boyfriend. He skimmed over it while she told him the whole story. Her niece had known the woman and had filled in the details. They had been on the phone for nearly an hour.

The woman was pregnant, and she had fought with her boyfriend over the baby. He wanted her to have an abortion, but she was refusing. He was drunk and a little high, and then he kicked her in the belly and stormed out of the house. When he finally dragged himself home in the middle of the night, she had pretended to be asleep. She waited a half hour or so, she said, and got out of bed. He awoke and asked what she was doing. Going to the bathroom, she said. But wait, I have something I want to show you. At that, she picked up the shotgun she had loaded and set in a corner. She made sure he saw her, and she shot him. Neighbors heard the shot and called the police. They found her in the kitchen, dressed and ready to go. She didn't resist. She told them everything that had happened.

At the police station, she told them everything else that had happened.

When she was eight, she had seen a group of teenagers fooling around behind an abandoned building. They were lighting fires and teasing each other with burning sticks. She went home. An hour or so later she heard sirens. When she and her mother ran over to the scene, she remembered what had happened earlier. Several houses were ablaze. Two ambulances were being loaded. There was a nearby policeman trying to control the crowd, and she walked right up to him and said, "Mr. Policeman, Mr. Policeman, I know what happened," and she told her story. The boys were soon identified. They were arrested, and the talk was they were going to get sent away. In the meantime, though, they were released in custody of their parents awaiting a hearing. It didn't take them long to figure out how they'd been caught. Only one person had been around when they'd been playing.

They found her. Five of them. They took her to a nearby riverbank densely overgrown with trees and bushes, near a busy highway overpass where the truck noise was so deafening no one would hear her if she screamed, and they raped her. All five of them. They beat her. They told her she was going to die and that no one would ever find her. Then, they left her. She managed to stay alive and stumble home.

Her parents screamed at her for causing so much trouble. They screamed at her for being a slut and told her no one would ever want her. They crudely cut off her hair with a pair of kitchen scissors and locked her in her room.

She never got medical care. She lay in blood-soaked sheets for days. They left food in her room and let her use the bathroom, but screamed at her not to leave a mess. Finally, after almost a week, her mother cleaned her up, the whole time repeating over and over that she must never tell anyone what happened or how she was treated. She was to say she'd fallen down a riverbank while the family was camping. Her mother evened up the crude haircut and dressed her in clean pajamas. The next day she was sent back to school wearing jeans and a boy's flannel shirt. She was coached again in the story. The school nurse asked her about her injuries and examined the visible bruises and cuts, but never verified her story. No one questioned why the little girl now only wore boy's clothing.

Life after that wasn't much better. Her parents' frequent rages had already left a number of scars on her body, but now they became even more frequent and more abusive. They called her a slut and told her she'd better behave or they'd really give it to her. When her body started to mature, her father started molesting her. She cried out the first few times, but her drunken mother never responded. Then, she stopped resisting and lived with it. When she was sixteen, she ran away. A relative in another state let her move in, and she was finally able to live without abuse. She graduated high school and trained as a practical nurse. She found and kept a job. Her life wasn't rosy, though. She drank a lot. When she dated, the men invariably turned out to be abusive and manipulative. As soon as she realized what was happening, she'd ditch them and return to her solitary life of work and gin.

At the urging of a co-worker, she joined a church, hoping to find some peace. She slowly began to enjoy the services and hoped she'd found an answer. She asked the pastor for counseling, and they immediately began sessions. He was eager to help, but seemed overwhelmed by her story. Finally, one day, he blew up as she related another tale of her childhood abuse and told her he had no idea what to do for her. She stopped going to church.

She was alone again. More boyfriends. A few beatings. A lot of drunken sex. Still, she managed to hold on to her job. Finally, she met Joey, the one man who seemed decent. He didn't beat her. He didn't scream at her. He didn't take her money or expect her to buy him things. They moved in together and she began to hope she might finally have a good life. He wasn't always home; he liked to spend time with the boys, he said, and she didn't mind having a few nights to herself to rest. He had a relentless sex drive, and it seemed like they were always in bed. That wasn't so bad, she figured. She didn't know at first sex was about the only reason he wanted her. He did spend a lot of time with the boys, but she eventually found out they were often picking up women at bars, for variety and for the sport of it.

And Joey wanted no part of a baby. When she got pregnant he told her she had to take care of it right away or he'd leave her. They fought over it often. Finally, one drunken night, they had the big fight and he hit her, over and over, breaking her nose, bloodying her face. Finally, he kicked her in the belly. And that was it. When the man she had thought would give her peace turned into another bully, she knew what to do. She wasn't going to stand for that kind of treatment anymore.

Her lawyer was going to plead a battered woman syndrome defense and was advocating for a sentence that focused more on treatment and rehabilitation than jail time.

It was a chilling story. Charles could barely stand hearing it. He stopped Tricia a few times to ask for details.

"Do you think Harry would mind if I left for a while?" she asked when she was finished.

Charles didn't much care what Harry would think.

"Go, take as much time as you need. I'll man the phones myself, and I'll deal with Harry."

Tricia went out to her car, and Charles paced her reception area.

How could anyone treat a woman that way? How could you brutally beat a woman for being pregnant? He paced feverishly. He knew, though, he was avoiding the real question. How could anyone rape an eight-year-old? How would you, even? Those boys needed to be locked up for the rest of their lives. They didn't deserve to live.

But Charles couldn't dismiss them so easily. He knew them. He'd heard two different guys at SAA meetings admit to molesting children. They'd done their time. They were trying to get back to a normal life. They were heavily supervised. One wasn't allowed any contact with his family at all. Both wore ankle bracelets. Both had to keep police notified where they lived. Their names and photos were available online on a website devoted to protecting neighborhoods from predators. And both were ordinary men.

Their ordinariness was the hard part. They could hold conversations, tell jokes, laugh. They held down jobs and supported themselves. They were not evil ogres living under a bridge stealthily eyeing passersby for their next victims. What was it that made it possible for them to do what they did?

They talked about overwhelming urges, of being obsessed with the thought of the girls in their homes. Both said they never meant to hurt the girls. They managed to blame the girls for their violence, for "making them" have to hold them down and hurt them. On some level they expected the girls to cooperate and were angry and hurt when they wouldn't. They didn't see the girls at all. All they saw was young flesh that would satisfy their needs.

At least that's what Charles got from it. He could never fully understand. But he did see one thing: what they had in common, all of them, the guys at the meetings, the boys in the paper, the boyfriend who'd been killed—none of them truly saw the women they were abusing. Women for them were a tool to satisfy whatever their needs were. How could anyone see a live, breathing woman as a pair of pliers, as a piece of wood on a lathe, as a piece . . . of ass?

A piece of ass. He'd used that phrase. Not seriously, of course. Never seriously. But, back in college, talking with his friends, he'd often commented on what a nice piece of ass some woman was. He had never forced himself on anyone, but he sure could be persistent. He could wait a couple of months to get someone in bed. True, he didn't get every woman he tried for, but he got enough of them, and he got what he wanted, and he eventually moved on. Find 'em, feel 'em, fuck 'em and forget 'em. How many times had he heard that one? And every time he'd felt revulsion at the crudeness of the slogan. He prided himself on his decency and patience with women. And yet, he realized, it was all a facade. The difference wasn't so much in kind, but simply in method. He used patience to get what he wanted. His frat brothers were aggressive and relentless. Others, like the guys at the meetings and the boys in the news story used violence.

It was clear to him: he had never seen women either. He had only seen his own desires. When he was hanging out in the commons back in college and spotted a woman with long, lean legs, a nicely shaped chest and a cute face, he wasn't seeing her at all. He was running through a checklist in his mind: legs, check. Breasts, check. Smile, check. Ass, check. It was as if he was taking an intangible inventory of body parts he'd decided were sexy and desirable. He was collecting baseball cards. He was going through another kid's stack of cards and reciting, "Need 'im, need 'im, got 'im, need 'im." If the litany of "need 'ims" was good enough when he checked out a girl's body, he'd go after her. She was just a collection for him. He collected body parts. That's all it was.

Even when he was visiting the adult stores right before everything came apart, it was the same. He didn't know or care about the women in the films. He wanted to see good body parts. He wanted them visible, on display in exactly the right combinations. The women were props, platforms on which to hang breasts, legs, labia. Do-it-yourself dolls.

Over the years, he'd played with a lot of dolls.

And Ellen? She was the one who would listen to him and be quiet if he needed quiet. The one who was always glad to see him. The one who could keep him entertained. Looking at it that way, it was pretty clear why he had married Ellen.

She wasn't just a doll, she was a great pet. She fit herself right into his life, and he could bring her anywhere. God. No wonder she'd grown distant over the years. She'd gotten tired of being petted and played with when it was convenient for him. She wanted to be let off the leash to run free. She had been quietly scratching at the door for a long time.

A couple was coming in. Larry was busy with another client. He'd have to approach them.

Wonder who held the leash in this couple?

****

Charles grinned broadly as Janelle opened the door. In his arms, a dozen red roses greeted her.

"Oh, Charles, how nice!" She took the roses from him and allowed their fragrance to surround her.

Charles saw her delight as she closed her eyes.

"I wanted to surprise, you, sweetheart," he said. Janelle placed the roses on an end table and turned to face him. He took her in his arms and kissed her deeply.

"And that's just the beginning. I have a wonderful evening planned out for us. We're going out. And, here's the good part, you don't even have to get dressed! First stop is the women's shop on Fifth. Remember that jade dress you saw in the window last weekend? You couldn't get over how the fabric shimmered in changing light. Well, we're getting it! Then we're off to Vasco's for dinner and dancing. It's going to be perfect!"

Janelle was overwhelmed.

"What's gotten into you?" she asked. "Where did all this come from?"

"I want to be the best I can possibly be for you, is all," Charles said, beaming. "I don't ever want you to be dissatisfied.

"And, you know how you said your car's been making a funny noise lately?" he went on. "I'll drive it home tonight and leave you mine. I can have the guys at the shop check it out tomorrow. We'll get it taken care of, no problem.

"Anything wrong here in the apartment? Faucets dripping or anything?" He was searching the room eagerly.

"No, everything's fine here, Charles. Stop prowling around the place and look at me. What's going on?" Janelle had disentangled herself from him and was standing a couple of feet away, arms crossed over her chest.

"Nothing's going on; I'm trying to make you happy," he said.

"By taking over? I have an appointment for the car on Friday. I want to keep it. I like my mechanic, and he likes my car. He thinks it's great that I've kept it going for so long, and he's proud of it. I like seeing him. He always gives the car a good going-over and he's fair and honest with me. Thank you for trying to help, but I can take care of my car myself."

"But, this'll be so much easier! You won't have to do a thing!"

"I can handle it. Charles, if I didn't know better, I'd think you were feeling guilty about something; but you haven't done anything. Have you? About to leave town for a year or something? What's going on?"

"I'm not going anywhere, sweetheart, I never want to leave you."

"Those roses have guilt written all over them. Roses, a new dress, the car, and offering to fix my whole life for me? What gives?"

"Janelle, honey, nothing gives. Get your coat and let's go."

"I can't just get my coat and go, Charles. You're sweet to want to buy me that dress, but I don't want it."

"You loved it!"

"I loved it, yes, but what I loved was looking at it. I thought the fabric was fascinating; it appealed to the artist in me. But that dress wouldn't work; I don't like wearing anything that low-cut, and I think the waist would be in the wrong place for me. Besides, I can't wear it off the rack. It'd probably take me half a dozen tries to find the bra that would work with it, to begin with, and I'd have to bring along two or three pairs of shoes to try, and I don't have a bag that's right for that kind of dress. Besides, where do you think I'd wear it? Even Vasco's isn't that posh on a weeknight, and do you think they'll have dancing on Wednesday? And we have to go to work tomorrow. What are you thinking?"

Charles drooped as she scolded him.

"I wanted to make you happy."

"Like this? This isn't you. It's like you read some cheesy magazine article on how to satisfy women.

"Remember back in the beginning when we said we weren't going to play by the rules?" Janelle took a few steps away from him. "This is why. You act like this and I feel like I'm dating a cardboard cutout instead of a man. Treat me naturally. Treat me like you have been."

"But that's not enough!"

"Have I seemed disappointed?"

"No, but I don't want to treat you like just another woman. You're not, you're so special. I don't want you to get dissatisfied or think I don't treasure you. I don't want you to feel ordinary."

"Acting like this doesn't make me feel special. It makes me feel like you're writing a script for me, and I don't like my part much. You haven't missed a cliché."

Charles sank into an arm chair.

"I guess so. How could I not see that? I did everything but bring you chocolates."

"Thank god it's not Valentine's Day." Janelle sat on the arm beside him.

"It's okay, Charles. It's a simple mistake. We all make them. It's over. Let's get back on track and have a real evening together, all right? I was planning on taking some books back to the library. How's that for a night on the town?" She was smiling again.

Charles put his arm around her hips. He squeezed her thigh gently and settled his head against her.

"And Charles," Janelle went on, grinning, "You don't have to bring me flowers to make up for this."

Chapter 7

HARRY WAS being odd. That was nothing new; that was his way of being. But he was being odd differently this morning. He seemed nervous. He was bustling around the office doing nothing in particular, sticking his head in everywhere, giving orders.

"Charlie, you gotta straighten up your area, clean off your desk. A messy desk makes people think you won't get the details right. Nobody wants to deal with a slob. Clean it up."

And with that, he was gone. Charles examined his desktop, with its two baskets for paperwork, nameplate, keyboard and monitor. The pad of notes he was working with. Not much to be messy. His filing cabinet had nothing on it. His shelf of catalogs and car magazines was tidy. The carpet was vacuumed. He had no idea what Harry was talking about. He didn't even have a coffee cup at the moment.

A minute later he heard Harry chewing out Brian about the plants arranged in the corner of the showroom. That's not Brian's responsibility, he thought. Harry did that himself. Something was up. Maybe he had downed too much coffee, Charles thought. Maybe it's just Harry being more Harry than usual.

He went back to the sales agreement on his screen. He filled in blocks one by one, making sure he didn't overlook or misplace anything. He even made sure his notepad was angled nicely on the desktop. Then he heard Harry talking in a loud, hushed tone to Tricia. It was weird, like a stage whisper designed to suggest privacy although everyone in the audience could hear it.

"Tricia, honey," he said. "I gotta go to a meeting down at the bank to set things up for the next sale. They're getting pricky about letting us pre-approve loans. Some federal something or other. Anyway, I gotta go. There's a guy coming to work on the computer system. He shoulda been here two hours ago. Can't get anybody to do anything anymore. Here's the key to the store room. He shouldn't interrupt what you guys are doing. Something's weird with the backup system is all. So, let him in, let him do his thing, and be sure to lock up when he goes.

"Sure, Harry. I'll take care of it. Hope everything goes well at the bank."

"Bastards. Like I don't make them enough money; they gotta get pricky on me."

Charles heard the back door open and slam shut.

Harry usually didn't get nervous when people were late. He might get angry, but not nervous. Something else must be up. What?

"Who knows," he said to himself, and went back to his screen. "Who knows."

****

It was time to take Laura to school. The university was about three hours from her home, two from Hartleton.

Laura had been obsessing about the move all summer. She wanted everything to be right. She spent hours texting with her new roommate, making sure they could bond before they actually had to live together. Once, they met on campus for lunch and to shop for curtains and a throw rug. It all seemed very strange to Charles, who had barely brought more than his clothes, stereo and favorite albums to school. But, times have changed, he realized.

They had arranged it all reasonably. They had Donald to help load the car at home. Ellen would drive Laura to the university, and Charles would meet them to help unload. He'd been duly warned not to wear ugly shorts, and he knew right where and when to meet them.

Of course, the plan didn't hold. The onslaught of new students and their families, their vans and station wagons and U-Hauls didn't quite fit neatly on campus. Charles had to park far away and walk to the dorm. Ellen and Laura had to wait in line to get in the nearest parking area, and the August weather made the car start to overheat. They switched off the engine and waited outside every time they were at a standstill, getting in to move ahead ten or twenty feet, then getting out again to wait. They kept Charles apprised by cell phone, so he wasn't too worried about being late himself. Finally, they made it into the lot, and the long process of unloading began.

"Hi sweetie," he said, when he saw Laura approaching, carrying a lamp and her laptop case. Ellen was awkwardly holding the microwave oven. "Hi, Ellen." He took the oven from her. she sighed in relief.

Ellen looked droopy. Nice, though, he noticed. She was wearing a pair of khaki Capri pants and a loose-fitting top. Her hair was swept back into a pony tail that poked out from the back of a university baseball cap. "Thanks for meeting us," she said, as if there had ever been any question.

"Hi, Dad. It took forever to get in here. I can't believe the stupid car was overheating like that. We had to get in and out like a dozen times. I'm dripping."

All Laura's teenage cool was being put to the test, and she was on edge. It was how she looked right before a game, he realized. She was on alert, checking out the other girls, making sure she fit in. She had on a casual pair of shorts and a printed T-shirt, sandals, and a long, dangly necklace. She looked like she had thrown her clothes on in a second, although Charles knew the outfit had probably been planned for at least a week.

"All ready for the big day?" he asked. He smiled at her.

He was so proud.

"Of course, daddy," she said, and rolled her eyes with the requisite teenage angst. "I'm ready. I'm a big girl, you know."

"Don't I know it," he grinned. He led the way into the dorm, and then followed Laura as she expertly navigated their way to her room. Third floor, facing a large field bordered by maple trees.

The ferrying of boxes, clothes and odds and ends took about two hours. It wouldn't have been so bad if they didn't have to wait every time for the elevator and if they could have brought the car closer. Get used to it, Charles thought. Four years of this.

When it came time to say good-bye, he held back and let Ellen make her farewell first. She hugged Laura for a long time, and they spoke back and forth even longer. He gave them their privacy and felt glad they had such a solid bond. When it was his turn, he had trouble holding back tears.

"This is it, baby," he said. He hugged her gently. "You're ready for this. You can do it. I know that. But still," he paused to collect himself. "It's still hard."

"I know, Dad. I'll be all right.

"You will," he said. "I know you will. Call me if you need anything. Let me know how things are going." He paused again. "I love you, Laura. Make a good life for yourself here."

"I will, Dad, I love you, too."

With that, he pulled away from her. He held both her hands and gave them a squeeze.

He walked back to Ellen's car with her. The sun was still beating down.

"She's a good girl," he said. "She'll be fine."

"Yes, she is. Reminds me of when I got to college, full of energy and ambition. She's ready."

"Makes me feel old," he said. "She's growing up. That means we are, too."

"I suppose," she said. "I do feel older, but seeing her like this gives me energy, too. In a way, I feel like I'm on this journey with her. I hate losing her, but I'm excited, too."

They walked on in silence for a while.

"You've done a good job with her," Charles said. "You were always a great mother. I want you to know I see that."

"You did all right yourself," Ellen said. "Not all fathers are as involved as you were with her. I always liked the way you could tease her and make her feel loved without putting her on the spot."

"Yeah, it was easy when she was daddy's little girl, but once she got to those terrible teenage years I guess I wasn't cool any more. But we worked it out."

"You did," Ellen said, and they returned to silence.

"So, you're dating someone," she finally said. "Were you planning on telling me?"

"Yes. And yes. It's pretty new. I wasn't planning it. I didn't go looking for her, but one day, she showed up at the dealership and we hit it off." He was staring straight ahead.

"I figured I'd better tell the kids right away. I would have told you the same day, but you weren't home when I picked them up, and the idea of calling you with that news didn't seem right. The next couple of times you either weren't home or were busy, and I didn't do it. I didn't know what to do."

"I know. I was upset when the kids told me, but I realized you have your own life to live. We didn't know how to be married, and now we don't know how to be not married. I guess we muddle through it somehow."

"I guess."

"You look good," he said. "Things must be going well."

"They are. I loved getting Laura ready for college this summer. Donnie's fine. Work is fine. It's overwhelming sometimes, but I like feeling like I'm actually doing something. I make decisions and we get results. I like seeing women coming in, working out, getting fit and feeling better about themselves." Her eyes sparkled.

"Are you seeing anyone?" he asked. He wasn't sure he wanted the answer.

"No, not really," she said. "I've had some offers. I went out for drinks with a couple of guys, but they didn't seem right. I don't know if I'm ready. I'm not worried about it. I'm enjoying having my own life and making my own decisions."

He stopped and looked at her again.

"I never wanted to hurt you, Ellen. I never wanted to disappoint you."

"I know. I was so angry at you. So hurt. I couldn't understand why I wasn't enough for you. I couldn't understand why you had to go somewhere else to get satisfaction. But, eventually, that faded, and I guess . . ." She gazed off in the distance. "I guess I finally realized neither of us was very happy."

"No, I guess we weren't," he said.

Silence.

He reached out for her hand. She took it. He knew the feel of her hand so well.

"I don't know what went wrong. I'm trying to figure it out. I'm trying to figure a lot of things out," he said. "But one thing I know. You're a good woman, Ellen. You always were. You deserve a good life. If I couldn't give that to you, I hope you can find it."

"Thank you," she said. "I've tried to figure it out, too. I'm glad you're doing better. For so long you looked broken down, and I worried about you all alone. I don't know how you managed."

"It was hard." He said. "A lot of it is still hard. But it's working out." He squeezed her hand. He felt awkward sharing this moment with her.

"Well, let's check out that radiator," he said, and the two of them continued walking.

****

Charles was in the midst of his morning start-up at the office. This time, however, he had trouble focusing on the newspaper. Harry was acting nervous again, running around, grumbling, moving the displays slightly, complaining to Tricia about everything, including the "bullshit goddam weather," that would keep customers away. Tricia mostly tried to ignore him, but when she had to, she'd answer in simple, short sentences, with a lilt to her voice and, Charles imagined, a smile on her face that must be driving Harry crazy.

He put down the paper and picked up a magazine. He still wasn't able to focus, but at least he could read captions and short sidebar articles. It had more variety of coverage. Color. As he was turning a page, he stopped.

A full page vodka ad leaped at him. On it, a tall woman was featured in an elegant evening dress, black, with plunging neckline and a slit way up her thigh. She was focusing on a man whose back was to the camera, facing out a window at a night city skyline. Her attention was clearly on him. She was handing him a martini. Everything about her seemed sexual; clearly, she was offering much more than a drink, and she seemed completely submissive, like she'd do anything he asked. The thin slice of revealed thigh, the shadow of her cleavage, more hinting than revealing, the expression on her face, were all sexually charged. It was a classic "sex sells" ad. But what caught Charles' attention was her skin. Her skin had been digitally altered so as to render it completely textureless, completely clear, so smooth and glistening that it was more like plastic than skin. This woman was being offered as appealing because she wasn't real. She was like a life-size doll, but definitely, completely, suggestively, anatomically correct.

He quickly thumbed through the magazine, and sure enough, the women in most ads looked preternaturally young and perfect. There were exceptions: ads for hormone replacement therapy and investment firms, ads clearly aimed at a more mature audience. But most ads presented doll women. He had never noticed before.

Harry was bristling again. Charles heard him bark something at Tricia and slam his office door. He figured she could use some positive interaction and walked over to her area.

"He's in rare form today, isn't he?"

She glanced up from her monitor. "I wish it were rare," she said. "He's been nasty for a week or so. A change from his usual, irritating self."

"He's always been a pill, Trish. He'll get over it." She swiveled her chair around to face him.

"How's Laura doing?"

"Got a call from her last night. She's fine."

"She sounds like a good kid. If anything goes wrong, you're not far away. You can still take care of her."

"I suppose."

"Kids sure do put you through the wringer, don't they?"

"How's your girl?" he asked.

"Don't start," she said. "Teenagers. God created teenagers to make parents willing to let go."

"Wish it worked that well."

"Well, you got a good one. Darla's a handful. If it weren't for my hair salon I'd be all gray."

"They do get over it, Trish."

"Yeah, but will I?"

"Hang on. She's good practice for dealing with Harry. Don't let him upset you. His bluster is all about him, it's not about you. He'd be doing it whether you were here or not."

"I know. I let him blow. It all passes by."

"Way to go. Well, I suppose I ought to actually do some work." Charles went to the break room, poured a new cup of coffee, and returned to his desk.

Soon, a woman came in to look at a mid-sized car. She was in her thirties and dressed in casual business clothes. She said she was in real estate and needed a car suitable for her clients.

"My old Honda's not big enough," she said. "And it's getting a little ratty. I need something nice that's comfortable for two adults to ride in, but not too big or fancy. I don't want them to think I'm getting rich on their commissions. Not that I am," she added.

"Don't I know it," he said, feeling on familiar territory. "Needs to give the impression you're successful enough to know what you're doing but not too successful. Has to be big enough to be comfortable, but not showy. If they could make a Lincoln Town Car look smaller and more ordinary, it'd be perfect, right?"

"Exactly." She seemed relieved that he knew what she wanted. It was a tough bill to fill, but he had a couple of possibilities for her. As they were talking and walking around the various cars, he was able to learn more about her. She was clearly doing well, but apparently new enough to the business to be unsure of herself. She was probably around Janelle's age, mid to late thirties, trim, and stylishly dressed. Again, nice and proper, but not too showy, carefully trying to avoid giving the appearance that she made too much money. Her face moved gracefully as she examined the cars and responded to his playful chatter. It was like watching a musician playing a finely tuned violin, as enjoyable as the music itself. Her conclusions and questions were sharp and focused, and they made Charles think about his answers. She had a warm smile and provocative eyes. Her very manner invited you to want to know her better. Her body seemed fit and able, healthy and relaxed. She's at ease with her body, and that's rare, he thought. Yes, she invited attention. She was attractive in the best sense of the word; she attracted you to her. Charles felt that attraction.

What he didn't feel, he noticed as she slid behind the wheel of a sleek, steel-grey convertible, was desire. When he saw her legs revealed, he was struck by the fact that although he was definitely noticing her, he felt nothing sexual. He simply liked her and liked talking with her. He'd like to go on talking with her. He'd enjoy knowing her better. And that was it. All the old patterns that used to play in his head, the ones that judged appearance and marked the results on a scale of desirability were gone. He was truly seeing her, and he liked her, and he liked himself better for being able to see her that way.

She liked the convertible. It was large enough and respectable enough for her clients, but she liked the idea she could let the top down and feel young and adventurous when the mood struck her. She said she had one other place she was going to check out before committing, but Charles was sure she was hooked. She needed to feel like she'd done her shopping and been careful. More so, he could see she enjoyed talking to him and trusted him.

It seemed that she responded well to being taken seriously. All these years I'd been thinking I knew how to handle women, he thought, and it turns out the best way to handle them is not to handle them.

****

That evening, Janelle was busy, so Charles was on his own. He thought he needed some time to think, so he picked up a sandwich and some fruit and drove to a small overlook park to eat and watch the sun set.

For one thing, he realized, even doing this was a huge change. Six months ago, he would have been home, eating pizza, idly watching TV, waiting to be tired enough to go to bed. He didn't care enough to make or buy food he enjoyed. Now, he saw meals as an opportunity. He was tasting food as he hadn't in many years, going back even before the raid.

He also enjoyed having some time alone. Six months ago, time alone was the enemy. That's when his thoughts turned on him, replaying scenes with the kids to remind them how much he missed them. Now, his mind was clear and dealt more with the future than the past.

He sat down at one of the picnic tables, then got up and settled under a large maple tree. Its leaves rustled quietly in the breeze, and he could hear an oriole scolding somewhere above. He could see the valley stretching below him, houses looking small and serene. Cars seemed like miniatures on an elaborate movie set. He could see the river winding its way toward the horizon.

After the woman with the convertible had left, he had spent the rest of the day in wonder. Every time customers came in, when he went to the corner for lunch, afterward as he picked up his supper and drove to the park, he was noticing the women. A curious glance, an intent focus, a casual, yet solid walk, a tone of voice. Every woman he met seemed to have something intriguing about her.

He was in love, he thought. But that wasn't all of it. The thought that a fifty-year-old woman could be childlike in the way she answered a question had never occurred to him. That an overweight woman could have an engaging smile had been lost on him. That an interesting comment could invite further conversation was new. He quietly went over a list of encounters during the day.

There was the waitress who plainly took an extra moment to make sure she got his order right, who looked right at him and listened to the details. The bank teller who complimented him on his tie. The customer who was worried about gas mileage in an SUV because she didn't want to be hurting the earth. He enjoyed the fact that her whole body relaxed and her voice softened when he told her she could get four-wheel drive in an ordinary size sedan. He enjoyed that she was so careful about her choices and her values. He felt like he gotten to know her that afternoon.

He thought back to his succession of women when he was young. Why was it he always got bored after a few months at most? At the time, he didn't think much about it. His only concern was how to get from one woman to the next with the least trouble.

No wonder he lost interest. He'd never had any real interest to begin with. So what was there to lose? That was probably why he never got too upset when a girl broke up with him. Nothing to lose. Nothing to begin with.

And that's what was different about Janelle. She was the most engaging person he knew. She wore her interests and her ideas on her sleeve for anyone to see. She did whatever she did with passion. She spoke with conviction, and he liked her ideas. Even if things didn't work out between them, he was glad he'd met someone like her. It was good to know people like her existed in the world.

He stared at the river for quite a while. The sun was beginning its final descent to the horizon, and the light was turning golden. Delicate shimmers danced across the river's surface, making it seem almost gilded, polished, and cherished.

Its lazy motion suggested life, always moving forward, through tragedy, success, loss and attainment. Every place on the river was different. Here it moved quickly, here slowly. Here it was smooth and unbroken. Here, the golden swirls and vortexes revealed the presence of rocks under the surface. He watched it for a long time. It soothed him.

Gradually, he became aware of something else. He was watching the river double back on itself, one great serpentine loop reaching back along its length, for quite a while flowing opposite itself before recurving again on its inexorable path to the sea. He was struck by that formation. How could it reverse direction while still flowing the same way? Moreover, how could he have never noticed before? He'd been watching it over an hour and not noticed. He'd been here with Janelle several times and not noticed, yet it had been right in front of him.

The river reversed direction, and yet it moved on, different, yet the same.

The current wound on, the waves and eddies swirled, the sun played down on them, and Charles felt like he was swept up in fresh waters taking him slowly to a future beyond his view.

Chapter 8

THE FIRST hints of fall were in the air, so Janelle and Charles were relishing the last summer warmth before she was swamped with work at school. They'd gone to a small open-air café where they shared an interesting bottle of cabernet and a seared salmon salad. An incredibly flakey Napoleon pastry finished off the meal, and they'd taken a walk to help digest. Janelle was wearing a lacy top over a shimmery camisole, and the effect was stunning. Charles felt alive and drank up every word she spoke and savored every touch of her hand.

They went back to her place, and soon they were in bed. Janelle was on top of him, teasing him with her tongue and playing her silky hair against his skin. He caressed her and kept trying to roll her over so he could tease her in turn, but she kept pushing him down, playfully, but forcefully.

His eyes were closed, and he was totally wrapped up in the sensations of her body surrounding his. They soon found a gentle, rolling rhythm, and he got lost in it. After a while, he opened his eyes and found she was turned slightly away. He was holding her close to him, enjoying her weight on his frame, but her eyes were averted. He loosened his hold on her, and she arched her back, bringing her head directly over him, her expression strangely . . . vacant. Her body was still moving rhythmically, and he noticed it was exactly in tune with his movement. He shifted himself and slowed, and she was right with him, her expression unchanging, still strangely passive.

When they were finished, and after they'd lain together for a while, the image of her expression returned.

"Janelle?" he finally said.

"Yes?"

"Was that all right?"

"That was great. Wasn't it for you?" She sounded concerned.

"You know you always thrill me." He paused. "But, you seemed, I don't know, a little off."

She straightened under his arm.

"Off?"

"Like you weren't enjoying yourself."

She stiffened. This is it, she thought.

"No, don't worry about it. I'm fine."

He was quiet for a while.

"Are you sure? One time, I looked up, and you seemed like you were somewhere else."

"Oh, that was me with you, the whole time. Couldn't you feel me?" She wiggled her bottom to emphasize the point.

"Oh, I sure could. All over. But, you're all right?"

She wanted a way out of this.

"You sure seemed to be enjoying yourself," she said. "That's all that matters. It took you five minutes to get your breathing back to normal."

"At least. Sometimes I wonder if I'll ever recover."

"See? It's all fine." She pressed her bottom against him.

"But still. You're sure?"

She rolled over and propped herself up on one elbow. She ran a fingertip up and down his chest, leaning against him.

"You're a great lover."

"But . . ."

"No buts. Don't worry about me. I'm totally happy. This is all I could ask for." She kissed him.

He let her kiss him, but pulled away quickly and sat up.

"You didn't seem to be enjoying it when I was inside you."

"I love giving you pleasure. I love making love with you. I love the intimacy, and I love the way you touch me. You're so attentive and so gentle. But, when you get right down to it, the actual thing, the sex part, I don't get too turned on by it. It's how I am, I guess."

He looked crestfallen. She knelt beside him.

"Really, Charles, it's not you. I've always been that way. I love the intimacy, the passion. I love it. I can't tell you how much. The foreplay thrills me, but, for me, it's not foreplay, it's what I enjoy."

"You don't like having me inside you?"

"It's not that I don't like it, but it's more the intimacy than the sensation. Don't worry. I love making love with you."

"Janelle, I feel awful that I never noticed before. Why didn't you tell me? I'll do whatever you need to make you feel satisfied. I just never . . . You get me going so hot and heavy, I don't notice anything except how good you make me feel. I'm sorry, sweetheart." He still seemed bothered. That wasn't all of it, she knew. He was worried that he wasn't a good lover. He was feeling inadequate.

"Don't worry about it. I sort of plan it that way. I try hard to satisfy you so you won't notice. I don't need orgasms. It's not a big deal. Sometimes, I think I'd be as happy snuggling and cuddling instead of making love. That's the part I like. I'm always afraid I'll be a disappointment if we make love."

Janelle knew he was confused. She searched his face for signs.

"That's why you were so understanding when I couldn't," he said. "In a way, it was a relief for you."

"Yes," she said gently. "But that's not all of it. I was happy to be with you. To know you wanted me."

"But glad you didn't actually have to go through with it." He turned away from her. She could see the tension running through him, even in his back. His muscles were tight.

"It's not like that, baby. I never 'go through with it.' I always like it. Just not in the way you probably think. I like giving you pleasure, I like seeing the look of love in your eyes. I like feeling your touch. You're so tender. You touch me like you love me."

"I do love you."

"I know. It shows. This has nothing to do with that. It's me. It's the way I am. I'm not a whole woman somehow. But I'm at peace with that, and I love making love with you. Don't let it bother you."

But it did. She could see it. And, to be honest, it bothered her, too. She wanted to enjoy it. She wanted to feel like a whole woman. But it wasn't going to happen. And now he knew.

"Baby?" he said.

"Yes?"

"Hold me." He turned toward her and reached for her. She melted into his arms. He held her tenderly, yet firmly, and she rejoiced in the feel of it. He had turned toward her. He still wanted her. She might not lose him. She might be good enough.

They were silent for a long while. He lay down, and took her with him. She lay curled against him, her head on his chest.

He still wants me, she thought. We got over this.

At least he never asked me why.

****

September arrived.

Janelle's life revolved around the young lives under her care. As a special projects director, she was involved with more students than any of the regular teachers, working with kids on art projects, community projects, research projects, and most of all, as with every fall, Charles learned, Shakespeare.

A hallmark of her school was that the fifth graders, the highest grade in their academic world, put on an annual production of a Shakespearean play. When she'd first told him about it, Charles had inwardly groaned. He immediately began hoping the performance would conflict with some unavoidable event at work so he could be spared the agony.

One of the teachers made a summer project of adapting a play every year. She would whittle out some of the subplots, simplify the main issues, and pare down the key speeches to their essence. The language of the play would still be Shakespeare's, but the play would take barely an hour, the speeches would be shorter, the ideas simpler, and the kids understood. This year they were doing *Macbeth*, and as Janelle talked about the project and described the kids working on it, he was drawn in. Soon, he was involved in set construction.

One day, as he was diligently painting flats in the background, he heard the kids working on their lines and talking about the scene, and he was amazed.

"How could he make the ocean red? That's nuts."

A girl's voice answered him. "He's not saying his hands will make the ocean red, he's saying he feels like if he washed his hands in the ocean, the blood on his hands would turn the whole ocean red. He knows it won't, he's saying how guilty he feels. Like how afraid you are about what'll happen if you fart. Except, you might be right. I've smelled your farts."

"Oh," the boy said. "Why didn't you say so in the first place?"

The girl was about ready to push his face in. What amazed Charles was hearing two ten-year-olds arguing about Shakespeare. He had to admit, this project had something going for it.

Janelle had explained to him that they started the project by telling some similar stories that the kids might relate to. In this case, they started with a powerful warlock and what would happen if someone tried to kill him to take over. Over a week or so, they acquainted the kids with the realities of medieval kingdoms. This was part of their history program, but it was all in service of eventually staging the play. They saw pictures of Scottish castles and read the basic story of the real Macbeth. Finally, the teachers told them how the play went and they talked about why each person would do what they did. Then, they were ready to start reading. The kids wrestled with the language and the teachers kept at it till the kids understood what was going on. Every kid was involved. Even kids who weren't going to be on stage were creating costumes, props and lighting, so they had to understand it all. Every scene had its own director, and every kid had to serve as a director for at least one scene. The kids' English, history and science classes were all tied in to the play.

"Science?" Charles asked.

"The play has a lot of references to animal behavior and weather and such. The kids have to know what they mean."

Charles liked seeing the kids grapple with their lines and with each other. He had never dreamed they could take on so much responsibility and be so mature. His respect for Janelle grew and grew.

Their relationship was growing well, too. After that first discussion, their lovemaking changed. They were taking it more slowly, more carefully.

Janelle trusted that she didn't have to be an amazing lover for Charles to remain interested, and so she stopped working so hard to drive him wild with passion. Knowing she enjoyed the connection and touching of foreplay, Charles learned to savor simple touches and kisses. She learned to allow him to. One time, he simply kissed and kissed her belly. At first, she didn't feel much, but gradually, her skin sensitized, and soon she was writhing with delight. When he tried to move on to her breasts, she pushed his head back down so she could enjoy the new sensations even longer. She, in turn, paid attention to his body in ways she'd never explored before. She kissed his hand and teased the softer, inner flesh of his forearms with her hair. They held each other and kissed each other endlessly, and making love was no longer about working him up to a fever pitch and climaxing. It became more of a celebration of their physical selves. They reveled in being.

****

Life went well.

Laura was adapting beautifully to college. She sounded pleased with herself whenever Charles saw her. Everywhere they went, people would say hello as they passed, and Charles was glad she had so many friends. She liked almost all her classes, and was managing to tolerate her dull Introduction to Psychology course. She said it was too basic and too theoretical, and the teacher was scarcely interested himself. But, she was doing well on tests, so she wasn't too upset.

Donnie was developing into a first rate high school jock. He was leading the school team in goals scored, and he occasionally had Saturday matches, so Charles got to see him play from time to time. The boy was getting good. He was team captain and could probably count on a scholarship somewhere.

With Laura away in college, Charles saw only one of them each week. They alternated evenly, unless specific events required a change. Sometimes he managed to watch Donnie play on Saturday and meet with Laura on Sunday. By November, both had met Janelle, and both liked her. After some initial awkwardness, Janelle's engaging personality and humor won them both over. They no longer saw her as an amorphous threat to their mother or themselves, but as a warm-hearted woman who was clearly good for their father.

Shakespeare was flourishing in the Cumberland Valley Primary School. Charles helped craft armor, swords, stone walls, and tin foil covered "silver" drinking goblets. Janelle was always busy helping kids with lines and fleshing out their characters. It was a huge project. It still tickled Charles to hear kids arguing about why Macbeth had to repeat himself and couldn't just say "tomorrow," or which ingredient of the witches' broth was ickiest. He had fun finding rubber frogs and newts and other props.

He and Janelle were inseparable, so far as schedules permitted. Even on some days when one or the other was exhausted from work and unable to do much more than collapse on the coach, eat and go to bed, the other would provide supper and a tender massage.

They had become fond of massage. Janelle had told Charles how she depended on it to stay grounded. Once in a while she would treat herself at a local spa, and it was one of the chief pleasures of her life. She loved being able to relax and allow someone to work out all the tensions from her muscles. It felt luxuriously self-indulgent, but she also noticed she was better able to face the stresses of daily life afterward. She said if she could afford one every other day she'd be a new woman. After she goaded Charles for a while, they arranged for a couples massage one day at her spa. Charles felt reluctant. The whole idea felt foolish to him; he didn't see the point, and he felt odd about having another woman touching him. He finally agreed, and afterward he felt completely relaxed. He and Janelle drove to a nearby park and lay on the grass for a while, silently watching clouds drift by. Then, they enjoyed salads and tea at an outdoor café. At home, they made love and then slept till evening.

Soon, they were massaging one another regularly. Janelle found some books on bodywork, and they practiced basic techniques. They learned to identify the hard masses that held physical tension and gently work each one out until the knot released and became normal soft tissue. Charles was amazed at how hard the nodules could become. Sometimes they were sensitive, and it was hard for him to inflict pain on Janelle, but they both knew the final result would be worth the brief discomfort, and he learned to press on. Janelle's massages were equally good for him. His knots, though larger and harder, tended to release more easily and were rarely as painful.

Charles was surprised by the fact that he quickly learned to spend an hour or more massaging Janelle's naked body without getting aroused. At first, more than one session was cut short by a powerful passionate urge. But after a month or so, and especially after noticing how therapeutic and important the massages were, he found himself able to simply lose himself in the gentle rhythms of working out Janelle's tension, giving himself over to the soothing music they played and enjoying the intimacy of being in such close contact with her. Gently kneading the soft tissue of her body and discovering its range of shapes and textures, he found delight in tracing her muscles and feeling their shape beneath his hands.

He soon became more intimately aware of her body than he ever had while making love, and he learned the joy of giving. In fact, as he gave more and more of himself, he discovered he was receiving a gift just as valuable: a genuine selflessness that made him feel more connected to Janelle than he had ever felt with any other woman. More than once, he mused that if for some reason he could never make love with her again, he could still feel that same intimacy through massage and touch.

One day, while working on Janelle, she seemed to relax more deeply than usual. While working on her inner thigh, he came across a particularly hard and painful knot. He was trying to work it out gently, but still, it was painful. Suddenly, she shouted, as if in terror, "No! No!" and broke into tears. He immediately took her in his arms and held her, quietly rocking her. "It's okay, it's okay," he kept saying, utterly confused.

Gradually, she calmed down. She stayed cuddled up in his arms.

"I don't know what that was," she said. "It just came out. I had this flash of fear, and I was shouting out to protect myself. I don't know why." He held her.

"Are you all right?" he asked.

"I think so. The fear is gone." She spoke quietly. "Maybe we should try going back to working out that knot and see what happens."

"Are you sure?"

"No, but let's try." She lay back down again, spreading herself on the padded mat. He carefully went back to working on the spot. At first he rubbed gently around the area, then located the hard lump again and began kneading it.

She tensed up. He could hear her breathing tighten.

"You all right?" he asked.

"Yes, go ahead," she answered, her voice thin and controlled.

He heard her gasp a few times, but eventually the knot softened and he could feel her tissue was back to normal.

"How was that?" he asked.

"The fear was back," she said. "Gut-level, animal fear. I don't know of what. And rage. It was like I was reacting to something happening right now. I don't know what was going on." She had turned partially toward him.

"What do you want to do?"

"Go on, let's finish up. Let's see what happens."

Nothing happened. The rest of the massage was peaceful. They were both concerned, however.

It happened again the next time. In a different spot, but the same sort of sudden, inexplicable response. Janelle didn't know what had come over her. It was an intense flood of emotion, as clear and powerful as if she were being attacked by a tiger. Except for the rage. She plainly felt rage. She had no idea what was happening.

Both times, it was as if she was taken over by some outside being that filled her with simultaneous feelings of fear and rage. She couldn't explain it. That it happened during massage confused her. She had come to see massages as precious time when she could forget the outside world and all its demands. She found herself feeling her body more and more fully. The sensations of Charles' hands on her were getting more and more tangible, and she trusted him. She allowed herself to feel fully whatever he was doing. For that trust and confidence to morph into pain, fear, and rage bothered her. What was happening?

They hadn't made love either night. They were both too distraught.

That Friday, they went out for fajitas and beer. It was a simple end-of-the-week celebration. The school week was over, and it was one of the Saturdays when he didn't need to work either. The meal was simple, but pleasing, just what they needed. They indulged in dessert, sinfully delightful margarita cheesecake.

After the meal, they needed to walk and work off some calories, so they strolled around town, looking in shop windows, going in and browsing at a couple of places. The air was cold, so they welcomed the warmth of a small gourmet kitchen store and a gift shop.

When they got home, they rushed through the cool air to the warmth of her apartment. They selected a movie and settled into the couch. Janelle snuggled up against Charles, and they relaxed. He gently stroked her arm and enjoyed the feel of her hair against his face. After a while, they kissed. And again. She squirmed around to face him and they kissed deeply and long. In a moment, they were in the bedroom, Janelle teasing Charles with her tongue on his chest, both growing more and more eager. He was too excited to wait, it had been too many days, so soon he was on top of her and guiding himself in. He had just penetrated when she let out a sharp cry, screamed, "No!" and pushed him off her. He was afraid he'd hurt her in his haste and quickly rolled to the side, seeing her curled up in a ball, shaking.

"Janelle, what is it? Did I hurt you?"

"No, no, please no," she was saying quietly, rocking slightly back and forth.

"Janelle, come here, baby, what is it?" he tried to pry her arms off her knees, and she struck out blindly at him.

"What is it? What happened?"

She melted into him, again curling up, head in his lap. She was crying.

He let her cry. He held her and stroked her arm. She felt hot and damp on him, her body burning with intensity.

Gradually, she calmed down and stopped crying.

"It wasn't you."

"Thank god, but what was it? What's going on?"

"I don't know." Her body shuddered with each breath. "You're not disappointed?"

"I'm sure not thrilled," he said, "but I'm not disappointed."

He held her, and eventually she calmed down. They lay together for quite a while, lost in their thoughts.

Janelle was afraid. *What's he going to think? Who would want to sleep with a woman who screams when he makes love with her? God. What's he thinking? I can't stand this. I can't even control my own body. What's he thinking?*

Eventually, they fell asleep.

****

They spent Saturday morning being studiously nice to one another.

Charles made omelets, and Janelle made blueberry muffins. They had a leisurely breakfast, then went for a walk. They talked pleasantly about their weeks and what lay ahead. They had the whole day to themselves and decided they'd go back to their original pizza restaurant, the one where they'd eaten after Charles had pitched in at the school fair, and afterward to a movie. They shopped for some new towels. Janelle said she absolutely couldn't continue using the ratty old ones he'd taken with him from his house when he moved out. She said they were so worn out it was like trying to dry yourself off with a handkerchief, and they made her feel dirtier than before she'd washed. They found some plush, cotton towels, thick and rich, and Charles admitted she was right.

They went home, and when Janelle asked what they should do till dinner time, Charles responded with a strong, full body hug. He ran his hand down her back and began caressing her bottom, pulling her toward him. His awakened desires ran deep these days. Janelle responded by kissing his neck and melding her body into his. Soon, they were on the living room floor, cushioned by its deeply piled rug, and Janelle was using her mouth to excite him further. She straddled him and began to guide him inside her when her face suddenly contorted, and she let out a single cry.

"Eep!"

It sounded strange. Her face was still contorted, like she was enduring great pain, but still, she lowered herself onto him.

The sight of her pain drove all desire out of him. He struggled to sit up and hold her.

"Janelle, baby,"

"I'm sorry. I tried."

"No, I don't want you to be hurt."

She curled up against him, hiding her face.

He's going to leave me, she thought. How much more can we do this? I can't stop it. I can't. At least I could pretend to have a good time before, I could be pretty convincing, but this hurts. Oh god, it hurts.

Finally, she calmed down. She could feel her body relaxing. He was still holding her, stroking her back gently. She felt her strength returning. She opened herself up and turned to him. She pushed him down on his back and stroked his chest. She gazed deeply into his eyes and smiled.

She bent down and started kissing his chest, using her tongue to tease him, running down his sternum till she reached the softer region of his belly. She reached out with one hand to stroke his penis.

"No, baby, no."

He began to get up. She pushed him back down without stopping and moved her tongue further downward.

"No, I mean it."

He gathered himself to sit, more forcefully this time.

"Please, Charles, let me."

"No."

"But I don't want to disappoint you."

"Sweetheart, the last thing on my mind right now is being disappointed. I'm worried about you. I don't know what's happening."

"I don't either, but that's no reason you should have to go without."

"No. We need to work this out."

"How?"

"I don't know," Charles said. "We need to do something to take care of you. I'm afraid to try massage. I'm afraid to touch you. I'm afraid of what it'll do to you."

She nodded.

"How about a long, warm bath? Would that help you feel better?"

"I don't know."

"Let's try it. Come on, I'll get it started for you."

He went to the bathroom and turned on the water. He found some bath salts and added them, swirling the pink powder in the tub. She clearly needed nurturing, and he didn't know what else to do. When the water reached about eight inches, he shut it off and went back to the living room.

Janelle was balled up at one end of the couch, wrapped in a throw blanket. He knelt beside her and kissed her forehead. She attempted a smile.

"Come on, baby. It's all ready." As he helped her up, he noticed the candles on the coffee table. He walked arm in arm with her to the tub and steadied her as she got in. Then he went back to the living room, brought in the two candles, arranged them in the bathroom and lit them.

"Would you like me to stay?"

"No, I think I'll drift away better if I'm alone," she said.

"Sure thing. I love you." He kissed her forehead again and went out.

In the living room, he sat staring out the window. What was this all about? What was causing all this pain? Why were massages suddenly dangerous and sex a mine field? He had no idea what to think or do.

Janelle, meanwhile, allowed her body to respond to the warm bubbly bath. The water felt familiar and reassuring. She felt her muscles relax. Her mind, however, was as tight as ever. This is it, she thought. Once is a fluke. Twice is a pattern. What will he think? Why is my body turning against me? She felt her abdomen tighten. Why can't I have some peace?

****

They didn't try to make love again that day. Once Janelle got out of the bath, she said she felt tired and went in to take a nap. Charles watched some TV, but soon fell asleep on the sofa.

When suppertime came around, without speaking of it, they both concluded their pizza restaurant was not the place to go and ended up in a small steakhouse instead. They ate quietly, then went to a movie. Janelle leaned against Charles the whole time. He enjoyed her warmth.

When they got home, they went to bed. Charles noted that she came to bed in flannel pajamas instead of her usual thin nightgown. She snuggled against him, and he admitted he preferred even this to being alone, but he had some trouble getting to sleep.

The next week crawled by. Charles had three nights scheduled at work. Janelle had a meeting one of the other nights and rehearsals the remaining one, so they contented themselves with talking on the phone.

Charles noticed himself being curt with customers that week, and he had no patience at all for Harry.

One day, when Harry came in to talk about the Monday night football game, Charles let him blather for a while, then said he didn't care and that Harry should go bother someone else.

Harry let out a few choice expletives and wandered off, blustering the whole way. Soon, Charles heard him haranguing Brian and felt relieved to be off the hook.

What was he going to do about this? What was wrong with Janelle? It was like her body was turning against him. He thought longingly of when her body seemed like a living, breathing invitation. Now, she was a danger zone. Who knew what was going to happen next? What if he was damaging her in some way and she wasn't telling him? Imagine having to call an ambulance sometime and explaining that one. No, sir, officer, I didn't attack her. She wanted me. She just started bleeding all of a sudden.

Something was wrong. They had to figure it out.

He didn't know where to turn.

****

Janelle was retching.

She was in the bathroom, her body racked with spasm after spasm, long after she had expelled everything in her stomach. Still, she retched, and Charles could hear the pain she was enduring as her muscles tightened and tightened.

He felt helpless. All he could do was kneel beside her and try to keep her hair out of the mess. Her body was burning hot, her face reddened. She was heaving uncontrollably.

Finally, she leaned back from the toilet bowl and rested against him, crying. Tears streamed down her already wet face, mingling with the sweat. He reached out for a hand towel and tried to pat her dry. She pushed his hand away.

After a moment, she struggled to her feet. She seemed weak. He supported her as she tried to wash her face. Her hair was stringy with sweat and soapy water, her eye bloodshot and puffy. Finally, she reached out silently for a towel, and Charles handed her one. They hobbled back to bed. Janelle lay down, curled up in fetal position, spent. Charles sat next to her, one hand on her shoulder.

It was a week later. They had enjoyed their Saturday afternoon. The local history museum had a new exhibit of medieval art, armament and crafts, and Janelle was thinking of taking the kids to see it on a field trip. Charles wasn't much of a museum person, but he had gotten so wrapped up in the Shakespeare project that he actually found many of the exhibits fascinating. They spent a long time looking at the clothing, and he made a few quick sketches to refine the knife designs they were using to make props. They had a light lunch in the museum's café, then spent the afternoon reading and napping in the park. Leaves were quickly changing on all the trees, and they enjoyed spotting the variety. Charles had always seen fall as a sad time, because it meant the onset of winter, but this time, he was enjoying it. Each change, in the leaves, the shortening days, the feel of the air, thrilled him. He was wrapped up in the details of change.

They managed to forget the previous week's turmoil and had a great day. Dinner was at a family-run Italian place, small and bustling, noisier than he would prefer, but a friendly bustle. People were enjoying themselves. When they had trouble choosing their dinners, the waitress asked them a few questions and quickly recommended a baked ziti dish that sounded mundane but offered a zesty variety of flavors. They drank an earthy Chianti and had a great time imagining they were in Italy in the Renaissance, soaking up the best of that nascent European culture.

They went to a movie afterward, and once again, Charles felt like he was a teenager out with his best girl. Janelle wore a trim dress that showed off her body gracefully and tastefully. The fabric felt soft and inviting when Charles placed his hand on her thigh, and she held his hand in hers tenderly.

When they arrived home, Janelle gave him a big kiss and wrapped her arms around him. He lingered in the feel of her embrace, noting and cherishing every point of contact, feeling her body through his, her foot, her thigh, her belly, her cheek, her hair. Soon, he was excited, and when Janelle took him by the hand and led him to the bedroom, he did not resist. His fears were washed away by his passion.

She must be okay, he thought. She obviously wants this.

Then, after delicious fondling that roused his excitement even further, she lay back and pulled him on top of her. He carefully guided himself inside and felt the first warm rush of pleasure.

Janelle shrieked.

She positively shrieked, short, but loud, and she was scrambling, pushing him off her, and rushing into the bathroom, making odd guttural sounds and violently throwing up into the toilet.

Once again, Charles was befuddled. Her whole body was convulsing with every effort, and he felt like he'd ruined her, he'd destroyed this precious woman.

He knelt beside her. He tried to do what he could for her. After a while, they were back in bed, Janelle facing away from him, and Charles, physically excluded from her world, feeling lost and helpless.

"What was it, baby? What was going on?"

She didn't answer for a long time. She stayed curled up against him in fetal position, face covered by her hair.

He asked her several more times. Each time, she was silent.

Eventually, she began to speak.

"I never had anything like that happen before. It wasn't you."

"Thank god; I didn't think so. But what was it?"

"I never had to throw up like that. It's, well, I suddenly saw something. Something I'd tried to forget."

"You saw something? What? What do you mean you saw something?"

She was silent again. She twisted around for a moment, so her face was even farther from him.

"I know why I had those reactions during the massage. I know what happened. It's the same thing tonight, but worse. Those times, I had the feelings and didn't know what they were. This time, I had a flash of memory. I know what it was." She was having trouble speaking. "I don't know why it's happening now, though. It has nothing to do with you."

"What is it?"

Her voice sounded contorted. She was fighting back tears.

"I never told you why," she paused, "why I don't like sex so much. I guess I'd better do that."

154

Charles was quiet. He could see this was hard for her. He didn't want to make it harder.

"It was a long time ago. I've tried to put it out of my mind for so long. I thought I had. I don't think about it anymore. So much else has happened. I have a whole new life. And I have you. I thought it had nothing to do with me now, but I guess it does. It's not gone. I guess the past is never gone."

She went silent again, collecting her thoughts.

Then, she began to tell her story.

Chapter 9

"I'VE TOLD you about my brother," she said. "I told you he's a computer genius and lives on his own, mostly with his computers and games. His only friends are fellow gamers. But that's not all of it.

"Buddy's a little different." She paused again, and Charles settled in to listen. He could see this wasn't going to be a simple story.

Even though Buddy was a year older than she was, she had always felt like his big sister. He had a mild form of autism, so mild many people didn't even notice at first. He didn't quite look you in the eye, and he always seemed tilted away slightly, like he wasn't really paying attention. He could talk with people pretty easily for a few moments, then he'd bog down and lose the drift of the conversation. A lot of people assumed he was mildly retarded until they heard him talking about any of the topics that interested him: computers, baseball, and tall ships. Suddenly, they'd think he was a genius and absentminded or something. Neither assessment was true. The fact was that he was never completely comfortable around other people and didn't see things the way they did. His world was different from other people's worlds and ran alongside it, a step or so out of kilter.

Buddy was intuitive with computers and could figure out software and hardware glitches quickly and easily. They were interesting puzzles to him. So he'd gone to a technical school and quickly found a job with a major software manufacturer working on its helplines. He didn't get impatient with customers because his autism kept him from tuning into their frustrations.

They could rant and rave and complain, and he'd wait for them to cool off, and he'd go into his diagnostic mode and calmly guide them into figuring out what was happening. After a few days of practice, he was good at it. In a few weeks, great, and after a few months, he was the best they had. He had his own apartment filled with a big screen TV, a computer center, and a corner devoted to making models of tall ships. He used a bus to get to and from work, had a number of online friends, and he was happy. Buddy had done well for himself.

"I really love him," Janelle said. He's such a special man. It's like he lives in a happy world untouched by the social nonsense most of us have to deal with. He's always busy with his games and his models. You'd think he'd be lonely, but that's only because of our expectations. He's fine."

She went on.

In his younger years, though, things hadn't gone so well for Buddy. He was functional enough that he spent most of his school day in a regular classroom. Outside class, at recess, or before school, when things were less structured, it wasn't so easy. There was always someone who thought he was weird and wanted to pick a fight. Janelle quickly assumed the role of being his protector. Soon, no one picked on Buddy while she was around, and if she wasn't around and she heard about it, she'd confront the perpetrator the moment school let out. She wasn't big, but she was fearless, and the way she'd find out unerringly who the creep was and where he'd be right after school was uncanny. She'd find him and tell him off so pointedly and determinedly that few ever harassed Buddy again.

The most nerve-wracking year of her young life was when he moved on to high school while she was still in middle school. Suddenly, she couldn't protect him, and she worried. The school officials were great; they made sure his day was well-structured and safe, and even between classes and after school, not much went on that bothered him. He kept to himself, and when what few incidents did take place got back to her, she still managed to track people down and set them straight.

The next year, when she started high school, Janelle was relieved for her brother, but nervous for herself. She worried about her clothes and her hair, gossiped with her friends about boys, went to soccer practice and tried hard to impress the older players. She was a typical ninth grader. All was well.

Then, about a month into the year, things got even better. One day, while chatting with her friends at lunch, she saw a couple of the older guys from the football team talking to Buddy. She immediately felt herself switch into vigilance mode to keep an eye on them while still maintaining her own conversation. Buddy was smiling. The football players were smiling. Soon they were laughing, and Buddy was laughing with them! She looked even closer, and she was sure they were all laughing together; the older boys weren't being mean.

"Who are those guys talking to Buddy?" she asked. Kelsey turned around to see, and when she turned back to answer, her eyes gleamed.

"That's Steve Braun and Mike Dominick," she said, "two of the biggest hunks on the team! Don't you know who they are?"

"No, I guess not. I've only seen them with their helmets on. What are they, seniors?"

"No, juniors. We get to drool over them two whole years. They're so hot."

"Well, I hope they don't get out of line with Buddy," Janelle said. "Seems like he's having a good time, though."

She went back to her lunch and listened while Kelsey and the others ran through the football roster deciding who was hot and who they hoped would ask them to Homecoming. Janelle had her own opinions on the subject, but she couldn't keep her mind from drifting back to the unusual social scene taking place across the lunchroom. She made a mental note to keep track of these two.

For nearly a month, she saw that the two good-looking guys seemed to go out of their way to say hello to Buddy, to joke with him in the halls, and to make him feel welcome. In fact, she also noticed an improvement in the way other kids treated him. Being accepted by two such well-known guys seemed to raise him a few steps in the pecking order. All this was good, so far as she could tell. She didn't understand why it was happening, but she was so busy trying to get her own high school life in order she welcomed the relief of knowing Buddy was in good hands.

About a week later, as she was trudging home after a particularly grueling soccer practice, she noticed Steve and Mike hanging out off to one side of the parking lot. I should talk to them, she thought, and thank them for being so good to Buddy. Wouldn't hurt to be seen talking with them myself, anyway. She ambled over in their direction.

"You look beat," Mike said as she drew close. He had made the first move!

"Beat down, drug down, and brung down," she said. "Hard practice. I guess you guys know all about that."

"Today wasn't so bad," Mike said. "They ease up on us the day before a game so we have energy when it counts."

"Cool. Gonna win tomorrow?"

"Bam," Steve said. "We're gonna stomp 'em."

"Great. Hey, guys, the reason I came over here is I'm Buddy O'Brien's sister, and, well, I've noticed how you guys have kind of taken him under your wing lately. I wanted to say thanks; he's been happy for the past few weeks. He doesn't have many friends up here."

"Hey, Buddy's great. He's a lot of fun if you get to know him. He's different, but he's cool," Steve said.

"Yeah, we like him," Mike added. "No problem; we like the guy."

"Well, anyway, that's all I wanted to say. Good luck tomorrow," Janelle said, and she began to turn away.

"Hey," Mike said, as she turned. "We were about to go over to Steve's house and get a pizza. Want to come along?"

She couldn't believe it. Steve and Mike were asking her to hang out? Juniors? She was going to hang out with juniors? With these two? Kelsey's gonna die!

"Um, yeah, I could do that," she said. "I'll have to call home to let them know I'll be late."

"No problem, come on, I have my car here."

As they walked toward Mike's car, Janelle walked casually, she hoped, over to the pay phone by the building. She couldn't believe her good fortune. She'd only been in the high school a couple of months and already she's about halfway up the social ladder! Maybe more! This was amazing. She was scarcely able to speak coherently to her mother on the phone. There was no problem with her getting home late. Her mom was glad she was making friends. The boys pulled up, and she climbed in the back seat.

Mike and Steve played their favorite songs on the car's audio system as they drove toward Steve's house, singing along loudly and poorly, goading Janelle to join in. She did when she knew the songs, and even though she was alone in the back seat, she felt like she fit right in and was totally accepted by the gorgeous guys up front. She was in heaven.

After a frightful rendition of some hip-hop tune she didn't know, Mike pulled into a driveway of a large, shady house in an upscale section of town.

"Come on in," Steve said, as he exited the car. Janelle grabbed her backpack and gear bag and followed.

"You can leave them in the car; we'll give you a ride home," Mike said, following Steve up to the door.

Janelle followed meekly, but excitedly. She didn't know what to expect; she wasn't sure what to talk about, but she knew this was going to be good. The guys were still singing and laughing, and she followed right along. Inside, they passed through a lavishly furnished living room with thick, soft carpet and went to a huge kitchen with stainless steel appliances and a beautiful stone floor.

"Want a drink?" Steve said, opening the fridge door. He rummaged around and handed Mike a can of beer. Janelle was surprised for a moment, and only managed to stammer out a simple, "Do you have a ginger ale or something?"

Steve smiled wryly at Mike and rummaged around again. He emerged with a cola and handed it to her.

"Best I could do."

"That's fine," she said, and popped the top. She was surprised they were drinking beer at all, let alone in front of her and in his parent's house. Steve must have noticed her surprise.

"My folks are out of town for a few days. They travel a lot. They have their own consulting company and have to go meet with clients all the time." He smiled again at Mike.

"So, what you wanna do?" Mike asked, returning Steve's smile.

"I thought we were gonna get a pizza and hang out," Janelle said, still off guard.

"I'm not quite ready to eat yet," Mike said, still grinning. "You wanna eat, Steve?"

"No, I'm not in an eating mood," he said. "I think we're gonna have a little party, though."

"Huh? What d'you mean?" She was starting to feel tense.

"Well, it's like this," Mike said. "You know how we've been nice to Buddy lately? Well, I didn't lie, we actually do like the guy. We really do. He's a nice kid."

"Yeah," Steve added, "A real nice kid. Like you."

"And," Mike said, "We've had fun talking with him and making him feel welcome in our school. That's been fine. But, well, it's a little more complicated than that."

"You see," Steve said, "We like Buddy, like I said, but if we're gonna keep on, you know, looking out for him like we have been, we have to get something out of it, too."

"Yup," Mike said, putting down his beer and taking a step toward Janelle. "And that something is you."

"You see, we sorta noticed you right away when you came over to the high school. You've, well, you've been growing up nicely, and when we were checking out the new freshmen, we saw you right away. And Mike here, he said, isn't that the girl who's always taking care of her brother? I bet she'd do anything to keep her brother safe."

"And so, we had this idea," Mike said. "We started being real nice to Buddy, you know, showing him, and you, how good high school could be. Of course, it can be real nasty, too. I hear some kids hate coming to school 'cause of how they get treated here. Some guys can be real assholes. Just for the fun of it. All they need is a victim. Someone like Buddy, well, he's got victim written all over him. Imagine what it would be like if some of the guys on the team started picking on him. There's almost fifty of us. You think anyone's gonna stand up for him against us? If we beat up on him, every asswipe in the school who wants to look tough is gonna join in. That's a lot of guys. You think you can take them all on? Against us? Yup, things could get real bad here for Buddy. Real bad. Real fast. Tomorrow, maybe."

"And all you have to do to stop it . . . is keep us happy," Steve said. "That's not much, is it? It'll be easy, for you. It'll be a lot easier to keep us happy than to try to keep an eye out for him like you have been. Trust me. If we treat him well, everyone's gonna treat him well. You watch. Even teachers are being nicer to him, aren't they?"

Janelle's head was spinning. She couldn't believe this was happening. Were they really threatening to hurt Buddy? He couldn't take it; he didn't understand meanness, he was so naturally nice himself. She'd always kept him safe. Were they going to go after him and get everyone else in school to join in if she didn't . . . What? If she didn't . . .

"What?" she croaked. "What do you want?"

"Oh, not much," Mike said. "Not much at all. Sometimes, we get to feeling needy, that's all. We want you to take care of us. Make us feel welcome."

"You'll like it," Steve chimed in. His voice lower, softer, yet firm. "Who wouldn't like it? Don't worry."

"Naw, nothing to worry about. We won't make you do anything you wouldn't like."

"Come on," Steve said, "I'll show you," He handed his beer to Mike and closed the distance between him and Janelle in a couple of easy steps. He put his arms around her as she started to back up and he held her to him.

"No, stop, what do you want?" Janelle cried out.

"Just what you've been wanting the minute you first saw us," he said. He started stroking her back, at the same time pulling her closer to him. She felt the hardness of his body against her and the strength in his arms. She also felt an unaccustomed hardness lower down, and suddenly, she knew. She struggled against him, trying to push him away, but he had her in too close for her to get any kind of leverage, and anyway, he was too strong for her.

"Come on, baby," he said. "You don't have to fight. You don't have to worry. I'll be good to you. Haven't I been nice to you so far?"

He held her tightly, and she kept struggling, crying out for him to stop, to let her go. He wouldn't. He held her till her struggles slowed.

"That's better. Now you be a good girl and you're not gonna get hurt. Be a good girl and your brother's not going to get hurt either. Be nice to us and we'll take care of him. That's the way it is. You decide."

He tightened his hold on her. She looked over at Mike through her tears, saw his looming size a few feet away and realized she had no chance. She let out one more gasp and collapsed in Steve's arms. He picked her up and carried her down a flight of steps to a carpeted rec room.

"I'll be up in a bit," Steve called up the stairs. "Then it's your turn."

And that's how it began.

The guys were true to their word. Buddy continued to be the mascot, more or less, of the football team, and as a result, he was accepted everywhere. Janelle never saw him happier. He never noticed she was worn out and depressed. Her parents asked about her haggard appearance, but she explained it away with stories of how grueling practice was and how hard her classes were. She told them she wasn't sleeping well, so they took her to the doctor. He gave her some sedatives, and the pills helped put her out at night. They didn't stop the dreams, however. Janelle woke more often than not to images of being pursued by wild animals, being held prisoner by primitive tribes of warriors, being adrift at sea. She woke up exhausted, sweating heavily, breathing hard, and gritting her teeth. She broke a tooth, and her dentist made her a mouthpiece to wear at night. It's pretty common, he said. Don't worry about it. That's what the doc said, too, about the sedatives. A lot of kids have anxiety in high school. It goes away after a while. These will help you get some sleep so you can learn to cope with it. Her teachers didn't seem to notice anything was wrong. Her friends did, but she put them off the same way she did her parents. No one knew. No one saw.

She went to the school nurse frequently that year complaining of abdominal pain, and the nurse would make her lie down for a while. She would ask some vague questions about what she'd been eating, but she never asked the right questions. No one did. No one ever asked if she was being forced to have sex with two cretins who didn't even like her. They didn't, either. In school and at the mall, it was as if they didn't even know her. After the first few times, they didn't even bother to talk to her very much. In the beginning they acted like they were friends, but after a while, that seemed to be too much trouble for them. In and out, that's all they wanted. In and out. At least it wasn't too often. It wasn't every day. Not even every week. But it never went too long before one or the other would lean in close in the hallway and say, "Today. After practice" and she'd have to be waiting. When Steve's parents were away, they'd go to Steve's house. Sometimes it was Mike's house. Sometimes the back of the car in some secluded area.

It was never very long, or very rough. They were true to their word. They weren't interested in beating her up or making her do anything gross. All they wanted was sex; in and out, quick and dirty. That's all she was to them, their own little cum-dumpster, as she heard one of them say, and that's exactly how she felt. Twice, only twice, as if that made it better, they brought along someone else. The first time it was Steve's cousin who was visiting from Ohio and staying for a week. They'd told him they'd treat him. The other time it was some friend she'd never seen. They were drunk. It was Sunday afternoon. Steve called and said she'd better get over there fast if she knew what was good for her, and when she did, they shoved her down the stairs to the rec room where the other guy, a buff six footer, was sprawled on the couch watching TV. He didn't even talk to her, he just grabbed her and pushed her down on the floor.

Two years of that. Two years of pain and degradation. Through it all, she had to see them in school, not flinch as they walked by, see them talking with Buddy and even hanging out with their girlfriends, and she could never say a word, never catch their eyes, never even acknowledge she saw them. It made her sick. She couldn't believe how they could even have girlfriends while they were doing what they were doing to her. She couldn't believe they could walk down the halls and act like regular guys. She hated it every time they got some kind of recognition or praise. She hated it whenever the football team won a game, and she secretly celebrated whenever they got trounced. School became hell to her, but she endured it. Home was no better, as she had to pretend to be all right and to keep coming up with excuses for when she had to "take care" of them.

She was terrified she was going to get pregnant, and so she started making regular pilgrimages to a free clinic located on the other side of town to get birth control and to get tested for STDs. Every time she had to listen to the woman lecture her on having safe sex and having respect for herself and her body. Every time she awaited test results with fear. Luckily, they were always negative. She was ok. She wasn't pregnant. One time, she wanted to scream when Mike muttered at her afterward, "You'd better be clean, you slut. You give me anything and I'll kill you."

Then, it was over. They graduated. They went away for the summer. Then they went to college. That first year, she lived in terror. When Thanksgiving neared, she was afraid they'd be home and want her to "take care of them." Nothing. The same at Christmas. Nothing. Spring break, the following summer, nothing. They seemed to have lost interest in her, and it was over. Not that she felt relieved. She was still on guard all the time. She still felt betrayed by everyone at school, the football team, the teachers, the nurse, her friends, her parents, everyone who never noticed what was happening to her. School was still hell for her, but at least the hell was purely emotional. The physical part was over. She could stop worrying about being pregnant. She could stop worrying about AIDS. She could stop making excuses.

Buddy, of course, was fine. He got through those two years on top of the world. The following year, he went to the technical school to start his computer training, continued for two years afterward to get his certificate, and then he was on his own, working, living in his own apartment, watching baseball games and building ship models. Buddy was fine. At least, she could claim that victory. She'd gotten Buddy through school unscathed. She had carried him through on her back.

****

Charles was literally speechless.

He had no idea what to say. As Janelle was telling her story, his emotions boiled. Rage, disgust, sympathy. He had no idea Janelle had ever been through anything so vile. She seemed too solid, so pure, so decent. This picture did not fit in with the woman he knew at all. He sat holding her and stroking her hair. She still wasn't facing him.

Then, in a small voice,

"Do you hate me?"

The simple question went through him like a bullet.

"Why would I hate you?" he asked. He was too confused to say anything else.

"Because you know now. Because I'm such a slut. How could you still like me?"

Now he was even more confused.

"You're not a slut, baby."

"But I've had sex hundreds of times with boys I didn't even like. I've had sex with boys I didn't even know. I'm a slut."

"Janelle, whatever you are, you're not a slut. You're not responsible for what they did to you. They are. They did it. They're the sluts. They're lower than sluts. They're rapists and criminals. I can't stand the thought of what they did to you. I can't imagine anyone doing that to anyone."

She turned slowly toward him. Her face was still reddened and worn. "You don't hate me?"

"No, baby, I don't hate you." He took her face in his hands. "I love you."

She reached for him, and he held her to him, feeling her convulsing with tears.

When she calmed, he asked, "Is that what happened tonight? You remembered that?"

"Yes."

"But why tonight? Why now? You said you hadn't thought of it in ages. Why now?"

"I don't know. But that's what it was the other times, when you were massaging me. It was the same feeling, the same emotions came over me. It was overwhelming, but this time I saw what was causing them, and I had to throw up."

"I didn't hurt you?"

"No, no, I don't think so." She was crying again. "But it seemed like feeling you inside me triggered something, and I was back when one of them was doing it and it hurt and they didn't care and they did it anyway. I hated them. That's what hurt. I couldn't stop them."

"It's okay now. It's over. You're with me. Nothing's happening."

He held her. Gradually, she stopped shaking.

"And you're sure you don't hate me?"

"No, I don't hate you."

"That's what I was afraid of. That's why I was so afraid when I told you I didn't like sex. I was afraid you wouldn't want me anymore if I didn't like it, and afraid you'd make me tell you why, and you wouldn't want me because I was a slut."

"No, I want you, I love you. Why do you keep saying that?"

"That's what they kept saying. 'You slut,' they'd call me. 'Be ready, slut,' one of them would say when they wanted me. They were always taunting me with that. The time they brought their friend in they really let me have it. 'Here, she's our own private slut, but you can have a piece. Here, take her,' they said."

"They were animals, baby. You didn't do anything wrong. You were a kid who didn't know what to do. I can't believe no one noticed. You had to be devastated when it was happening. No one noticed?"

"No one. Well, they did notice some things, but they never put it together. I kept hoping someone would ask. If someone had asked, I could have told them, I think. I know I kept hoping, but no one ever did. That bitch at the clinic kept lecturing me about being responsible. She thought I was a slut, too. I felt like one. I could hardly walk down the halls at school; I felt like everyone was looking at me and calling me a slut because I was sleeping with two different guys at the same time."

"What do you want to do?"

"About them?" she asked.

"No, I don't imagine we can do anything about them, now," he said. "I'd like to find them and put them behind bars, but I doubt we can. I'm more worried about you. We have to take care of this. You can't be breaking down in tears every time we try a massage or to make love. We need to take care of you."

"What would we do?"

"I don't know. But let's start by making sure that nothing physical is wrong."

"I don't think you hurt me."

"It's a place to start."

"What do I tell the doc?"

"Tell him you're having pain with intercourse. Tell him you want to make sure nothing's wrong."

"Charles, I don't want to have to explain any of this to anyone. I didn't want to tell you."

"We have to do something."

She glanced around the room, unable to focus on anything. Finally, she said, "You're right. I'll try."

"In the meantime, let's not try to make love again for a while. We'll be careful with the massage, too."

"Thank you," she said, "for not taking it personally. I was so afraid you'd hate me. Who could want a woman who throws up when he tries to make love to her?"

"Someone who knows you," he said, and he held her close.

Chapter 10

"So, CHARLIE boy, you been holding out on me!"

Harry looked expectant. He was leaning into Charles' cubicle, hanging from one hand hooked on the doorway.

"What, Harry. What do you mean?"

"I mean Tricia tells me you been going out with that babe from the school I gave the car to, what's her name?" He had a sly grin on his face.

"Janelle. Yeah, we've gone out a few times."

"I don't blame you, Charlie, and let me say it's about time. Time to get back in the saddle, if you know what I mean. You been moping around here for two years; it's time you got some fun back in your life."

Charlie nodded. Harry was in rare form.

"I don't blame you one bit. Man, the day she came in here for a donation I about shit myself. She is one hot woman! I'd a gone after her myself, but Mary's got a nose on her like a bloodhound. She'd smell some other woman on me in a second. Don't think I didn't wasn't tempted, though, let me tell you. She was nice!" He put a heavy emphasis on the "nice," drawing it out to emphasize his meaning.

"I know, Harry."

"Man, Charlie, you're one lucky guy. Why do you think I donated such a sweet ride? You think I'm that into her school? No, man, I started trying to impress her right away, like I was a big man. Before I knew it, I was telling her about that convertible, and whammo, there it was. Oh well, it's a good tax write-off, anyway."

Charles hadn't realized he had donated the car to impress Janelle. He'd always thought the gesture was uncharacteristically generous, and now he understood why. He didn't like the thought of Harry drooling over Janelle, twirling a cigar in his mouth and leering at her.

"Well, she sure appreciated the car, Harry. It's a good school; they do wonders with the kids. I'm glad you donated it."

"Probably didn't hurt your maneuvers, eh boy? I bet you swooped in and took all kinds of credit. No problem. Glad to help. You needed to get laid, my friend. I'd thought so for a long time. If I'd ever talked you into going to the nudie bar, I was thinking of slipping one of the girls a few bucks to be extra nice to you, but you'd never go. I'm glad you're back in the saddle, Charlie boy. It's about time."

Charles winced at the thought of Harry paying some dancer at the sleazy men's club to "be nice" to him. He didn't like Harry's teasing any more. He used to think Harry was a fun guy. They were fast friends years ago. What happened? How'd he get to be such a sleazeball?

"So, how is she? She as hot as she looks? Come on, you can tell me." Harry's grin widened.

"Harry, I'd appreciate it if you didn't talk about her that way."

"Oh, the lad's serious about this. Excuse me, I thought maybe you were trying to your feet wet, but no, you're diving right back into the ocean. Charlie, you already did the wife and family thing, you did the respectable thing. It's time you had some fun. If me and Mary ever split up, I wouldn't be shopping for another wife. I'd be playing the field. Pick up a few grounders. Catch a fly once in a while. Have some fun, then move on. No more bein' tied down. No sir."

"I'm not tied down, Harry. I like her. I like being with her."

"Oh, well then, if you 'like' her that changes everything. Shit, Charlie, I'm not saying you should hang out with women you don't like; I'm just sayin' you don't need to be getting tied down already. Take your time."

"I am taking my time, Harry. I'm not rushing into anything. I like this woman, and I'd appreciate it if you wouldn't talk about her like we're back in college screwing around."

"Okay, okay, I can take a hint. Geez; you don't need to wet your shorts about it. I was just bein' friendly!" Harry stepped into the room. "Hey, why don't you bring her to the Thanksgiving party? I'd like to say hello to her again and this time get to know her, all right? I'll behave, I promise."

"I'll do that. But behave. I don't need to be wiping off any drool stains when you're done talking to her, all right?" Charlie grinned. He liked putting Harry in his place.

"Done. I'll bring my own bib." With that, Harry took off down the hall.

The Thanksgiving party was another of Harry's eccentricities. He said he didn't want to have a company Christmas party because people are always so busy in December and because he didn't want everybody getting testy about buying presents. So instead, in mid-November before the holiday frenzy started, he had a Thanksgiving party. Big meal in a private room at a nice restaurant, live band, good food, good drinks. It was a little over the top for a company of this size, but he said he wanted his people to feel appreciated. Besides, it was a write-off. Harry seemed to have more write-offs than Charlie figured the feds strictly allowed, but that was his business.

Yes, he'd bring Janelle to the Thanksgiving party. It was still almost a month away, but yes, he'd like to go and enjoy himself. He also smiled at the prospect of showing Janelle off. She was a catch, he had to admit. He was lucky to have her.

****

"Well, I've been having this weird thing," Janelle said. "I don't know if this matters, but my boyfriend and I try to do massage on each other, you know, for relaxation."

Janelle stumbled onward with her story. This was her first experience with a midwife, but her gynecologist hadn't had an opening for weeks, and the nurse on the phone said the new certified nurse midwife they'd added to the practice could handle most conditions. Bonnie seemed kind and receptive, and Janelle had to admit she felt more comfortable talking to a woman.

"I don't know why I'm telling you this. It's not a GYN thing," Janelle paused, checking for a response.

"Well, you started," Bonnie said. "Go ahead."

"So, we were doing massage, and he started working on this knot on my thigh, and it hurt. Suddenly, I was overcome with fear. I felt this incredible fear, and rage."

"All right. What else?"

"That happened a couple of times. Then, Friday night, that's what I came in about. We were," she hesitated. "Well, we were having sex, about to have sex, and he started to enter me, and it hurt. I mean it really hurt. I screamed. I couldn't help myself. And then I was in the bathroom throwing up," Janelle finished, feeling sheepish. "And so, I was, we were afraid he'd hurt me or something. We wanted to find out. That's what I called about."

"I see," Bonnie said. "I guess we should have a look. Hop up on the table."

Bonnie did a few routine checks, examining Janelle's eyes, ears and nose. She listened to her heart and her breathing. She pulled out a shelf at the end of the table. "Here, swivel around and lay down," she said.

Janelle lay down. Bonnie pressed into her abdomen and pubic area with her fingers.

"That's all good. It's time to see what's going on inside. Take off your jeans and underwear. You can cover yourself with this," Bonnie said, handing her a green blanket. She turned her back and started making notes in Janelle's chart.

Janelle lay down.

"Scrunch up and lay flat, with your bottom as near as you can to edge of the table. Put your feet in the stirrups."

Janelle did so. She glanced up and saw a picture of a galloping horse on the ceiling.

"What's with the horse?" she asked.

"That's so you can think of a different kind of stirrup," Bonnie grinned.

Janelle laughed.

Bonnie took a speculum out of a warmer drawer.

"First, you're going to feel my fingers touching you." She gently pulled her apart and began to insert the speculum. Janelle felt her whole body tense up. Her knees closed involuntarily. She breathed a little faster.

"I'm gonna need you to relax," Bonnie said. "I can't do this until you relax. Let the muscles between your legs get soft."

That worked, and Janelle lay quietly, examining the chestnut horse on the ceiling, letting her muscles go soft.

Bonnie continued with the exam, and Janelle was surprised at how little it hurt.

When she was finished, Bonnie removed the speculum and started taking off her gloves.

"All right, you can get dressed now," she said and turned away.

"Wow, that didn't hurt at all," Janelle said as she pulled her jeans back on.

"Good, that's what I like to hear," Bonnie said. "Now, I suppose you want to hear what I found. Well, for starters, the good news is nothing's wrong inside. Nothing is injured," Bonnie said. "But that doesn't mean there isn't a problem."

Janelle felt her anxiety returning.

"This is the first time this happened?"

"Yes."

"You and your boyfriend getting along pretty well?"

"Yes. He's wonderful. I've never felt so loved and appreciated."

"Good. That's great. Congratulations." Bonnie paused. "Well, from the way you described it, and the way your body tried to clamp shut when I went to examine you, I have to ask you something else." She was looking right at Janelle, still pleasant and open, but no longer smiling widely. She was intent.

"Have you ever been sexually abused?"

The question hung in the air for a moment.

Then, Janelle was crying, her chest convulsing with sobs.

Bonnie leaned forward and took her hands.

"I thought so. It's not that uncommon. You shouldn't be embarrassed about this. It happens more than you'd think. I gather it's not happening now?"

Janelle shook her head no.

"Good. I didn't think so. When was it?"

Janelle was reluctant. She had never told anyone about this other than Charles. She couldn't believe she was about to tell a complete stranger. But they had to get to the bottom of it. She needed to move forward. She pulled herself together and answered. She choked down her tears.

"High school."

"Oh, my," Bonnie said, and handed her a tissue. "An unresolved experience like that can surface years later, with as much pain as if it had just happened. I've seen it in a lot of women, especially that clamping shut. This isn't my area; I can't treat you for this, but I can make a referral. I know a woman who's done a lot of work with women who have been abused. I think she could help you."

Bonnie's face was still earnest.

"Really. You're not physically damaged, but you have some emotional healing you have to do. If you don't do anything about it, the pain will keep on coming back, and as you've already found out, emotional pain can be as real and as debilitating as physical pain. You need to take care of it. Your body is asking for healing. This woman can help." She rummaged through a drawer and produced a business card. "Call her."

"I will. Thank you, Bonnie. Thank you."

"That's what I'm here for. That's what I can do. Now it's up to you. You need to take care of yourself."

When Charles arrived that night, Janelle was beside herself telling about the visit.

"When she asked if I'd been abused, I broke down and cried all over again," she said. "I so wanted someone to notice. Someone, just once. She did. She noticed."

"That's great," Charles said. "I'm so glad you went to see her. Did you call the other woman?"

"As soon as I got home. I have an appointment for next Thursday."

"I'm so proud of you for facing this."

"Thank you. I don't know what I'd have done if you'd gotten angry at me or turned away from me."

"We're figuring this out, together, baby," Charles said. "We can, and we will."

He held her, for a long time.

Never, in his whole life, when he thought about being in love with a woman, never, when he was first getting to know Janelle, had he imagined being here, in this place, facing the deepest fears and pains of another person's soul. He had no idea how to navigate these waters or where they would take him. What if Janelle could never have sex again? What if she couldn't get over the pain she carried? What if he could never massage her again without her crying out in fear and rage? He didn't know. But there was nothing else to do. Wherever it was they were going, they were going together.

****

Macbeth went off without a hitch. The kids gave three performances, one at school, and two at night for parents and friends.

Charles was backstage for all three performances. It hadn't been easy to get off during the day, but after some good-natured ribbing, Harry let him go. He had his hands full making sure props were ready for the next scene, changing sets, and keeping the kids quiet. It exhausted him, but it was fun.

When he saw the whole production, he was again amazed it was being performed by children. The kids did more than get through it; they nailed it.

As the play unfolded and Macbeth's fate started closing in, the kid playing him looked positively frightened. When he heard his wife had killed herself, he collapsed on the floor to give his "tomorrow and tomorrow and tomorrow" speech, and Charles understood it for the first time. He'd never dreamed he could be helped to understanding by a fifth grader.

Well, a fifth grader and some remarkably talented teachers.

Every audience loved the show. All three performances were first rate, and Charles did not tire of doing his part. When it was all over, they had a huge party for the kids in the cafeteria with pizza, cake and ice cream. The parents were exuberant over what their kids had done, and the kids themselves were pleased beyond measure. Charles did catch some cattiness among some of the parents who thought their own kids didn't have large enough parts, and he did see a couple of fathers holding back, unable to join in the celebration, but all in all, the mood was triumphant, and the kids were exuberant. Charles couldn't have been prouder of Janelle.

"Charles, come here, I want you to meet someone." Janelle motioned to him. He put down the soda he'd been pouring and walked on over.

"These are Shawn and Barb Miller. They're Tim's parents." Tim had played Duncan. They were both smiling broadly.

"Glad to meet you. Tim's great. I couldn't believe a little guy could get a handle on a part like that. He was amazing. Smart kid. I liked talking to him while we worked."

The two parents brightened at his compliments. He began to sense how Janelle could get a huge reward from this job. All the teachers and directors at the school tried to involve parents as much as possible, and Charles could see why. He began to wish he and Ellen had put their kids in such a school.

"Hey, Charlie!"

Mike Schroeder was calling him over to meet his parents. Mike was one of the boys who didn't want to be onstage, so he'd done a lot of set work, instead. He and Charles had gotten to know each other pretty well.

"This is Charlie, he helped us with the scenery," Mike said, and Charles shook his parents' hands.

"Mike can sure use a hammer," he said to them. "My right-hand man." They beamed.

The party wound down. Charles helped clean up and put things away. This is where I came in, he thought, remembering how he'd pitched in at the school fair the previous spring. This is nice. This time, it feels like I belong.

Charles was eager to give Janelle her own reception at home. He hoped she would be able to relax. She'd been so wrapped up in the play she often went without enough sleep. The hours had begun to wear on her. He planned on devoting the weekend to letting her decompress and recover. No big plans. Tonight, he had cheese, fruit, and a bottle of her favorite wine. They would nibble, they would sip, and they would relax.

****

Janelle came home from her first meeting with the therapist full of hope.

"Victoria says I have posttraumatic stress disorder, and she thinks she can help."

"PTSD? Isn't that what soldiers get?"

"Yes, she says it's from unresolved trauma from when those boys abused me."

"Well, gee, I think we'd figured that out already. Is she going to predict yesterday's weather for us too?"

"No, no, come on, listen. I'm not sure I remember it all, but she says it's like this. She says whether or not something is traumatic doesn't just depend on whatever happened, it depends on how you react to it. That's why some people can go through some absolutely awful stuff and they're fine afterward. Other people have smaller events but they're traumatized. It's not what happens, it's how your body and mind process it.

"She says if you study animal behavior, it all gets pretty clear. If a cat catches a mouse or a rabbit and starts shaking it around, the animal gets scared to death. Its body makes it go kind of catatonic. It shuts down. She says the old 'fight or flight' thing is only partially true; it's really 'fight, flight, or freeze.' A lot of animals freeze. Then, if something happens so the cat drops the rabbit, once the danger is over, it'll lay still for a moment, start to wake up, and go into sort of a frenzy where it bucks and kicks, then he runs off and he's fine. That bucking and kicking works out all the adrenaline that was running through its system. It purges the adrenaline, the fear and the pain, and then he's fine.

"Victoria says if something happens to you, say, you get attacked in an alley, there's more going on than you can process, and the experience gets frozen into your memory and even your body.

"When something happens, like what happened with those boys, all the pain and fear gets bottled up. It doesn't get worked out. It doesn't get expressed. She said that's probably what happened with the massage. We were finding masses of stored up pain and releasing them. That's why I'd feel the pain just as if it was happening."

Charles was lost.

"You mean you were feeling twenty-year-old pain?"

"Yes. Exactly."

"But, we found those knots all over. Your back, your legs, your arms. You mean they were beating you all over? You didn't tell me that."

"No, they didn't. That's the weird thing. She says the location of the pain has nothing to do with where it was originally inflicted, or at least it doesn't have to. It's a matter of where it got stored."

"So, why didn't it come out at first? Why didn't it come out when you got professional massages? Why does it only come out with me?"

"She's not sure. She thinks maybe I finally felt relaxed enough with you and trusted you enough to let it out. She says my body has probably been waiting for a chance to let it out for years, but needed a safe place to do it.

"Charles, please. I need you to be with me on this. She says the only reason I'm on the edge of healing may be because I feel safe enough to try. It's been a long time, Charles. I want to be rid of this. You may not like hearing me scream, but trust me, this is better than going on like I had been.

"She says I never processed the pain or the emotions. The emotional stuff and the knowledge of what was happening is kind of like the rabbit thing. It needs to be processed or it all gets tucked away somewhere inside, waiting to get out.

"That's probably what happened when I started throwing up. I was feeling the sickness I felt when it was happening. That was the disgust I felt. It was old emotion surfacing."

"So, what, we need to get you sick again?"

"Well, that's one way. It's pretty much based on making you relive what happened and act out how you felt at the time. She says it gets pretty brutal.

"But she uses a new technique; it's only been around about twenty years and isn't totally accepted, but she's been using it for six years and she's getting good results."

"What's that?" Charles was afraid of what she'd say. None of this sounded very promising.

"It's a strange name: Eye Movement Desensitization and Reprocessing. It's based on getting the brain to reprocess what happened years ago. We focus on the feelings I have now based on what happened, and she does this hand motion thing and I follow her hands with my eyes, and somehow that triggers the brain to process all the old emotions and release their power over me. We also work on letting go of old ways of seeing what happened and replacing them with new, healthier ways to see them."

"Sounds weird."

"She says it feels weird, and looks weirder, but she swears it works."

"How long will all this take?"

"Depends. She says I'm lucky, in a way, that it happened when I was a teen. She says early childhood stuff is a lot harder to deal with. Kids don't understand what's happening, and can't remember or express it very well. They also have more years of maladjusted behavior layered on top of it.

"But it's not so good that it happened a lot of times. She said if it had been a single event, not terribly long ago, she could probably take care of it in about ten sessions. If it had happened when I was a kid, it could take years. She's not sure how long it'll take, but it could be a year or two, or more."

"A year?" Charles was shocked. A year of therapy? What were they supposed to do in the meantime, put their lives on hold? Would he be allowed to touch her or be with her? Would she be screaming and retching?

"At least a year." Janelle sounded sympathetic. "I know what you're thinking. I don't know how this is going to affect us. But she thinks she can help, and I know one thing. I can't go on like this. I can't bear thinking that if you touch me I'm going to end up screaming or vomiting. I have to do this. I have to try."

Her eyes were pleading, but resolved. He could see she meant it. She was going to do the therapy no matter what he decided. It seemed like the only choice he had was whether he was going to stay with her while she did. Could he? Did he have that much dedication? Was he man enough to stand by her through such a painful process? He had no way of knowing. All he knew was one choice had no Janelle in it. The other choice might have Janelle in it, but maybe not, and maybe a Janelle different from the one he knew. Which would it be? What did he want?

He wanted the most resourceful, surprising and loving woman he had ever known.

"Let's do it," he said.

She shifted over on the couch to curl up in his arms.

"Thank you," she said. "I knew you'd stay with me."

He held her, and he realized she knew him better than he did himself. There hadn't been any choice at all.

****

"So, this guy, this big loser of a guy gets out of the car, and you can see the whole thing lift up like six inches when he gets out of it. This guy had to be 400 pounds; I couldn't believe it."

Kenny was telling his story to a small group near the hors' d'oeuvre table.

"So, I'm wondering how to tell him why he keeps chewing up tires. He's somehow shoveling his mound of fat into this compact car and he wonders why it keeps needing to be aligned. It's lined up fine when it's empty; it's when his fat ass is in it that it gets out of whack!" Kenny laughed. "I thought maybe we needed to have him sit in it while we line it up next time."

"Or maybe put a load of bricks in the passenger's seat," grinned Ted.

Janelle was forcing a smile. This wasn't her kind of humor, but she was trying to be nice at Charles' company Thanksgiving party. He'd been around the service guys for years, so he was used to their stories.

He steered Janelle away from the group and they ran into Tricia.

Charles smiled broadly as he introduced them.

"I'm so glad to finally meet you," Tricia said.

"And I'm happy to meet the people Charles works with," Janelle said. "He says you have the patience of two saints the way you hold the office together."

"It ain't easy," Tricia smiled. "Sometimes Harry can make a dead man jumpy, but I have his number. Next to him the other guys are a piece of cake. Charles here is a gem. You got a good one."

Janelle smiled at the compliment. Charles was uneasy. "Oh, I try to keep the peace," he said.

"Keep the peace, put a lid on the boss, fill in when he screws up," Tricia said. "You do a lot more than keep the peace, let me tell you. Life's been a lot easier since you came on board. Harry's such a piece of work. One minute he's all seriousness and work and figures, the next he's wandering out for a beer in the middle of the afternoon. And you never know when something's gonna set him off."

"Don't I know it," Charles said. "He was the same way in college. But then, I didn't work for him; I could tell him to shove it and walk away if he got out of hand."

"So far as I'm concerned, you still can," Tricia laughed. "It'd do him good."

"Say, Janelle," she continued. "How'd you rope this guy in? I thought he was going to rot away the rest of his life in his cubicle till you came along. You put some life in the old boy."

"It wasn't too hard," Janelle smiled. "In fact, he more or less roped me in. Conquered me with kindness. He did so much for me and the school I figured I owed him. Pretty sly, I guess." She was enjoying teasing Charles.

"I figure you still owe me about fifty-seven back rubs and quite a few beers. And, now that you mention it," Charles said. "I aim to collect."

Janelle laughed. "I bet you do."

"Now, now, Tricia said, "Let's keep it civil in here! I don't want you two over in a corner necking next time I turn around!"

The three of them sat down together for dinner. Charles was glad Tricia and Janelle were getting along.

"Janelle!" Harry's voice boomed over the background music.

"Hi, Mr. Fleming," Janelle said, starting to get up as he approached.

"No, no, sit down, relax," Harry said. "And it's Harry. Only lawyers call me Mr. Fleming, and only when they're trying to screw me. You aren't trying to screw me, are you?"

Janelle took him in stride.

"No, Harry, I'll leave that to the lawyers. They can do it in their briefs."

Harry laughed. "Not a pretty picture. Not pretty at all." He slapped Charles on the back.

"I'm glad to see you here; I told Charlie he'd better bring you along. He's a lucky man to land a woman like you. I told him so. Glad to see you here. Make sure you have a good time. The drinks are on me!" he said, and in a moment, he was on to the next victim.

The rest of the evening went well. Janelle hit it off with Brian and his wife, and they had some pleasant conversation with the rest of the guys. When the band started, Charles timidly took her to the dance floor and was pleasantly surprised that he wasn't completely hopeless. Janelle was patient with him.

"Trust me," she said. "I've had worse. I don't need you to be a great dancer, just to have a good time."

So they had a good time. Charles liked the slow dances best, because he had a chance to hold her and feel her body move against his. He craved that contact, no matter how often he held her.

She was wearing a simple velvet dress that wasn't tight or clingy but still accentuated her trim figure. Her necklace and earrings made her face seem to sparkle with their brilliance. She was stunning.

When they got home, Janelle turned to him as soon as he took off her coat. She reached out and pulled him close. He was so handsome in his suit; she rarely saw him dressed up. He had seemed confident and happy, and she was struck by the difference in his demeanor from the day they met. He had looked so tentative and out of place. She knew the change had a lot to do with her, and as he held her, she let her body move with his caresses. In a minute, she raised her face to be kissed, and when his lips met hers, she felt their touch through her whole body. She gave a shiver. Then, she took his hand and placed it on her bottom.

"I know you wanted to do that all night," she murmured.

"It was hard not to," he said, and he gave her a squeeze.

"I bet that's not all that's hard," she whispered in his ear.

"Would you . . ." he began.

Before he could finish, she had taken him by the hand and started leading him to the bedroom.

They made love for the first time in several weeks. Janelle reveled in the familiar feel of his hands on her. She felt warm and safe. His kisses and caresses aroused her. She let herself float in the feelings. Finally, she took him inside, and there was no pain. No pain and no nausea.

Maybe, she thought. Maybe, this will work. And she settled back to enjoy his passion.

****

Charles awakened slowly the next morning. He felt the November sun on his face and rolled over. Next to him, Janelle was curled up under the covers, only a puff of hair exposed. He placed a hand on her back and watched her for a few minutes.

Soon, she stirred. He heard a rustle of covers and saw a few tentative movements. Finally, a face emerged. She smiled when she saw him.

"Good morning, lover," she said. "Sleep all right?"

"Better than all right," he grinned. "You know how to get me going."

"It's not hard," she said, and giggled, remembering her opening line from the night before.

"Not after that workout," he said.

She scooched her way over to him, struggling with the covers. Finally, her warm, soft skin was against his. The sensation was almost a shock, it was so good. He pulled her closer and rolled her over on top of him. She purred with delight.

"But," he said, "things can change." He started kissing her cheek, and his hands ran down her back and pressed her against him. Desire started filling his body, and he felt the surge enlivening him.

Janelle arched her back and pressed her cheek into his kisses. She rolled off him, and Charles followed her, caressing and kissing her gently, but passionately. She let out a few gasps, and soon, she was on top of him again. She carefully lowered herself onto him, and her eyes turned upward. They widened, and panic rushed in. She let out a yelp and was off him in a second, sitting up, facing away, holding her belly and looking sick.

"Oh no," Charles said. "Are you all right?"

She sat, rocking back and forth.

In a while, she said softly, "It happened again. I'm sorry. At least I didn't need the bathroom this time."

Charles sat beside her, one hand on her back, feeling the waves of nausea run through her. He had no idea what to say. After last night, he had hoped the trauma reactions were over. He had thought the therapy was working. But, no, once again, her body was closing up against him as if he were one of the high school worms who'd hurt her. What could he do?

After a minute or so, when she seemed to calm down, he went into the kitchen and started making coffee.

At least I'm good for something, he thought.

****

"Come on, dad, we were just having fun."

Donald was gobbling down pizza at a record pace.

"I know, Donnie, I know. It's your senior year. You feel on top of the world. You should enjoy it. But you have to realize, there are some limits. Your mother is worried sick."

"Dad, do you expect me to be calling my mommy in the middle of a party?"

"No, but you could tell her where you're going. You could tell her when you'll be home. And, by the way, on school nights, that should be eleven."

"Dad, I'm almost eighteen."

"Yup, almost. Not yet. And even when you are, you're still living in her house. She's still your mother. She has rights, too, and one of them is to not have to worry if you're out somewhere killing yourself."

"Let's not get too dramatic, dad."

"I need you to promise this, Don. Either you or one of the other guys stays straight all night, or if you're all drinking, you stay put till morning. I know I probably can't get you to stop drinking, but we need to know you're safe."

"Dad!"

"Yes, dad. I'm still your father. I need this from you, or you won't be allowed out at all, and no car privileges, ever. This is not negotiable."

"Right, dad. But this sucks."

"It can suck. It can suck through a whole long and healthy life. That's what's at stake, Donnie, it's not about rules, It's about your safety."

"Yeah, yeah, dad. I promise, all right?"

Donald went back to scarfing pizza. Sausage, pepperoni, hamburger, extra cheese.

"But one thing, dad. I'll be eighteen in a couple months. You know what that means!"

"You get to be eighteen and still be home by eleven on school nights?"

"No, dad, I mean, yes, dad, but that's not what I'm talking about. I get to go to the T-Bird!" His face lit up triumphantly. "We're already planning it. Tom and Joe'll be eighteen by then, too. It'll be amateur night on my birthday. Girls from the college show up!"

Donnie's face was glowing.

"Oh, right. The 'gentlemen's club.'" Charles said. He wondered how he could pack all he'd learned in the past few months into a few nuggets of wisdom.

"Listen, Donnie, I don't want this to be old fuddy-duddy day at the pizzeria, but I don't want you going."

"What? Dad, come on, I'll be eighteen. I'll be legal!"

"I know you'll be legal, but I don't want you going," Charles said quietly.

"All the guys go! We're planning it! Come on, dad, this isn't like the thing you were involved in, this is all straight and out in the open, come on."

Charles winced.

"I know it's all legal. But that doesn't make it right. I don't want you drooling all over the girls."

"Come on, dad! We're gonna save up so we can tip them like crazy! You get to put it in their thongs. Dave says it's a rush!"

"I don't want you staring at those girls, treating them like they're just a show."

"Dad, they are a show. That's the whole point! They like doing it. Why do you think they even have amateur night? The girls love it; they get a charge out of turning on a whole roomful of guys. It makes them feel hot and sexy."

"They might get caught up in the excitement, Don, but trust me, no woman will like having strangers staring at her and talking about her like that. She might not realize it at the time, but she won't."

"Are you crazy, dad? If she likes it, she likes it. They're happy, we're happy. What else is there?"

Charles felt frustrated. This wasn't going well at all. How could he tell Donnie the girls were getting caught up in a fad that was turning everyday girls into strippers? Back when he was a young guy, he would have scarcely believed it.

He gave up. Youthful exuberance knew no bounds. He couldn't fight an entire culture.

"Well, think about it. But that brings up another topic, as long as I'm being Mr. Prude."

"Now what?"

"You are being careful, aren't you?"

"Dad, I told you we'll make sure someone's straight to drive."

"No, I don't mean that. I mean with girls."

"Dad!"

"I'm serious. You have to be careful. Don't take it for granted, don't assume you'll be lucky. Don't assume the girl's taking care of it. Condoms. Every time. No question."

"Gee, dad, anything else you want to tell me? How to brush my teeth?"

"Don, I'm serious."

"Yes, I know dad. Don't worry. I'm being careful."

"Good."

Charles was taken aback by the apparent admission that Donnie's been having sex, but he knew it was inevitable. At least he had some sense. Or maybe he only had enough sense to lie to his father.

"Anything else, dad?"

"Well, now that you mention it, I think you need to rethink your hairstyle."

Anger flashed over Donnie's face, then he realized Charles was kidding.

"All right. I'll go to the old guy's barbershop tomorrow and get a nice crew cut."

"Good. That'll look great. The girls will go wild over it."

They ate the rest of the meal in peace. Charles didn't know if he'd accomplished anything, but he'd given it the old college try.

Ironic, he thought. The old college try: trying to get his kid to be different from the way he was.

Fat chance.

****

"Geez, come on, guys. It's not funny anymore."

"No, I'm serious, John. All kidding aside. I'm wondering how it goes, you know? One of these days I'm gonna get married again, and I want to be ready. I screwed it up once, and I don't wanna do that again.

"So, seriously, once you got that ring on her finger, did she put out more, or was it like taking a cold shower? I mean, she licking your stick like she used to? This is important."

Bill and Eddie erupted in laughter. Charles could hear them plainly over the cubicle walls. It was late morning, and business was slow, so they had time on their hands, and Charles hated it.

Sounded like John wasn't having much fun, either. He had decided to marry the woman he'd been dating, and ever since he made that announcement, Bill and Eddie were all over him. They kept asking for more and more stories of his fiancé's sexual acrobatics. Now that he was planning on marrying the woman, John wasn't so anxious to share details with his buddies. They, on the other hand, were having a blast.

"Eddie, shove it up your ass. I told you I don't want you talking about her like that."

"You never told us about that one. She like it up the ass? You can tell us." Bill and Eddie erupted again.

"Johnny, you gotta come clean. It's good for the soul, man, you gotta get this off your chest. You can tell your old buddies."

He heard John stomp by them, retreating to the break room. Bill said something to Eddie in a hushed voice, and the two of them burst out laughing.

Just good old boys, Charles thought. Just out for a laugh. What's the harm? Who cares if they talk about a woman like that? Who cares what they think? They're not doing anything about it, right?

Right. Those old familiar thoughts passed through him like a recording. How many women had he dismissed like that? How many times had he treated women like a video game?

****

"Damn!"

Charles had stopped to pay a toll on the turnpike, and he couldn't get the window on Janelle's car to close.

"Damn it! It's freezing!"

It was mid-December, and the first real chill of winter was upon them. They were on their way home from going to a Monet exhibit Janelle had wanted to see. They'd had a pleasant drive to the city, a good lunch at an authentic Spanish restaurant, and a couple of hours at the exhibit. Charles wasn't terribly interested in art, but he'd had a good enough time. When Janelle explained something about what was going on with the paintings, why Monet used such vivid pastel colors and the unusual brush strokes, he found he actually had some curiosity.

Now, however, it was dark and cold and the damn window wouldn't go up.

"Pull over," Janelle said.

"What?"

"Pull over."

He did, and she got out of the car. She came around and opened up his door. She knelt beside him and fiddled with something by his left foot. He had no idea what she was doing.

"That should do it," she said, standing. She reached down to his armrest and pushed the button. The window went up.

She went back around to her side and got in. He stared.

"What did you do?"

"Sometimes these old Swedish cars get finicky," she said, fastening her seat belt. "The fuses get tarnished, then things stop working. The first rule is if something electrical goes wrong, get out and spin the fuse around. That rubs off the tarnish and might get it working."

Charles was flabbergasted.

"A friend told me about it years ago. I should replace that fuse, but I don't want to fiddle with it in the dark. I'll get to it later. One time I was cruising along at seventy and the engine quit. Miles from an exit and in the middle of the night. I pulled over, got out, fiddled with fuses, and away I went."

Janelle kept surprising Charles. When they were on their way out of the museum, she had squealed in delight as they passed an exhibit of ship models. They had to go in. She was fascinated and kept talking about things Charles had never heard of.

"Look at the tackles on that! Incredible detail. The sail is actually bent onto the jackstay with little lashings! How'd he find thread with that texture?"

He had no idea what she was talking about. She reminded him her brother had a hobby of making model ships, and she'd learned a lot from him. She might have to take Buddy to see the exhibit.

"He'd love it," she said. "He'll find something wrong with every ship, though. He's particular like that; no matter how good a model is, he loves finding other people's mistakes. He'll be looking at one, suddenly laugh and point out where the main brace isn't routed correctly and would end up fouling on a stay."

She was delighted. Charles had no idea what she'd said. She was a wonder.

They drove on. It would be nearly eight before they got home. They'd probably be too tired to do any massage. Probably stop for a quick supper, go home, and go to bed. It was just as well. Charles was beginning to tire of the whole massage process. These days, they found painful knots in Janelle almost every time they tried it. He hated hearing her shrieks, and always offered to stop, but she always told him to go on with it.

"It hurts, but it's helping me. I almost always get bursts of emotion when you work on a trigger point, so I know I'm releasing a lot of old stuff. It's therapeutic. You have to go on."

He did, but he didn't like it. He couldn't believe how she'd actually reach out and embrace something so obviously painful. Why go through all that agony?

She was faithful to her therapy. Once a week. Her insurance covered part of it, but the copay was substantial, and it put a real crimp in her budget. "It's worth it," she'd say. "I think this is working."

The process had started out with a few sessions mostly designed to get Victoria familiar with Janelle's case and her way of thinking. Victoria also taught her how to deal with emotional outbursts and releases.

"She says I can expect to get these sudden feelings out of nowhere. That's part of their being released and processed. She says it'll be disturbing when it happens while I'm at work or driving or whatever. She's showing me what to do so I can cope. She also wants me to record when it happens and what I'm feeling and anything I remember so we can talk about it."

And sure enough, she started to have releases at the oddest times. Charles soon learned they might not get through a shopping trip or a movie without her suddenly stiffening up, her face absorbed in something he couldn't see. She'd tell him about it and write it down.

All that happened after the real therapy began. Janelle described the process to him. He never quite understood how it was supposed to work, but she seemed convinced it was helping. She would talk with Victoria about whatever their topic was for the session. Her pain with sex, for instance. They'd discuss what she felt and what memories it triggered. They'd try to find a way to put the old, painful feeling into words. Then they would replace it with a new, healthier response. The idea was to process the old statement enough that it no longer felt true and to reinforce the new statement until it did.

The therapy seemed almost like voodoo to Charles, but Janelle was very hopeful. She'd had several sessions already, and she felt like she was making progress.

"Any idea how long it's going to take?" he asked once.

"No, I told you Victoria said it could be a few months or a few years. We won't know till we get there."

"Um." He rarely had much to say about it.

"Victoria says I'm a good client. She likes the way I'm always willing to go right to the heart of a problem, right for the painful stuff. I want to solve this. I've been enduring it for too long."

The next day, winter began. It started snowing while he was at a movie with Laura. They emerged to a couple of inches on the ground. He got her back to her dorm and drove home in the snow. He arrived around seven, talked to Janelle on the phone, and settled in for a microwave dinner and a movie. His old routine, before Janelle, had been lonely and empty. Now, his life was full, but he wasn't sure what it was filled with. Janelle was still exciting, but an enigma, and he never knew how a day was going to go. Donnie was starting to be a problem. Laura was doing well, but growing more and more independent. Where was it all going?

Chapter 11

"SHE'S DRIVING me crazy."

Tricia was visibly tense. Charles had offered her lunch because she looked especially bad. He'd been noticing for a long time, and thought it was a shame, because he had come to like Tricia.

"Your daughter?"

"You know how electronic these kids are, right? Internet, cell phones, texting, cameras on the phone, movies on the phone.

"Well, a while ago, Darla was fooling around with her friend Sandy online. She was playing around with a web camera so they could see each other while they chatted.

"Then, I guess she got goofy and she pulled her shirt off and took a shot of herself naked from the waist up. She told me she got all giggly, and her friend got all giggly, and the friend said she should put it on her web page."

"What?"

"That's what I said, but she put it on a special area where she could control who saw it, and she only put that one friend on the list. She was having fun, being daring and all."

Charles was uncomfortable with where the story was going. But so far it sounded pretty innocent; kids fooling around like kids always did.

"Well, that part's not too bad. I did stuff like that when I was a kid, but without the internet. So, the friend thought this was pretty cool, and when she got online with another friend of hers, she sent it to her friend. The friend shares it with another friend, but this one doesn't like Darla so much. This friend posted it on her own page, but put it in the totally public area so anyone could see it. She titled it "Hartleton's biggest ho" or something like that."

"She did what?"

"You heard me. Soon, it's all over school. Darla's finding copies of it slipped in her locker or between pages of her books. Copies are pasted to walls everywhere. The photo got forwarded all over school from kid to kid, and some of them were pasting her into real porn pictures and sending them around, too. Darla's devastated. She wants us to move so she can get away from all this. She can't get through a day of school without having to deal with it one way or another.

"I don't blame her," Tricia went on, her face looking more and more defeated. "I'd want to get out, too. I have no idea how she can even face those kids. But we can't move. We don't have the money; this house was a big stretch for us."

"I'm sorry," she said. "I didn't mean to lay all that on you, but I'm at my wit's end. I have no idea what to do. I'm sorry."

"No, no," Charles said. "I can listen. No wonder you've seemed worn out lately. I bet you're not sleeping much."

"No, I can't. Too upset. And all the phone calls. Every smartass in the school is calling to harass her or to ask her out. The ones who know her call her cell phone; the others call the house. Imagine picking up the phone and hearing, 'Hey slut,' and knowing it's your daughter they're talking about."

"No. I can't imagine. What are you gonna do?"

"I don't know what to do. We've talked to the school, and they've promised to take action on anything they see, but so much of it is behind their backs, and by phone, and out of school."

"How's Darla?"

"I have to fight with her to get her to go to school every day. Her grades are shot. She comes right home and hides in her room. All I hear from her anymore is either crying or yelling. She hates me because we won't move and because I can't fix it."

"This is awful, Trish. I don't know how you're holding up."

Tricia had put down her sandwich. She was turning her glass around on the table, leaving an expanding wet ring on the placemat.

"I'm at the end of my rope."

"Do you think she'd do anything stupid?"

"You mean any more stupid? Like hurt herself? No, I don't think so, but she's miserable. We're all miserable."

"I bet. Still, keep a good eye on her. Kids think everything's the end of the world."

"Of course, she doesn't see that she did it to herself. She's blaming her friend. She won't talk to Sandy at all, and they used to be so tight. She actually got in a fight with a kid at school one day. I had to go in and get her."

"So that's why you cleared out early a couple weeks ago," Charles said.

"If only she hadn't sent the damn photo in the first place," Tricia's lower lip was trembling.

"Or taken it. This stuff used to happen when people took shots of each other and the drug store guy made some extra copies, but it didn't get all over town in an hour. Kids today aren't any dumber than they ever were, but the mistakes get bigger faster. They have no idea what can happen till it does."

Charles paused a while to poke at his food.

He glanced up. "This sucks. No question about that. It's awful for her and for you.

"So, now that it's happened, what do you do? All you can do with a mistake is set it right if you can, pick up the pieces, and learn from it. There's nothing to set right here. The big thing is for her to learn from it. I expect she's already figured out she shouldn't be posting any more photos on the web. That's a no-brainer. But has she figured out she shouldn't be doing the same in retaliation? That'll make it worse. It'd start an online gang war, with friends on both sides joining in."

"No. We've talked about that. She wanted to post some kind of page against that girl, but she didn't."

"Good. That leaves one thing. And this is the hard one." He hesitated. He wasn't sure how Tricia was going to take what he was about to say.

"Now, she has to endure it. She did what she did, and she has to live with the results. You can bet she's never going to do anything like this again. She'll try to stop other people from doing it, too. Someday, sooner or later, it'll blow over. And, yes, from time to time, the photo will resurface. But, if she gets tough now, she'll be able to handle it later.

"What she can do, I think, is not slink away when someone brings it up. Instead, she should bring it out. If she finds a copy in her locker, she should say, 'Hmm. Another sleazeball loser.' If a guy makes a snotty comment to her under his breath, she should call him on it. 'What was that? What did you say?' They're all counting on her slinking away. That's what makes it fun. Don't let them enjoy it. Make sure every kid who tries to put her down ends up on stage himself.

"You can't control how other people will react or what other people will do; all she can control is what she does. She can go on acting like she's defeated, or she can stand her ground. Whichever she does is going to become her life for a while. That much is her choice. That much, she can do."

Charles doubted he'd ever said that much to Tricia in a whole day. Tricia looked confused.

"You're right," she said quietly. "We've all been moping around, hanging our heads like dogs."

"Exactly. She did something stupid weeks ago, but that's over. The question is who's wrong now? And the answer to that is every kid who's dragging up that picture and making her squirm. They keep harassing her because it's fun and because they can get away with it. Most people know what's right and what's wrong, and they only do wrong when they think they can get away with it. Don't let them. Make noise. Draw attention to them. Get people to point a finger at them instead of at Darla.

"She'll need a lot of support from you and Tom. You're all she's got. But I bet if she talks to her real friends, they'll join in on her side, too."

"I hope so."

Tricia was twirling her glass again.

"Thank you, Charles."

"No problem, Trish. We're friends. Trust me on this one. Help her stand up for herself, and help to her be careful."

"I will."

They went back to the dealership. Tricia walked in to Harry bellowing he needed her right away. Charles found two voice messages. The outside world was back. He sighed, and picked up the phone.

****

Winter wound on. It was a cold one, so the long walks and beloved picnics and outdoor meals were over. Christmas came and went. Janelle took her brother home to see their parents. Charles brought Laura home in mid-December, then returned two weeks later to open presents. It went pretty well.

Business at the dealership was slow. Typical for winter. Charles had some time on his hands. Janelle was busy with change of semester work.

They spent more time inside, sharing the living room reading or watching movies on TV. They began a campaign of watching old classic films they'd never seen: *Lawrence of Arabia, The Great Escape, Citizen Kane.*

Janelle remained faithful to her therapy. She insisted on regular massage, even though the emotional and physical releases it brought were often painful for her. Charles gradually began to value the massages as much as she did; he felt more connected to Janelle through them, and he felt more a part of her healing.

Janelle's trauma reactions while making love were diminishing. They no longer feared her flashbacks every time they began, and when she did feel pain, all they had to do was wait for a minute to let the sensations pass. Charles gained more and more respect for her determination.

He was glad they could make love again without fear, and he was very glad to have passion back in his life. But knowing Janelle didn't seem to enjoy sex very much, he felt inadequate. She explained many times that she loved being with him, and she relished the physical intimacy they shared, but still, he often felt like he wasn't a good enough lover.

One night, he decided it was time to help Janelle feel the same excitement he did.

"Tonight," he said, "I want to please you."

"You always please me," Janelle said, and reached out to pull him toward her.

"No, I mean it, whatever you want, it's yours."

In answer, she pulled his face to hers and gave him a long, soulful kiss. He wrapped his arms around her and held her tightly. They lingered in the kiss, and their whole bodies danced.

When she finally released him, he began kissing her neck, as he knew she liked. She began moaning and writhing under him. He lingered. He kissed his way down her sternum to her belly and pressed in gently, exploring her flesh with his tongue. He teased her belly button, and stroked the length of her thigh. She was moaning deeply. He brushed against her mound of pubic hair and she shuddered with excitement. He traced along its upper edge with his tongue. She was shivering with delight. He moved downward, and suddenly, she gripped his head and pushed him away.

He resisted, but allowed her to move him slightly. He went back to kissing her along the edge of her pubic hair.

"Come on, baby, let me," he said.

"No, do what you're doing. I love that."

"You'll like it even better if you let me."

"No, don't."

"I'll be gentle."

"No, it doesn't matter."

"But baby,"

Janelle pulled herself up and sat.

"No, I told you, no. I won't. No."

"What is it? I thought if I took time with you and was very gentle, you'd see it could be good for you." He was leaning on one elbow, looking intently into her face, stroking her hip.

"Oh, is that what you thought? So, tonight was going to be whatever you thought I wanted? Not what I want? That's good, Charles. Thanks a lot. Anything else you want to tell me I want?"

He was surprised by the edge in her voice.

"Janelle, I just meant. . ."

She cut him off.

"You meant you were going to show me a good time. You were going to make sure I enjoyed myself. I know. *You* were going to take care of me. *You* were going to make me feel good. *You* were going to make me come. I know."

Janelle drew her legs up and clamped her arms around them.

"I told you about modeling during college, but I never gave you the rest of the story. When I got away to college, I thought the whole world opened up to me. I got away from my parents, and I got away from that town where I was always afraid someone was going to know what happened. I figured I could start out all over again.

"It was a whole different ball game. No one knew me, and no one knew my past. Suddenly, I was hot. Guys were sniffing around all the time. I was getting asked out right from the first day. The first day! Pretty soon, I was going out all the time. And, I liked it. Pretty soon, I figured out who had all the power. I did. I had what guys wanted. And, you know what? Those guys liked me. They treated me like I was gold. They wanted to hold me and be tender. The sex, I didn't need; I had enough of that to last a lifetime, but I loved the kissing and the tender, romantic touches. Of course, I couldn't keep a guy dangling on a string forever, so eventually, I'd sleep with him. They thought I was great. I learned what a guy wanted. You want moaning and groaning? I got it. You want me to thrash around? I can do that. You want oral sex?

I'm the best. Guys go crazy for that and they're so grateful afterward. I got the tenderness I wanted, and they got sex.

"But every now and then a guy would feel like he had to do more, like he needed to be the world's greatest lover, and he'd try to take over, like you did."

She hesitated. This was going to be difficult. She'd been holding back from him.

"Charles, I never told you I was married once, did I?"

"No." The news shocked him. She'd never said a word about being married. He knew there were large patches of her life he knew nothing about, and he didn't pry into them. He'd always figured she'd tell him when she was ready. But this? It was his turn to pull back.

"No, you never told me that."

"Well, I was. For almost three years. It didn't work out so well." She was avoiding his eyes.

"Wayne was a good man. I loved him. We met when we were seniors. I was getting tired of my party girl life, and he seemed very solid, very reliable. We kept running into each other on campus and always seemed to end up talking for a long time. He was funny. He was interesting. He could listen. It was only after we started really going out that he admitted we hadn't just run into each other. He had been trying to get to know me. He'd heard some guys saying I went through a lot of guys, and he was trying to figure out why. He said he thought it was because none of them could keep up with a bright girl like me.

"So, we started going out. Right before graduation, he asked me to marry him. I was astonished. I'd never thought anyone would want to marry me, and I never thought I'd care enough about a guy to want to say yes. Then Wayne came along, and I stayed interested. He was great. So I said yes.

"Things started out all right. His job was a good one. He was working in his father's investment house. He couldn't take on his own clients yet, because he was too young. People get nervous when real money is concerned, so he was working as an assistant, but he was doing well, so we knew it would only be a matter of time till he had his own clients and the money would start pouring in. In a way, I respected his father for doing that. He wanted Wayne to learn the business from the bottom up.

"We bought a house. Nothing spectacular, but it was ours. We were happy. At least, we were for a while. Eventually, Wayne noticed I didn't enjoy sex all that much. Like you did. It took a while, because I kept him busy with my bag of tricks. I kept him pretty much sexed out. When he noticed, he took it very personally. He kept trying to 'satisfy' me. He tried everything.

"Finally, he decided he wasn't going to 'take advantage' of me anymore. He said that when we made love, he was going to take care of me first, and if I didn't have an orgasm, he wouldn't do anything for himself. I didn't like that idea, but he insisted. He would start in on me, with his mouth usually, and keep at it. The first few times, when I gave up, he did too. He meant it; he wasn't going to let me do anything for him unless I had an orgasm first. So I learned how to force my body to come. It was awful. I'd be stiff as a board, every muscle straining, I'd be sore afterward, all over. But, I could come. Then we would have intercourse, and he seemed happier.

"Eventually, I realized I was right back in the same situation. In high school, I had to force myself to lay there while they did what they wanted to do. In marriage, I had to force my body to do what Wayne wanted it to do. Either way, what was happening didn't have much to do with me or what I wanted, and I resented the lack of control.

"So, when you start talking about wanting to please me, I don't believe it. I've been down that road. I don't want to go there anymore. Not even with you."

She could feel herself pulling away emotionally, as she always did when she had to reveal something she thought would bother him. It was like she was preparing for him to leave. Again. What was it about this man that made him so persistent? And what made her want him to remain?

"I guess I underestimated you," he finally said, quietly. "I had no idea."

"How would you?" she said. "It's my fault for not telling you sooner. But that's why I don't like it when you try to force me in any way. I won't allow that."

Charles had never thought of it as forcing her. He had thought he was helping her.

"So, what do you want?"

"I want to go on loving you. It's beautiful when you hold me, kiss me and caress me. And I do like having you inside, even though it's not the way you expect. I like the intimacy. I enjoy your pleasure. I really do. Let me enjoy that without expecting anything else. I can't put up with feeling forced in any way. Not now, not ever. I couldn't be true to myself and allow that. You understand?"

"Are you really happy with what we have?"

"I am. Maybe in time our lovemaking will become even better, but, yes. I'm happy."

Charles was confused. He felt that if for some reason his penis went numb, he'd never want to make love ever again. Or would he? He had to admit, all those times she had a spasm and couldn't take him inside, he liked holding her. He'd been surprised that he didn't feel frustration when he couldn't continue, but he didn't. They would end up lying together, holding hands, talking sometimes, sometimes remaining silent. And never, never had he felt cheated. He'd felt lucky to have a remarkable woman by his side.

"All right. I won't try. I won't do that again until you invite me. If you ever feel like you might be ready, let me know. Otherwise, I won't."

"And you're okay with that?"

"I am. Janelle, you keep surprising me. I never seem to know where we're going or what to think. But, somehow, I always feel like we're moving ahead."

"We are. I know it." She straightened out her legs and leaned over to kiss him. Only her lips touched him, and he felt every ounce of energy he had go into enjoying the savory sensation.

They lingered. Then, she pulled him over on top of her, and they made love beautifully and lovingly. It lasted a long time.

****

"You look distracted, sweetie, what is it?"

"Yeah, dad. I am.

The silence was disturbing. Around them restaurant noises continued. Voices drifted in and out from a dozen conversations. Glasses were set down, silverware clanked against plates.

But here, at their table, nothing was being said. Their weekly dinners weren't always fun. Laura was growing up without him. It no longer occurred to her to fill him in on all the details of her life. He knew the big picture, the main events, but he was losing touch with the day to day flavorings, and he knew it. He wondered how long she'd bother to fill him in at all.

"What is it?"

"Well, you know I've been working at the donut shop a few blocks from my dorm."

"Yeah, I know. Your boss treating you all right?"

"Yeah, he's fine."

"He working you too hard?"

"No, he's fine."

"So, then. . ."

"Well, you know we get all kinds. The roughest part of the job is dealing with crap from customers: 'I said I didn't want any cream-filled in that dozen!' 'Can't you make sure the box doesn't smoosh the frosting on the chocolate ones?' It goes on and on."

"I'm sure it does. Some people are too fussy, I get that, too, you know. You think people are fussy about donuts? Try showing them a car with carpet a shade off what they're picturing in their head."

"No, dad, that's not it. I mean, yeah, I know that happens to you. I know it's part of the job. I try to do what I need to do and ignore the crap. That's not it." She pushed some rice around her plate. He watched her fork for a moment, then returned to her eyes. They seemed darker today. Brown eyes can look so sad, he thought. What's wrong with my little girl?

"I can handle all that." She stopped playing with her rice. He could see the muscles in her neck tighten. She took a deep breath. Her eyes shot up to meet his.

"It's the men. I can handle most of them. Most are lonely guys who are trying to have some fun with a pretty girl. That's no problem. But some of them are . . . so . . . gross."

"Gross? You mean ugly?"

"No, I mean gross. What they say. This old guy was in yesterday, I mean, he had to be almost sixty. Gray hair, the works. Nice clothes, nice suit. But when I'm getting his coffee, he leans over the counter, real far. I mean, real far, so he can talk to me quietly. He says, 'Hey sweetie, see that black beauty in the parking lot out front? That's mine. Wanna go for a ride sometime?' I can't believe it, and he's not even looking at me; he's staring at my chest. You should have seen his face. Gross." She shook visibly, and returned to pushing rice on her plate.

"That shit happens all the time."

She wasn't in the habit of swearing with him. He tried not to react.

"What do you mean, honey?"

"I mean with all of them. Young guys, married guys with their wives beside them, wrinkled grandfathers, staring at my chest, not even trying to pretend they aren't. And the things they say." She was flowing, the words were pouring out of her. She was gripping her fork tightly, her wrists tense.

"The things they say," she repeated. "'Nice ass.' 'Hey, nice boobs.' 'I bet you can make your boyfriend shout, huh?' 'I got a huge éclair for you, baby. Want something you can really sink your teeth into?' 'I could think of some things to do with that frosting.' 'The donuts fresh? How about you?' 'When you get off work? I got some booze out in the car.' 'Ever seen the inside of an RV?' 'Bet you get tired on your feet all night, how about we get you on your back?' 'You got nice lips, baby, wanna wrap them around something hard?'

"Last week some guy came in, and when I went to get his donut, he laid some skin magazine on the counter. When I turned around again, he pointed to it, and said, 'Damn, girl, you look just like her, don't you think? Your tits are bigger, though, I bet, huh? How about we go and find out?'"

Her grip got tighter and tighter, like she was trying to drill through her plate with her fork. Charles didn't know what to say to her. He'd never heard her talk this way before. He didn't even know what she wanted. Did she want advice? Did she want him to cry out and vow revenge? Did she just need to tell him? He couldn't tell; he didn't know her well enough anymore. He couldn't protect her from all the jerks in the world. He couldn't take her in his arms and make her a little girl again and make everything okay.

He knew he wasn't getting it. There was something else. Something she hadn't said.

"Keep going, honey. I can't stand to hear this, but I know I have to. What is it?"

She pushed down hard with her fork. No movement, just force, raw force. He wondered if she'd shatter the plate.

"Why do they do it, dad?"

"Why? I don't know, some people are like that, some people don't know what the limits are. Some people . . ." He was flailing about helplessly.

"No, dad. Why me." It wasn't a question. Now he was seriously puzzled. And worried.

"Why you? Don't they do it to the other girls?"

"Yeah, they do it to the others, but that doesn't matter. What matters is me."

Her eyes slowly raised, until they were almost on his. Almost.

"They like me because I'm pretty, so they think they can do and say whatever they want. And when they have sex with their wives or girlfriends they're thinking of me. And when they're done and go downstairs and open a beer and get online, they're thinking of me. And nothing would please them more than if they found a naked picture of me on a sleazy porn site. Maybe they'll find someone who looks like me and they'll download her and jack off, and they'll be gross and they'll think they haven't done anything wrong. It's disgusting.

"And dad," She put down the fork and stared straight at him. Tears glistened in her eyes—tears, and a solidity he'd never seen before, like polished walnut on a gunstock, gleaming, hard, and dangerous.

"That's what you did. That's what's wrong. That's why I don't want much dinner tonight."

She sat still, looking small, but looking defiant at the same time. She had been angry with him ever since the raid, and this was the first time she'd confronted him. He wanted to comfort her, he wanted to take care of his little girl, and he could do nothing. How had being pretty turned into such a bad thing? When she was little it was nothing but joy. Everyone always commented on how pretty she was, and she beamed when she heard it. Now, she can't bear it. He hated all those men. But she was right; he was one of them. He had taken all those women, and he had tried to take Janelle.

He looked in her eyes. She was so strong. She was so good. She was so determined.

And he was nothing.

****

"She hates me."

Janelle turned from her book. She was sitting in the sun by the living room window, curled up in her round chair.

"What do you mean?"

"She hates me. We were having dinner, and she burst into this tirade about how men look at her and how I was hurting women by looking at them. She hates me. She said she can't stand to think of me."

He slumped down on the floor in front of the couch. The sunlight flooded over him, leaving his face in shadow.

Janelle straightened herself to see him better.

"It can't be that bad. She doesn't hate you."

"She does. You didn't hear her. She hates me. She slammed down her fork and glared at me. I never heard her so angry in her whole life. I thought maybe I was starting to put it all behind me. I have you. I have a new life, and I've paid hard for it. Living with that guilt every day was wearing me down. I was starting to feel like maybe all that was over, and now, Laura hates me. It's like it all happened yesterday."

He looked defeated, and the desire to comfort him welled up in her, but she didn't give in to it. He didn't need her comfort. He needed her to listen to him.

"You sure she hates you?" she asked.

"She thinks I ruined her life."

Janelle struggled to focus on him. It was easier to go into her mind and imagine all the things she could do for him. She could gather him in her arms, kiss him, surround him with her warmth and melt away his pain. She could draw him out. If she got down on the floor with him, it would only take a few moments of her scent, her arms around him. With a few gentle kisses he'd melt. They'd make love. He would tell her he loved her, and they would move on with their day and they would be all right again. This moment would pass.

But it wouldn't work. She'd learned that much. Healing comes from facing the pain and moving through it, not burying it. She could soothe the pain from his wounds, but the infection would linger.

This was a huge decision for her, and he didn't even know what she was wrestling with; he was too wrapped up in his own needs.

"Janelle?"

"Yes?" She must have glazed over. She hadn't even noticed he'd raised his head. Several minutes must have passed.

"Thank you for not trying to fix this. I need to be with it."

She saw the gratefulness in his eyes. All he needed from her was her presence, she didn't have to divert him from his pain with her body; it was a moment for her heart.

She watched him sit and thanked him, oddly enough, for not wanting her. Gradually, her body gave up its sexual energy, and she noticed it also gave up its anxiety. She relaxed, she felt the sun again, and she breathed deeply.

****

"How's it going with Darla?"

Charles was having lunch again with Tricia. Their meals together were becoming somewhat regular. He was even getting teased by some of the other guys.

"She's doing better. The whole thing's pretty much died down. She still gets harassed once in a while, but not too often, and she's learned how to take it in stride. She sure seems to have toughened up in the past couple months. She's not half so concerned with what people think about her."

"I'm glad it's working out for her," Charles said. "Still, you don't seem all that relieved."

"Life hasn't been a bowl of cherries overall," Tricia said. She was chewing thoughtfully.

"What's up?"

"You really want to know?"

"May as well. Avoiding it doesn't help any."

"Darla's only been part of what's been bothering me. She's the most visible part. She makes sure you notice her." She put down her sandwich and took a drink of coffee.

"Her drama gives us something to talk about," she said. "Tom and me. We can always talk about what to do with her. Argue is more like it. He's all for clamping down on her and not giving her any freedom. He'd like her to live in school and her room. Me, I'd go crazy with her around all the time, and I figure she needs to get out and make choices, make mistakes and learn from them."

"No doubt," Charles said.

"I can see what he's afraid of. You know. You raised a girl. There's plenty to be afraid of. But I'm afraid of what happens when she leaves. If we keep her on a leash till she goes off to college, what'll happen when no one's guiding her and temptation calls from every direction?"

"Makes sense."

"I think so. Tom thinks I'm nuts. He goes on and on about drinking parties, sex, drugs, the whole nine yards. He wants to protect her. And he's right, but I don't think shutting her in is the way to deal with it."

"No one ever said parenting is easy," Charles said, "or that parents would agree on it."

"Well, that's only half of it," Tricia said. "I think we argue about her so we won't argue about other things."

"Like?"

"Like," Tricia stopped and took another sip of coffee. "Not wanting to spend much time together. Disagreeing about nearly every decision." She paused, "Not doing anything in the bedroom anymore."

She picked up her sandwich and took another bite, using it as a shield between them.

Charles recoiled. This was exactly the kind of thing he'd tried to insulate himself from for years. Talking about Tricia's daughter was one thing. Talking about her sex life was quite another.

"What do you think is going on?" he asked.

"I don't know," Tricia said. "We don't seem to connect anymore."

"Did you ever?" he asked. That question came from out of nowhere, but as soon as he'd asked, he knew where it came from. His marriage. Janelle's.

"Of course! We were in love once," Tricia said. "What do you mean did we ever?"

"I mean, did you really connect? Or were you having a lot of fun and figured it was connection? Did you ever talk about what you expected from each other?"

"Charles, you're scaring me. You're starting to sound like a daytime talk show host."

"All I know is that I didn't do that with my wife till it was too late. I think a lot of people get into marriage before they know what they really want."

"Well, we did all right. We were happy for a long time."

"But were you connected? Did you know him? Do you feel like he knows you?"

Tricia didn't answer.

Charles let her think for a minute. He fiddled with the last of his salad. He picked out the bits of spinach and radicchio. One olive remained. He deftly speared it with his fork and chewed it, savoring its sharp flavor and juiciness.

"Do we ever really know anyone else?" Tricia finally said.

"I'm not sure," Charles said. "I'm working on that one myself."

"What should I do?"

"I guess you talk," he said. "Don't assume things. Don't assume you know what he thinks or feels. Ask him. Listen when he tells you. Tell him what you think."

"I don't assume much," she said. "I know him pretty well."

"I bet you assume a lot more than you think," he said. "You don't know it because you never take the time to find out."

Now Tricia was chewing thoughtfully again.

"I guess," she finally said. "I guess it's worth a try."

"Can't hurt," Charles said. "Even if it does."

Chapter 12

JANELLE WAS trying to figure out the right shade of brown to mix in. Burnt sienna wasn't quite it, though Tuscan earth and Van Dyke brown were definitely out. She was trying to paint Shandra, a golden retriever she'd had as a girl, and she wasn't able to find the basic color of her coat.

Since Charles was going to be tied up all weekend with Donnie's eighteenth birthday, she had decided to take that large block of time and start a painting that had been playing in the back of her mind for months. She was basing it on a photo she had taken of Shandra one day when the two of them had been wandering all over a park, throwing sticks and racing after squirrels. It was the last time she could remember being totally carefree.

But the browns weren't right. She tried mixing in another variation of yellow.

Painting was nearly a lifelong hobby. She didn't paint often, but now and again, an image would work its way into her mind and hover until she got out the paints and a canvas and started in on it. She found the process relaxing, a different kind of mental activity, one that was almost completely intuitive and nonverbal; it took her away from her everyday world and thoughts.

Mozart filled the room, a CD of various pieces that she found soothing. The music quieted her usually active mind and allowed the creative portion free rein to dominate and discover. She was painting by a window that allowed the dim March light to wash over the canvas, balancing the yellowish incandescent indoor light.

She found a shade she thought might work and started filling in Shandra's back. She carefully directed her strokes to reflect the lay of her fur, even though little of this layer would show in the finished piece. She was preparing herself, warming herself up.

She wondered how things would go for Charles. She knew he'd be happy to see Laura; the two of them had reconciled after her outburst and seemed to be rebuilding their relationship. Donald would be a different story. He was getting increasingly uncontrollable and resentful. Turning eighteen wouldn't make him any easier to handle. And there was Ellen. She wondered who this woman was who had lived with Charles for so long and knew him so well. She wondered how they had been when they were in love. She couldn't help comparing herself to Ellen and wondering how she stacked up.

"I hope it goes all right," she said aloud, surprising herself.

She was worried about him seeing Ellen again, but she sensed there was more to it than that.

"Well, he's been off lately," she said.

She usually wasn't someone to talk to herself. She focused again on her brushwork.

He's been quieter, she thought. Slow to laugh. Almost cautious. Like he's afraid of saying or doing the wrong thing.

Was he getting tired of her? It would make sense. She was his rebound relationship. Rebounds never work. The guy gets his feet wet, starts to get his confidence back, then he's out the door looking for something real.

"He isn't doing that." She was starting to get used to the sound of her own voice in the empty room.

They'd been through too much. He'd grown too much. He'd helped her too much. This relationship was more serious than that.

She shook herself. He'd admitted it was hard to have her react as she sometimes did when they made love, but he'd also said he felt honored that he could provide the emotionally safe space she needed to face her trauma reactions. He had mentioned many times how massaging her pushed minor thoughts and worries right out of his head and made him more aware of his own feelings. She grounded him. What was she worried about?

He had a lot going on with his kids. Winter was a slow time at work. Winter's hard on everyone. Seasonal Affective Disorder. She'd read about it. The winter blues.

"Why can't I get this?"

She'd made a bad brush stroke and ruined the line of Shandra's back. Stopping made her realize she wasn't happy with the color after all. It was too much like wheat.

She picked up some Mars Yellow and squeezed a blob onto her palate.

"It's so simple; it's only a color. It's probably right in front of me."

Right in front of me, she repeated to herself. That's what Victoria says. The answer to everything is right in front of you. Every problem comes bearing its own solution. Whatever is missing in a relationship is what you're not bringing to it.

"So what's the problem?"

She knew the answer: she didn't trust Charles. She didn't believe he could love her the way he said he did. She didn't trust him. But why? The first time she had screamed during a massage, he'd looked horrified that he'd hurt her. But he didn't let it stop him. He worked on her patiently and calmly, and with such tenderness. The same thing when she had a flashback while making love. He had looked so confused and hurt the first few times. Now, he would hold her and comfort her until it passed.

How rare is that? What man can stop making love and be content with holding and comforting his lover? How much more proof did she need? Why couldn't she open up to him like he had with her, why couldn't she let go and ride the currents?

"Because he won't want me if he knows me."

That statement surprised her. He knew about her modeling. He knew about her abuse. He knew about her marriage. He had taken it all in stride. He never judged her. He'd told her about his past, and she was sure she'd heard it all. He was so open with her, so generous with his history and his inner fears and doubts.

She had told him about everything she had done. Every guy, every dumb decision, all her worst moments. She had shared it all.

Except.

She had never told him what she was. Or wasn't. She had never told him she wasn't a real woman, a whole woman. That she was incompetent. She guarded that nugget closely, held it tight to her heart. She couldn't share that one.

She put down her brush. She felt unsteady. The canvas blurred in front of her. She felt her heart slowing down, and she went into the living room to lie on the floor.

She felt the weight of Celia's presence within her. She felt the old pressure against her skin, stretching it, forming a growing bulge that mystified her with its independence. She remembered looking down, running her fingertips over her belly, amazed at how solid it felt, how smooth the skin, how complex the curves. She loved it. She couldn't touch it enough. She showed it off to her friends. She had Wayne photograph it.

She had been entranced by Celia. She swore she knew right when her baby was conceived. She had felt something happening. It was palpable. A change. Indefinable and indescribable, but a change. When she later missed her period and took the pregnancy test, that moment came back to her. That was it, she knew it. She had been able to think back and remember what was going on and figure out exactly what day it had been. March 23. Celia's day. The miraculous day of her beginning.

As the pregnancy progressed, Janelle grew more and more fascinated. She had little morning sickness, and she attributed that blessing to her love for her baby. She always knew it was a girl. Her girl. Her chance to shine. She had created a new life, and she promised herself she would take good care of her baby. Celia would be the most perfectly loved girl in the world.

As Celia grew, as Janelle's belly expanded, she became more and more enamored of her darling. Wayne was thrilled, too. He said he'd always wanted a girl and he was so happy and so proud of her for making one. He helped decide how to decorate the nursery and happily started painting and papering it. He helped pick out clothes, toys and bedding. He was a perfect father. His dissatisfaction with her lovemaking disappeared, and he bragged about his new daughter to all his friends.

And their world grew. Her joy grew. She was journaling every day about the new life within her. She tried several times to paint portraits of her daughter. The water colors shimmered with life and promise, but Janelle never felt she got the image right. She painted over and over again, one image following another as she tried to give form to the unknown life within her. Together, she and Wayne would hold her belly and coo to it at night, quietly singing their daughter into life.

The day she felt the first kick she felt so triumphantly alive she couldn't contain herself. She actually danced around the room, feeling Celia's weight moving to her rhythms.

From then on, Janelle had a companion. She learned her baby's habits and knew her personality, all from her faint stirrings.

One morning, she felt unsteady when she woke up. She couldn't put her finger on it at first, a little crampiness, almost like a menstrual cramp, so she figured she'd lain in an odd position and Celia had pressed on one of her organs too heavily. Or, maybe it was just another one of the new facets of her pregnancy. She couldn't tell.

The feeling continued all day. She noticed her discharge was runny when she went to the bathroom. She knew some variation was normal and didn't worry about it. In fact, she congratulated herself that she was having so few uncomfortable symptoms. She was sure her pregnancy was going well because she took such good care of herself and her baby.

The next day, though, she had pink coloration in her discharge and more crampiness. She called her doctor. The nurse told her to come in to the office, just in case, she said. Just in case. Probably nothing wrong. This happens all the time. We'll take a look, she said.

So Janelle went in, by herself. Nothing was wrong, after all. She waited nervously in the reception area, chatting with another woman about their bellies and names and plans and room decorations.

She was called in. She got on the table, and the doctor came in to examine her. Almost as soon as he began, his face changed slightly, and he stood up and took off his gloves.

"Janelle, we need to move you over to the hospital right away. I'm glad it's right across the street; we can take you over on a gurney, so you don't even need to get up. You're pretty fully dilated. That means your cervix has gotten soft and has stretched open wide. It needs to do that when you deliver, but now it should still be small and tight. The way it is, the only thing holding your baby in is the water sac, and that's not enough. We'll have to get you over there right away. At 22 weeks, if you want to keep this baby, you'll have to be very good. We're going to keep you on bed rest, head down, so gravity will help keep the baby in. We'll put in a catheter so you won't even have to move to pee. If your water breaks, we're going to lose the baby. I'm going to go and make the call; I'll send a nurse right in to get you ready."

And with that, he was gone, and Janelle was alone with the baby she loved so dearly and the body that was betraying them both.

They moved her into a hospital room. She called Wayne and he left work and came over right away. He was an angel. He sat with her and comforted her and did whatever she asked. She was determined to keep her baby safe, so she lay patiently on the bed and prayed. She would do whatever it took.

Wayne stayed by her bedside that night, holding her hand. The next day he had to leave her to go to work, but promised he'd call and be back right afterward. He was. That night, she told him to go home so he could get a full night's rest. No point in wearing him out, she said. The nurses could take care of her. He reluctantly agreed, and she settled in for a long, lonely night.

It took her a long time to get to sleep. Every noise in the hall startled her. Her mind raced. She tried to shut out her fears, but they kept resurfacing.

Finally, she slept.

She awoke to a dark room lit only by a few pilot lights from the equipment around her. She felt strange, she felt wetness around her legs and bottom, and as she gathered consciousness, she realized what it was. She fumbled for the call button, crying out at the same time.

"Nurse! Nurse!"

Soon, Emily, the night nurse came in and turned on the lights. She took one glance at the bed and her face stiffened. She stepped back out the door and called up the hall.

"Sheila? Could you bring me some nitrazine paper?

She turned back to Janelle.

"Come on honey, let's see what we've got." She gently lifted the sheet off Janelle and pulled it back.

"We got a little mess is what we got," she said. "Come on, honey, it'll be all right. We'll take care of it."

Sheila walked in. She handed the nitrazine to Emily and went to Janelle's side. She smoothed out the sheet beside her and smiled.

Emily went back to work. In a moment, she nodded to Sheila, who left the room. Emily looked directly at Janelle.

"I want you to stay still. Your water broke, so we've got to be very careful. Don't move. I'm going to tidy up, and we're going to wait together for the doctor to get here."

Janelle was terrified. She did as she was told. She lay perfectly still, not even talking. She wasn't going to do anything to hurt her baby. Nothing. She forced her breathing to be slow and deep. She tried to calm herself. She told herself it would be all right.

She felt pressure building up inside her. It grew. It felt almost like she was going to empty her bowels, but that wasn't it. She knew that wasn't it. The pressure grew. She fought it. She tried to clamp herself shut, but the pressure grew, and she felt herself pushing. She fought that, too, but her body didn't obey. She couldn't control it. She pushed.

Emily dropped the sponge she was using to clean her thighs and turned to face her.

"Oh, no."

Janelle felt something wet and warm moving against her.

"Oh my, oh my, Janelle, it's here."

Emily took a towel and reached down between Janelle's legs. She swaddled a tiny bundle.

"Janelle, honey, she's here, but she's so little. She's too little to make it. The doctor's on his way, but there's not much we can do. She's too little. Do you want to hold her? You can while we wait, or I can do it for you. She won't last long, though, no matter what we do."

Janelle couldn't believe what she was hearing. A few days ago she had a healthy daughter dancing inside her. Now?

She nodded slowly, unable to speak. Emily handed the bundle to her and helped her scooch up so she could see better.

Celia was perfect. She had miniature toes and fingers and fingernails and tightly sealed eyelids, and they were beautiful. She was a tiny little girl, hardly bigger than a can of soda, perfectly formed, perfect in every way, except she was dying. Her chest moved spasmodically. Her lips were turning blue. Her arms twitched. Her chest had the slightest rattle to it; she was too small to struggle much. Her eyes shuddered. Then, she lay still.

Is she still here? Janelle wondered. Is she still here with me? If she isn't, where did she go? Is she still in the room? Where is my baby? Where's my Celia? Baby, where are you? Stay with mommy, stay.

Celia lay unmoving.

After a few moments, Emily spoke.

"You can hold her as long as you want, honey. This is the only time you're going to have with her, so make the most of it. She's a beautiful little girl. Hold her. Talk to her and pray for her. I'm going to finish cleaning you up, and then I'll leave you alone. Do you want me to call your husband for you?"

Janelle nodded weakly. She was staring at her baby, examining every bit of flesh. She really was perfect. She had grown well. She was beautiful.

Twenty-two weeks. If only you'd made it a few weeks longer. They could have done something. They could have saved you.

Why baby? Why? Why couldn't you stay with me? Soon, she was quiet, even in her mind as the tears fell. There were no thoughts, no words for this. She felt the slight weight in her arms. She felt emptied.

She was still holding Celia when Wayne arrived. He strode quickly into the room, turned on the bright lights, and went straight to Janelle's side. He reached down and moved aside the blanket with one finger. She could see the tears welling up, his face fighting back the emotions. He looked at Celia for a long time. Then he plopped down into the chair.

He was silent for several minutes. Janelle could see he was struggling. It had all been dumped on him too quickly. He hadn't been there to see it, to feel it. She waited.

Finally, he spoke. His voice was very quiet, very slow.

"What did you do? Why didn't you do what they told you?" he paused. "The one important thing you ever did in your life and you screwed it up."

Janelle couldn't believe it. She had been holding her baby, trying to know her and love her, hoping Wayne would arrive quickly so they could say goodbye to her together and hold her together, but he was accusing her.

"I thought this was going to work," he said. "I guess not."

And he was out the door.

Janelle was shocked. How could he leave her? How could he leave their baby girl? Her mind raced, her chest heaved with sobs. Finally, gradually, she calmed down, and returned to simply holding her baby and talking to her. She told her about all her plans and dreams. She told her stories about dancing with her and painting her. Finally, she was ready to say goodbye.

"Goodbye, Celia. You were a good girl. You were mommy's best thing, the best thing I ever did. I'm sorry you couldn't stay longer. We'd have had a good life together. You go on. I'll see you when I get there. I will. I know I will. Goodbye for now, sweetheart. I love you."

Janelle was alone for a long time. Finally, the nurse returned and Celia was taken away.

Things happened quickly after that. The arguments. The fights. Wayne blamed her for Celia's death. She blamed herself. The doctor said her incompetent cervix might have been caused by any number of factors and he couldn't be sure what would happen if she got pregnant again, but the chances were good she'd have the same problem. He didn't know if she'd ever be able to have a baby.

She knew she wasn't going to have one with Wayne. His accusations were brutal. He wasn't violent, but he couldn't understand no one was to blame. He had to blame something, and Janelle became the target. When the doctor said the incompetent cervix could have been caused by a procedure done years earlier as a result of a chronic infection, Wayne said it was all her fault because she was such a slut and had been with so many guys.

The fights continued, and finally, he left. Janelle barely missed him. The quiet he left behind was better than anything she'd hoped to regain with him. She knew she'd never trust him with another pregnancy. She was so heartbroken, she didn't think she could face another one at all. She didn't want to find out if her body would betray her again. Six months later, she had her tubes tied and put an end to wondering.

She stayed in their old house for a few months, then found the job in Hartleton. She shook the dust off her feet when she left town and devoted herself to creating a new life and burying the old one. She had nothing to remember, nothing to care about.

Except March 23, the day her world had opened up. The day she kept for herself and cherished for herself as the one day she had created something beautiful and pure. The one day she never shared with anyone.

Even her beloved Charles.

Lying on her living room floor, paint-stained sweatshirt and all, she cried. She cried again for Celia, and she cried for the one man she'd hoped could finally love her if she would let him. Her heart had been screaming for someone to share her anniversary of joy with, to share her burden of pain, but once she left Jonestown, she had never told anyone. Celia was private.

She knew what was missing in their relationship. She was. She had never let him fully know her. She hadn't trusted him with her heart, and so he couldn't find his way in.

Her chest heaved with gut-wrenching sobs; she let out low, guttural moans that filled the room and drained her body of energy. The tears rolled down relentlessly. Her heart ached.

Eventually, the tears stopped flowing, and she remained stretched out on the floor, feeling her chest emptied of all the fears and tensions she'd been holding in. She could feel the hollow space where the pain had been, and she held on to that feeling. She explored it, probed the raw edges where it had been ripped free. She had let go. She had seen it and felt it. Now it was time to fill that void. She was ready.

****

Janelle was sitting on the floor, cross-legged.

"You said it was important."

She had called Charles while he was on his way home from taking Laura back to college. Her voice had been insistent, so he came despite how tired he was from the weekend. She sat quietly, collecting herself.

Finally, she drew in a deep breath and began her story.

It took a long time. She didn't know how Charles was going to react to this news. She plowed forward, knowing she had to tell him; she couldn't hold back any more. He was quiet. He listened. He let her tell the story in all its emotional depth. She started crying all over again, which made it take even longer. She could only get out a single sentence, sometimes a few words before she'd have to pause. Describing how beautifully innocent and pure Celia seemed in her few minutes of life took forever. Janelle couldn't put into words all she felt as she pored over every contour of her daughter's body. She struggled with every word, tears streaming down her face.

Charles sat quietly. He asked a few questions from time to time to make sure he understood, but otherwise he didn't interrupt. She could only bear to look up at him a few times; she was so wrapped up in her story and so afraid of his response.

When she finished, she stopped talking. She stretched out on the floor. She needed to wring herself out after that intense ordeal. Her back arched and her arms raised above her, reaching up and behind as her whole body formed a vaguely crescent shape.

She released her position and came to her knees just before Charles.

"Why haven't you told me this?" he finally asked.

"I don't tell anyone." She placed her hands on his ankles. "It still hurts too much."

They shared silence for a while.

"So, this is almost her anniversary, isn't it? She was conceived around this time of year?"

Janelle was stunned. Yes. This week, in fact. Wednesday would be her anniversary. Twelve years ago Wednesday, her Celia began her brief life. Somehow, Janelle had not allowed herself to notice the date. That's why she'd been on edge, that's why she was so dissatisfied and impatient lately. Even though her mind was refusing to think about it, her body and her heart knew it was Celia's time. She shook herself, confused. She had never forgotten before. Why now?

"Well, then, we'll have to do something for her. We need to honor her," he said quietly, looking right at Janelle.

"Can we?"

"We have to. It's too important to let pass by. I don't know what I would have done if I'd lost one of my children. I can't imagine what it was like for you. I don't know what I can do to help you, but I know we have to do something. Even though I never saw her, she's a part of both our lives."

Janelle looked up at him in surprise. He understood. Most people never even wanted to admit Celia had ever existed. Her own mother told her she had to get over it and put the memory behind her. "It's not like she was a real child," her mother had said. Not a real child? She had held her, loved her. She was as real as anyone could be. For a while, before she moved to Hartleton, she used to say yes when people asked if she had children. Yes, but she died. But when she'd explain, no one understood that Celia was her little girl and that she had lost her. But Charles did. He heard.

He sat down beside her and took her in his arms.

"We can have a ceremony. We'll light candles, and we'll talk to her. We'll wish her well and thank her for being here with you for the time she was. We'll remember her."

Janelle began to cry all over again. This time, though, the sobs were quieter, more peaceful. She remembered what her therapist said, not to judge tears or pain, but to listen to what they were telling her. So she calmed her mind and simply felt.

She held Charles closer to her and stroked his head with her hand. Gradually, she understood. These weren't tears of grief at all; these were tears of relief. Her heart was crying because it could finally let go and be at peace. She could drop her guard and let the tears flow; Charles could hear them, and he would listen to them. She kept stroking his hair and felt his arms around her. How could she be so lucky?

****

The next morning, Charles was doing his regular perusal of the local news when suddenly "The Stars and Stripes Forever" blared through the dealership's sound system at full volume. He nearly spilled his coffee.

Then, over the sound of the brass, he heard Harry.

"Come on ladies! Time to wake up! It's a new day, let's get a move on! Drop your cocks and grab your socks, it's time to roll!"

Harry was blustering through the whole place, popping his head into every cubicle, clapping his hands and shouting at them all like they were new recruits in Marine boot camp.

When everyone had made it out onto the main sales floor, he yelled back to Tricia.

"Okay babe! Cut the music!"

He turned to face them.

"All right, men, it's been easy duty for a while, but it's time to shake off the winter blues. We gotta get things moving around here! No more whining that no one's coming in! No more bellyaching. Your momma's not gonna bring in customers! Now, I want you all to get out there and hustle! Every name you have you think might be getting in the mood for a new car, call em! I'm gettin' a new hot convertible in next week, it's gonna be parked right here in front in the window, and we're gonna be talkin' springtime and summer cruisin! I don't care if it snows ten feet tomorrow! It's springtime in here!"

And with that, he began slapping guys on the back and talking them up. Charles endured his turn and made his way to the break room to get some more coffee. He'd do it. He had some names. He knew the drill. But his heart wasn't in it.

"Not that it ever was," he murmured to himself.

Janelle grounded him. She brought him to realize who he was and who she was. They had no pretense between them anymore, they'd shared their most shameful moments, and they'd learned how to truly feel their own emotions without interpreting or judging them. Together they had discovered what truly drove their lives, what they valued and wanted. When he was with her, social custom disappeared. What remained, distilled in its pure essence, was himself, and the miracle was that when Janelle saw his essence, she loved it.

Now, Charles saw events and activities differently. He no longer looked for what would be fun or entertaining. He sought what would be fulfilling and nourishing. He was astonished at all he used to value that now seemed empty and meaningless. Once, he had avoided many TV shows because they reminded him of his shameful sexual past; now he simply saw them as silly. He honestly could find no reason to be interested or entertained by people driven by vanity or greed. He felt no connection to that world at all. That was the world of shadow. That was the world of new cars.

He sighed, and wondered once again what else he might do for a living. His college degree was over twenty years out of date. He scarcely remembered anything he'd learned.

Harry was still haranguing the staff, making noise, doing what Harry did best.

Charles opened his desk drawer to get out his contact book.

****

Janelle lay back on the soft cotton sheets. Her skin seemed to glow in the shimmering candlelight, golden and warm. She was completely at ease, her eyes focused plainly on him, and she reached up for him.

He bent down and kissed her. Her tongue played on his lips and invited him further. They lingered, Charles almost shocked by how the sensation seemed to fill his whole body. He kissed her cheek and felt its softness against his lips. He brushed them lightly along her cheekbone and marveled at the miracle of her being. She traced a finger along his chest, and her touch thrilled him. Soon, he was exploring the delicate textures of her neck with his lips and tongue, feeling her flesh moving with his. She moaned, and he continued down her neck, along her collarbone and to her breast. He felt her breath deepen, and he lingered. Soon, a slow, driving rhythm grew between them. He reached down and traced the length of her calf, then moved upward and luxuriated at the smoothness of her inner thigh.

Finally, his fingers brushed her pubic hair and she gasped. Their rhythm deepened and their bodies warmed. They kissed. Her face and upper chest flushed. Her rhythm grew longer and more intense, her breath getting heavier and hotter. His fingers continued to caress her. Soon, her whole body joined in the rhythm, and it deepened and grew more intense. He felt her skin heating up, and she let out a cry, and her body arched and released several times.

Janelle lay feeling her blood pouring throughout her body. She still felt rivulets of pleasure radiating outward. She was hot, and out of breath. She could barely contain her emotions, and decided not to. She simply felt joy and love and gratitude washing over her. Eventually, her heart slowed down to nearly its usual rate. Her skin cooled slightly, and she could feel the rest of her body letting go of its flush and glow.

She rolled over to look at Charles. She gazed in his eyes and saw his love. She reached for him, and their damp bodies fit together.

"Thank you, sweetheart."

"For making love with you?" He smiled. "It's my pleasure."

"No, really, thank you. I never knew what it was like to have an orgasm while relaxed and present in my body, to want it and enjoy it and not need to make it happen or worry how you'll react. It was beautiful."

"It was. You're beautiful. We're good together."

"We are. Thank you, my love."

They lay together for quite a while. When it was time to go to sleep they blew out the candles and resettled under the covers.

They slept deeply and well. They were at peace.

****

"How's the egg salad?"

Tricia chewed thoughtfully.

"You know, it's good. I haven't had this in years."

Charles and Tricia had become frequent lunch partners at an old-fashioned, stainless steel diner that had straightforward, good food.

"Great."

"How's Janelle?"

"Tired. They're in the end-of-term homestretch. The kids are getting antsy to be outdoors in springtime and it's hard to get much done. But, she can handle it."

"I bet. She can sure handle you; it's like you're a different person these days, Charles. You always used to seem so hesitant and weak. Now, you're a presence, you draw people to you. I've seen it."

"She has a lot to do with that. I don't know how to explain it, but we tend to bring out the best in each other. I don't have to try to be like anything or anyone; I can think what I think and be what I am. She can, too. You know, sometimes, we don't even talk. She'll be doing homework, and I'll be reading, and an hour or two might go by without us saying a word, and it's fine. It's like we're so sure we know each other and care for each other that we don't need to prove it all the time."

Charles realized he'd run off at the mouth, and stopped. He took a bite of coleslaw. Good, homemade coleslaw, with fresh dill.

"That sounds wonderful. I wish I could find that." Tricia was staring beyond Charles, into the distance.

"Not going so well with Tom?"

"Well, that depends on what you mean by 'well.' If it means that we're patching things up and getting along great, no. 'Patch it up.' Sounds like what you'd do to a leaky tire."

"Oh?"

"No, I guess things aren't so good. We've tried a counselor. Not much use. We tried getaways. What we found out was when we got away, we didn't have much to say to each other. At least at home we have the practical stuff to talk about. Getting the cars serviced, weeding the garden."

"I'm sorry to hear that," Charles said. He put down his fork and looked in her eyes. "Anything I can do?"

"Actually, you've done a lot. I don't want to sound like you're breaking up my marriage or anything, but I think if it hadn't been for our lunches, it wouldn't be coming to this. I probably would have coasted along forever, not thinking about how I was or how we were.

"But, as I've seen you change and grow, and seen how happy you are, it got me thinking. I realized I wasn't happy. Haven't been for a long time. I guess I figured that's how it goes. You know, you get married when you're young and in love and don't know anything, and you stick it out. We didn't fight much, he wasn't hitting me or cheating on me, and that seemed like a pretty good deal. Better than a lot of women get. But not having problems isn't having a good marriage.

"And you know what? Lately I've been wondering if all the trouble we've been having with Darla isn't really about her. I wonder if she's been acting out all the pain she senses in us. I don't know if that's true, but I've read about that sort of thing, and she used to be such a happy girl. As I look back, her problems seem to match our problems. Gives us an outlet, too. If we're focusing on her and trying to figure out what to do about her, we don't have to think about us. Maybe that's crazy."

She went back to her sandwich.

The noise of the diner had disappeared. Charles heard only Tricia. Her face was all he saw. He saw the life in her eyes, the vitality hidden under years of suffering. He saw a beautiful woman.

"Well, do what you need to do. Don't make the mistake of staying together for Darla's sake. She already knows you're not happy. She might not like what you decide, but if you're honest and talk with her, sooner or later, she'll understand. Strong relationships endure, no matter what the circumstances. And, you know what?"

"What?"

"I bet one of the things she wants most is for both of you to be happy, you and Tom," Charles said. "Kids want their parents to be happy, even if they don't realize it."

"I think so."

"Like you want her to be happy."

Now it was Tricia's turn. "You know what?" she asked.

"What?"

"I want Tom to be happy, too. Even though we're not doing each other much good, I want him to be happy. He's a good man. He deserves it."

"Yes. So do you."

Tricia reached out and touched Charles' hand. At first, he recoiled inwardly. He'd spent so many years avoiding any kind of improper touch. But this wasn't improper. This was genuine. This was the touch of a friend. It was human touch.

He turned his hand over and held hers for a moment. He smiled.

"You'll be fine, Trish. Take good care of yourself."

"I will. You, too."

They dropped their hands and finished their lunch.

****

"Oh, come on, Dad. It's not the end of the world."

Donnie glared up at Charles standing stone-faced over him.

"No, but it's going to seem like it for a while."

Charles had had a good long time to think about how to handle this situation. The call had come first thing in the morning, when he was still shaking himself into life.

"Charles." Ellen sounded distraught.

"Yes?"

"Donnie's been arrested."

Charles had felt like he'd been punched in the gut. Donnie had been arrested with three of his soccer team buddies as they were driving home from a drinking party. All four were well over the legal limit for driving, and, of course, all were also underage, so the amount of alcohol was relevant only to the driver, who, fortunately, wasn't Donnie.

The police had given them the full treatment. Field breathalyzer tests. Handcuffs. Taking them to the station. Custody. Impounding the car. They weren't getting off with a light warning. Ellen got the news in the middle of the night. She

231

waited till morning to call Charles, but she wanted him to be there. He wasted no time. He got off the phone, left a message at the dealership, got dressed and got in the car.

He had had three hours to think as he headed back to Westbury. He knew full well how scary it was to be on the wrong side of the law. Doubtless Donnie's youthful bravado would protect him from some of the impact, but the helpless, animal feeling of handcuffs came back to him. He felt again the hard and unyielding steel on his wrists and remembered how vulnerable he had felt.

Donnie had been arrested in Westbury itself, whereas Charles had had his experience one town over, so at least they wouldn't be dealing with any of the same officers.

They would have to arrange bail. Donnie was an adult. Yay, eighteenth birthday. He was still sitting behind bars. What were they going to do with him? How much could they do?

True to form, Donnie was trying to take it all lightly. They'd been able to post bond easily; the amount wasn't very high, and he was home now, facing the full brunt of his parents' wrath. Unfortunately, Charles and Ellen didn't have much more than wrath at their disposal. Too bad parents aren't issued their own handcuffs, Charles thought.

"Really, dad, it's no big deal. It happens all the time."

"I don't think it happens all that often, Donald. You know, most kids manage to make it to adulthood without a police record."

"Yeah, that sucks. If it'd happened a couple months ago, the whole thing would've gone away on my birthday. Talk about bad luck."

Donnie still had no idea what he had actually done. All he cared about was the arrest, the legal consequences. Charles' resolve was firmed. It was time for a dose of reality therapy.

"The record isn't the point, Donald. The four of you were driving drunk."

"I wasn't driving."

"I don't care if you weren't driving, you were in a car with a drunk driver. All of you could have been killed. The way I see it, getting arrested was lucky. That was safe, at least."

"Yeah, I feel real lucky."

"Donnie, I'm serious. Have you seen how mangled cars get in a bad accident? I see them all the time at the dealership. Sometimes they have to literally cut the car in half to get what's left of the people out. It's not pretty. Believe me; you're lucky."

"We knew what we were doing, dad. Tony's used to driving after a few beers. He was fine."

"He wasn't fine. If he were fine, the cops wouldn't have pulled you over in the first place."

"Yes, dad."

Donald had shifted into his "Dad's gonna give me another one of his speeches" mode and would sit and take it till Charles got tired of trying to pound something through his head.

Ellen was already worn out. She'd been the one in the daily struggle to keep Donnie in line. She'd been awake all night, and she'd been the one to sign papers to put up her house to back the bond. She'd had a rough ten hours.

"Donnie," she said. "Don't you see? You're in so much trouble. You could have been hurt. You'll have a record. All this for a few beers, though I doubt it was just a few. All this." She stared at him.

"I'm sorry, mom. I'm sorry you had to get up last night. But it was all right. It was under control. If those cops hadn't showed up, I would've gotten home, no one would know, and everything would be fine."

"No, it wouldn't have been fine," she said. "It hasn't been fine for a long time."

"See?" Charles said. "See what you've been doing to your mother? Haven't we talked about that before? Doesn't she deserve better than this?"

"Yeah, dad, like you're the one to tell me what mom deserves."

The statement lay like lead on the living room floor.

"No, Donnie, I can't claim I've never hurt her. I know what I did to her, and it's the worst thing I've ever done. But when I saw what I'd done, I stopped, and I cleaned it up as best I could. Now it's your turn."

Donald looked up at him defiantly. He'd sensed an advantage, and he was pressing it. His competitor's instincts were taking over. It was time to speed past his father and score.

"Yeah, I see how you're cleaning it up. You leave town and get a nice new girlfriend. That's helping mom a lot."

Charles stood his ground.

"Nice try, Donnie. But let's stay focused here."

Donald hesitated a moment, then tried a different offense.

"Well, Tony says we're lucky. It shouldn't be too hard for a lawyer to get the charges reduced, or maybe even dropped. He's the one who's going to be in for it. At least I wasn't driving."

"No, you weren't driving. But, I suppose you're going to get used to that."

"What?"

"Well, an underage drinking conviction in this state means you can't drive until you're twenty-one," Charles said. "You know that."

"Yeah, but we can get out of it. Tony says all a lawyer has to do is go in and say what a great guy I am, show them my soccer record, tell them I'm going to college next fall, and they'll drop that part and make me pay a fine and do some community service."

"Oh, is that what Tony says?"

"Yeah, he says his older brother got picked up once. They got it all taken care of in about half an hour."

"Well, good luck with that."

"He knows who the lawyer was. You can call him."

"Like I said, good luck with that."

"What d'ya mean?" Donnie looked perplexed.

"I mean I'm not going to call him. I mean I'm not going to hire him. You can, if you want, and if you can afford it, but I'm not." Charles had never spoken so bluntly to Donnie, but he had decided on the ride over that he wasn't going to play guilt-ridden father any more.

Donnie stared at him.

"Dad, you have to. You have to get this taken care of. I'll work extra hours this summer to help pay you back, but you gotta call him!"

"No, I don't."

"Dad!"

"Right. I'm your father, not your fairy godmother. I can't make this go away. You've been telling us for a long time that you're grown up and you can make your own decisions, that we have no right to tell you what to do. Well, you made your own decision, and you got arrested for it. Now it's time to clean up after yourself—but it's not your room this time, it's your life. This is for real."

"Dad, I need my license. Come on, you want mom to have to drive me around all the time? How am I gonna commute to college next year? I was saving for a car; I was gonna have one in a few months. Come, on, dad."

"Well, I guess you'll have to go to school somewhere you won't need to drive. Lots of places are like that. Some schools don't even allow freshmen to bring a car."

"Dad, I'm already accepted at Hilltop. It's too late to apply anywhere else."

"No, I think some schools will still take applications. It is late. You might not get in, but you can try."

"So what am I supposed to do if no one takes me?"

"I suppose you'll figure it out."

Donnie looked shocked.

"You can't do this to me!"

"What, exactly, am I doing to you?" Charles asked. "Seems to me you did it all yourself. I'm just not stepping in and fixing it for you."

"Dad!"

"Dad. Not god. Not your savior. Donald, you make decisions. You get results. You deal with the results. You deal well, or you deal poorly, and you get more results. Welcome to life."

"Mom!"

Ellen gestured faintly at him, her face weary and wan.

"I've been trying to tell you this for a long time. You wouldn't listen. This is your mess; you have to clean it up."

"But I need my license! The fine's gonna wipe out all my savings! You can't do this!"

"I'm not doing this. Your father already said that."

Donald glared at her, then back at Charles.

"Thanks, thanks a lot. Are we done here?"

"Almost," Charles said. "You're responsible for your legal problems. You're also responsible for abiding by your mother's rules. Don't give her any more grief. It's time to be a man, Donald. Men treat people well. Men are responsible for what they do. Men think of others."

"Right. Gotcha," Donnie said, and he went upstairs.

Ellen had her head in her hands.

"I'm sorry I wasn't here last night to take the call," Charles said. "I'm sorry you've had to take the brunt of dealing with him."

"Sometimes I think it would have been easier if you were here," she said. "I wonder if he's been acting up because he resents being brought up by a woman, but I don't know."

"You've done fine, Ellen. He's angry. I suppose he deserves to be. I suppose I get the blame for that. I wish I could take the burden off your shoulders, though." Charles meant what he said, and he had apologized before, but it felt different this time. This time, he didn't feel like an immeasurable weight was burdening him down. Now, it was just the truth. He had acted badly, and he had hurt his children and his wife. He had to face what he had done—but he didn't have to be crushed by it.

"Ellen?"

She looked over at him.

"You've done well with Donnie and Laura, and I'll be eternally grateful. I know it's been an awful day for you, but, you know what? Underneath it all, you seem solid. You seem more yourself than I've seen you in a long time, and you seem satisfied. I always wanted you to be happy."

"Thank you. Thank you for saying that."

"I mean it."

"I know you do. And thank you for being here and standing up to Donnie."

"It's what needs to be done. Sooner or later he'll see that. Don't worry."

He got up and took the two steps toward her.

"So, would you accept a hug from an ex-husband?"

"No, but I'll take one from a good, dear friend."

She stood up, and he held her. It was a very good feeling.

Chapter 13

THEY'D BEEN having a bang-up week at the dealership. Spring had come late, but when it arrived, it was glorious. The sun shone brightly every day, and though the air was warm enough that everyone went in short sleeves, a cool breeze kept them refreshed. Families were picnicking, gardeners were preparing their beds, kids were anxious to be done with school, and people were buying cars. They were buying cars wildly. Convertibles were flying out the door, with family cars right behind them. Charles had never seen it so busy. Every day was crammed with customers, and he barely had time to keep up with his paperwork.

In fact, he couldn't, and one Thursday night, he was trying to put together the final details on an unusually complicated multiple trade-in deal when he discovered he'd left his organizer at work. They'd started using a new online contract preparation system about six months earlier, which made it possible for him to work on contracts at home, but the security system changed their passwords every week, assigning a random series of letters and numbers so they would be hard for someone to guess. Unfortunately, that also made them hard to remember, and Charles had taken to embedding them in a longer series of characters in his organizer. He had to go back and get it. The couple was coming in first thing in the morning, and he didn't want to take the chance of not having enough time to be ready before they arrived.

He playfully scolded himself for being forgetful, but in truth, it was such a grand evening, with a clear sky full of stars, that nothing could shake his good mood. Janelle was busy with a project anyway, so he wasn't losing time with her.

He kissed her goodbye and headed out to his car. Traffic was light, so he made it to the dealership in about ten minutes. He parked behind the building and was surprised to see Harry's car. Harry generally didn't work late. In fact, sometimes Charles wondered how much he worked at all; he mostly seemed to putter around and bark at everyone else to work harder. So it goes, he thought. He's the boss.

Charles got out of the car and took a moment to glance skyward. The stars were dimmed in town by all the surrounding lights, but he could still see the brightest. He picked out a few he knew and marveled briefly at the wonder of creation. Stars. Stardust. We are the stuff that dreams are made on, he thought. Janelle's got me quoting Shakespeare.

He unlocked the back door and stepped inside. The door to the storeroom was standing wide open, pouring light into the hallway. The brightness in the darkened building was startling. His eyes protested, and he wondered why the door was open. He never saw that room open. Harry always said there wasn't much in it but some old records and the computer server, so he kept it locked up.

"Harry?"

No answer.

He wondered what was going on, if something was wrong. He stepped over to the open door and peered in.

"Harry?"

Still no answer.

What he saw in the bright light wasn't the old metal shelves and dusty boxes of records he'd expected. One wall was filled with bright, new gleaming shelving loaded not with boxes, but with computer equipment. He recognized the brand name on the machinery, but not the machines themselves. Several horizontal cases, each with a single small glowing pilot light filled one row. They were about the size of full-size desktop computers. Nearly a dozen vertical cases filled the bottom row, all lined up, pilot lights gleaming. Wires ran along the back of the shelves and all disappeared into a large box mounted on the wall. Against a second wall were a number of monitors, all dark, and a couple of keyboards. An oak cabinet contained row after row of disks, more than Charles had ever seen in one place.

What was all this? The dealership's server couldn't be this large. Charles didn't know much about computers, but he knew a business the size of theirs wouldn't take nearly all this computing power. What was going on?

None of the monitors were turned on, so he walked over and pushed the button on the nearest one. It began its warmup sequence, displaying the manufacturer's name brightly.

In a moment, an image appeared. Charles couldn't believe it. It was a dark, dingy room, with bare, dirty walls and no furniture but a low, narrow bed with a thin mattress. On the bed he could see a large, flabby man pumping away relentlessly on top of a reed-thin woman. All Charles could see of the woman were her legs protruding around the man's fat haunches. The scene looked dank and filthy, it was poorly lit and shot from a bad angle. Finally, the old man finished and rolled over onto the bed. Charles was shocked to see that what he thought was a thin woman was in fact a child, possibly ten or eleven years old.

He punched the buttons on the other monitors. One by one they warmed up. On the original one, the child sat up and pulled on a dingy, torn t-shirt. The fat man lay panting. The child walked off camera.

The next monitor displayed a sequence of still photos, one appearing every few seconds. They featured young girls, very young, ranging from four or five up to some displaying the first signs of puberty. Some were in what were supposed to be seductive poses, though their age made the poses a mockery. Others were simply standing, cringing in front of the camera. Some were on their backs, legs spread wide open. A third monitor showed a small boy performing oral sex on an adult male, the camera focusing on his face, and the final one showed two men pawing a young girl who was struggling to get away.

My god, what is this crap? Charles wondered. What's going on here? Is Harry one of those perverts the cops were after back in Westbury? Is he buying all this garbage? My god, Harry! What are you doing?

He examined the room. At least fifteen, maybe more computer-like machines were running. He couldn't identify some of the other gear, simple metallic boxes with glowing pilot lights. All the wires. What did he need it for? Could he possibly be watching four different websites as he downloaded them? Why load more than you can see? Why so much? The capacity here must be staggering.

He stopped. All the units. All the wires. Four monitors. No. Harry wasn't downloading. He was supplying. All this. He was feeding this garbage to the world. Right here.

Charles was in the hallway in a second heading for the men's room. He pulled on the door to find it was locked. He turned to the women's room and yanked the door open. He barely made it to the toilet before he was retching, violently, into the bowl. He felt like his whole body was heaving, trying to purge the filth he had seen. It seemed to permeate his whole body, and he was trying desperately to get it out. He howled between retches.

"Damn!"

"Harry!"

"No!"

He heard a response.

"Geez! Who's in there? Who is that?"

Charles heard Harry's voice. The sound made him retch even more violently. His face was burning with anger and hatred. He tried to speak, but his voice was overcome by another spasm.

"Charlie! That you? What you doin', man?"

"Harry," Charles uttered the name in a gasp.

"Geez, man, you tie one on or what? You musta drunk a whole case o' beer. I didn't think you were the type, man!"

"Harry, you bastard," Charles gasped.

"Hey, I didn't force it down your throat, buddy, don't blame it on me! You better not be messin' up the floor, or Trish's gonna have your ass!"

He heard Harry out in the hall laughing.

"Holy shit, Charlie boy, I haven't seen anyone puke like that since old Jake downed a quart of scotch back in school! You come here to hurl? I was in the crapper taking care o' business and I hear you tossing your cookies! I tell you, Charlie boy, I was scared at first, till I recognized your sorry-ass voice callin' me. God. You musta downed a whole bathub 'o booze!"

Charles was finally able to stop. He hovered over the bowl for a minute to be sure, then gathered himself up. His gut and throat felt like they'd been worked over with a wire brush. His mouth tasted awful. He staggered over to a sink and rinsed it out several times, scooped some water in his hands and drank it down. He rinsed off his face. Finally, he turned around.

Harry was standing in the doorway to the men's room, leaning on the frame, grinning at him.

"Harry, you bastard."

"So you said. What are you bitchin' at me for?"

"I saw."

Harry's face darkened.

"Saw what?"

Charles stepped toward him, so his face was merely a foot away from Harry's.

"I saw what you have. I saw what you're doing"

Harry took a step backward, then gathered himself and advanced. He jabbed Charles in the chest with a pudgy finger.

"Now look here, Charlie boy, I don't know what you think you saw, and I don't much care. This is my place, remember, and I can pretty much do whatever I damn well please around here. Anything you think you saw, you saw without permission from me, and I'm still the boss. Got it?

Charles stood firm.

"What I think I saw? I think I saw some fat guy raping a little girl. I think I saw a boy giving a grown man a blow job. I think I saw two men molesting a child. There wasn't a whole lot of room for error, Harry. I know what I saw. That was some pretty raw stuff."

"So what. What's it to ya? What I do on my time in my place is up to me. You can get your righteous ass outta here."

"No, Charlie, I'm not going anywhere. What you do on your own time might be your business, but nobody has any business with anything like that."

"I woulda thought you'd be more open-minded on this, Charlie, boy. After all, you don't have a squeaky clean reputation, you know. You're lucky I took you in here after all you were messed up in."

"I wasn't messed up in garbage like this. They were attacking that girl!"

"It's a movie, Charlie. No one was getting hurt."

"Like hell. That girl was terrified."

"It's a movie, Charlie. Besides, I wasn't doing it. I'm right here, minding my own business."

"That what you call it? Harry, don't tell me you were sitting around looking at porn. Don't even try to tell me that. I saw all that equipment. You don't need half of that to be the biggest collector on the planet. You're supplying. You're the dealer. You're raping that little girl."

Harry's face turned red. He pushed Charles against the wall. He was speaking firmly and solidly, driving each word into Charles' face.

"I'm not doing any such thing. I'm a simple businessman supplying people with what they want. I don't make the shit and I don't force anyone to watch it. They come to me. So, shut your trap and get your ass out of here!"

He tried to shove Charles toward the door. Charles gathered himself and stood solid.

"Oh, no, Harry, don't give me that. You can lie to yourself, but don't even begin to try to pull it on me. You're pushing that garbage. If it wasn't for guys like you, they wouldn't be making those movies. They wouldn't be attacking those girls. It's you, all right. You might not be in the room holding the camera, but it's you. It's you! Harry, what are you doing?"

Charles was outraged. He'd never imagined Harry could do anything like this.

"Charles." Harry spoke calmly. His voice was measured and firm.

"I'm serious. This is none of your business. This has nothing to do with you. Up till ten minutes ago, you were perfectly happy here. If you know what's good for you, you'll go right back to coming to work, doing your job, and not thinking about anything else. Get your head on straight. Do what you need to do."

Harry was staring him right in the eye. Determination filled his face. He was as serious as Charles had ever seen him.

Who was this man defending the rape of girls? How could Charles not know this about him? How could he do it? Business? What business? Sex slavery?

He shook himself out of his train of thought and poked Harry back.

"No, Harry. I can't let this go. You have to stop. Stop now. I'll help you rip out all the equipment. Stop it now and it'll be over. No one has to know."

"Stop it? You serious? Are you fucking serious? You know what I make on this? You think this dealership is big business? Kiddo, I could get out of the car business tomorrow and I'd be fine. I make more money in that room than I do in this whole place. People are lining up for what I got. I don't even have to advertise. I put it online and they come to me. I'm not stopping anything, Charlie boy. You gotta be fuckin' kiddin' me."

"Then I'm gonna have to go the police."

"Oh, yeah, that'd be great, wouldn't it? The great kiddie-porn fugitive from fuckin' Westbury is gonna turn me in. The cops'd listen to you real good, wouldn't they? So, suppose they did. Let's think about what'd happen. Number one, you'd be out of a job so fast you'd think a fuckin' safe fell on your head. Not just here, either, Charlie boy. I got connections. You'll never sell another fuckin' car. No cars, no houses. What's left for you, Charlie boy? You got any other prospects? Besides, I got friends, you know. You don't run a business like this without knowing a few real hardcore computer guys. My guys are good. By the time you're done singing to the cops, I can have your hard drive here at the dealership so full of kiddie porn they'll lock you up for twenty years right beside me. They can have it on your computer at home, too. You think they can't do it? They can do anything. You and me, Charlie, side by side in the slammer. You want that?

Harry was steamrolling over Charles. "How do you think your family's gonna like this one? Last time you managed to convince 'em you didn't do anything. Think they're gonna buy that again? Dear old dad was guilty after all. He's doing it again. He can't stop himself. You think those kids of yours are gonna forgive you this time? Kiss that one goodbye.

"And how about that sweet piece of ass you been running around with? What's she gonna think?

"Remember when you brought her to the Thanksgiving party?" Harry's eyes widened. "We took some pictures that night. She looked real nice. Well, my guys could take that pretty face and stick it on some luscious body so good you'd never know it. We could have her plastered all over the net in about two hours. We post the pictures as freebies on half a dozen sites and in a few days she'd be everywhere. We might even get clever and get hold of some local email lists. Imagine parents at her school getting a nice email with a picture of her getting it up the ass. They'd love that, wouldn't they? Want every boy in school whacking off to your sweetheart? I can make it happen.

"No, Charlie boy, the thing for you to do is go home and forget you saw anything. Just go home. You don't have to do a thing. Not a thing. Pretend like it was yesterday and you didn't see nothin'. That's all. Anything else, and you're gonna wish you were dead. I guarantee it."

Harry was beaming. He was standing on the balls of his feet, leaning in toward Charles, hands in his pockets, like he held all the cards, he had all the advantage. One word from him, and Charles' life was over. Harry was right. His kids would never forgive him. If they thought he'd been lying to them the whole time, they'd hate him. They'd be right to hate him. Ellen would hate him. They'd have to go through it all over again. And even if he managed to beat the charges, they'd never trust him or believe him again.

And Janelle. How could he drag her into this? How could he do this to that sweet, loving woman who had finally opened up and learned to trust him? What would she think? How hard would she clamp her heart shut this time? How would she ever get over it? She'd never speak to him again.

"So, what d'ya say, Charlie boy? What's it gonna be? You don't think you can stick around here, I can get you a job at some other place not far away in a flash. You're a good salesman, you'll do fine. One word from me and I can get you in anywhere. You never have to see me again."

He could be fine somewhere else. He knew that. And he didn't have to do anything. Nothing. That's all he had to do. Nothing. He could do that. He was good at that.

And besides, it's not only him. Trish would lose her job. All the other guys. The guys in the shop. Everyone. And all he had to do was nothing.

Harry was expectant. His face still showed that arrogant assurance he always had. The attitude that whatever he did was all right and he'd come out on top.

Nothing. All he had to do was nothing.

Charles stood up tall and straightened out a rumpled sleeve. As he passed Harry, he said, "You are scum," and walked on by. When he got to the chill night air, he looked up at the stars watching over him in the sky. They seemed so independent and free. They weren't affected in the least by what he'd seen, by what Harry had done or said. They were bright, beautiful and free. Charles gazed up at them for a long time.

Then, he walked to his car and opened the door. He knew what he had to do.

****

Charles drove straight to Janelle's house. His mind was whirling with the images on the monitors and the thought of what had gone into producing them. He thought of Janelle posing for lingerie ads and photographers trying to entice her into doing some "other" work. He thought of Laura's friends. Of Laura herself. He thought of Laura as a seven-year-old and someone trying to force her, as he had just seen. He thought of all the kids at Janelle's school.

He thought of his own life. He was finally happy. He was doing all right financially, he had faced his own demons and left them behind. He had a better relationship with his kids and his ex, and he had the love of an astonishing woman who saw him as a beacon of decency and love. How could he risk all this? Harry was right. All he had to do was nothing, and it could all continue as it had been. He could get another job, never see Harry again, and put it all behind him. His life would be fine.

Except that it wouldn't. If he turned his back, he'd be helping Harry continue, and who knew how many other kids would be kidnapped, molested, manipulated, raped, killed. How many lives would be ruined so he could have his middle class happiness?

He arrived. He slammed the car door behind him and ran up the steps. He yanked the door open and quickly closed it. Janelle looked up from the papers she was grading.

"Charles. What is it?"

"Janelle. I have to tell you something. I'm about to do something that might harm you. You need to know."

He told her what had happened. He told her what he had seen, Harry's threats.

Her eyes were fastened upon him. He saw in them terror, and disgust, and concern, and, most of all, determination. She knew. He knew she would.

"Yes," she said. "I'm with you."

"Thank you, thank you, sweetheart. I had to tell you first."

"Go," she said simply. "Go."

He kissed her, turned and strode toward the door. He didn't think a phone call was good enough. He had to go to the police station; he had to tell them everything, and they needed to raid the place right away. They couldn't give Harry time to shut down and clear out. Two guys with a truck could empty the room of evidence in ten minutes.

He drove straight to the station. A duty officer looked warily up from his desk as he approached, bulletproof glass separating them. Charles felt the old fear return to him at the sight of the uniform, the gun, the nightstick on the table. He remembered being shackled and shoved against a squad car. His gut reacted, and he felt the fear welling up within him.

But this time, he wasn't helpless.

"I need to talk to someone, right now," he said. And he began his story.

****

The police reacted quickly. Charles told them they had to hurry, that he'd stumbled upon a massive child pornography supplier who was active right at that moment and knew he'd been discovered. They called for help from some neighboring departments, and a group of ten cars assembled a few blocks from the dealership. With some hasty coordination, they descended on the dealership from both sides. Charles rode with them, keys ready. As they pulled into the lot, sure enough, there was a truck backed up to the door. A man Charles had never seen emerged with a computer in his arms. He took one look at the flashing lights and stopped. He set the computer down on the ground in front of him and put his hands up. An officer rushed over to cuff him as two others covered him with their guns drawn.

They entered the building. Harry had seen the reflected red and blue lights and was sitting in a chair in the computer room. As the police stormed in, he faced them and said quietly, "I'll need to talk to my lawyer."

They cuffed him and escorted him away. Charles saw him being loaded into a squad car. One of the monitors remained on the shelf, and Charles walked over and turned it on. It was the two men and the little girl. One of them was holding her down as the other raped her. One of the police gagged. Charles turned it off.

"This is what he was doing. You won't believe what you'll find here. Do a good job and get it all. Shut this thing down."

He stood and let the police do their work. He rode to the station with one of the men and spent several hours telling them what he knew. He told them the whole story, including the threats Harry had made against him and Janelle. The officer told him they'd investigate it all carefully. Charles didn't actually have much information, but they wanted to know everything about his confrontation with Harry, what he'd seen on the monitors, and what was in the room. They asked all about the storeroom and how none of the employees had any access to it. Charles told them about the time Harry seemed anxious because the "computer guy" was coming. He told them about Harry's odd behavior. The whole time, he fought a lurking sense of fear. It all reminded him too much of when he was the suspect and they were asking him about his own activities.

He told all he could. They asked him about Harry's friends and business associates, about his hangouts, his travels. He held back nothing.

Finally, the officer said they were finished. He said they'd certainly need to talk with Charles again as they gathered evidence and thanked him for the tip. It had been a long, exhausting night for everyone.

Epilogue

IT WAS August. Two years had passed.

Laura was attentively working a braid tighter into Janelle's hair. She had already done and redone it twice, but she was working on it a third time. It had to be perfect. Janelle felt each pull and tug, and she smiled. Her eyes were closed, and she was surprisingly serene, breathing deeply and feeling the air fill her lungs over and over. Laura's hands on her were warm and sure, gentle, but firm. Janelle could feel the love in them and marveled that the two of them could feel so close.

So much had happened.

She remembered the night Charles had come home with an intense expression on his face she had never seen before. He strode right over, took her hand and guided her to the sofa. He told her what he had found at the dealership. His voice trembled when he told her what Harry had threatened to do to her; she could see the thought of it pained him. Yet, he wasn't asking what to do, or even for her blessing. He knew she'd side with him. Neither one of them could stand by and let Harry continue to abuse children.

When Charles left, she had remained on the sofa for a long time feeling strangely proud. She had been surprised that she had felt no fear. Harry had threatened her very livelihood, her reputation, her self-respect, but it didn't matter. She knew she could take whatever he threw at her and that no matter how bad it got, Charles would be at her side. She was proud of him, and of herself. She felt strong, and it took a while for that feeling of strength to sink in.

"Look down."

Janelle looked down, and Laura began working behind her. The gentle, sure touches continued.

"Thank you for doing this."

"Oh, I wouldn't miss it for the world. You know, when dad told me, the first thing that popped into my head was that I wanted to do your hair. It's so lovely and full. I wanted to get my hands on it."

Laura took a moment to lay her hands along Janelle's braids and let them rest for a moment. Janelle felt her warmth and relaxed into it.

"You know," Laura said, "that's when I knew it was all right. I was surprised. A few minutes later, I thought I should be upset, that I should get angry at him and at you, but that was just a thought. What I felt was that I wanted to help. Dad was so worried when he told me. He looked like he was afraid of what I would say."

"He really was worried," Janelle said. "He was devastated that day you talked to him about what he had done. He came home and cried. Knowing he had hurt you, I think, was the worst pain he'd ever had. He sat on the floor all by himself. I didn't know what to do for him. But later on, when you were getting along again, I was so happy for you both."

"Yeah, I was pretty rough on him. I think I needed to dump out all those feelings at once. They'd been building up. A while later, I was over it."

"I'm glad. You two are fine. And now I get to know you. Sitting here, with you working on me, I feel like you're an old friend. Is that all right? I know I'm supposed to be a stepmother or something, but I feel like you're my friend. I feel young, like I'm starting my life all over. Is that all right? Would you be my friend?"

Laura stepped in front of her and knelt down. She took Janelle's hands in hers.

"I know you make my dad happy. I've never seen him like this. Even before it all happened, he always looked like he didn't quite belong. He was a great dad; he cared so much about me, but he always seemed like part of him was somewhere else. Now he's more alive than I've ever seen him. Mom sees it, too. She's glad you asked her to come."

Laura squeezed Janelle's hands briefly. "You can be my friend," she said. "We can gang up on him if he does anything wrong."

Janelle smiled.

"You're all done," Laura said. "I've been done for a while; I just didn't want it to be over."

Now Janelle squeezed Laura's hands.

"Is it time?"

"I'll go see if they're all ready." Laura got up, and Janelle watched her leave the room. Alone, she breathed in the fresh summer air and counted her blessings. Everything had turned out so well.

Harry's threats had been hollow after all. They were never able to find out if he had been bluffing or if his lawyer had convinced him to behave and not make matters any worse. They were afraid of what the police would find on Charles' hard drive at the office, but it was clean. They all were. The whole pornography business had been confined to that one room. And what a business it was.

Harry had it all. He was one-stop shopping. The servers Charles found had material gathered from sources all over the world. He fed digital files from his storeroom through a dozen proxy servers in various countries. Every customer had a unique account. An elaborate system of electronic encryption kept the pornography invisible to law enforcement. Each download had its own encryption key, and the keys were constantly changing. The police said if Charles hadn't given them the source, they would have never even known what was going on, let alone who was doing it or how.

The scope of Harry's operation was staggering. Simple photos. Live video feeds. Movies of all kinds. Many of the children were clearly being forced to perform. Some films involved child prostitutes and their customers, and he even had live webcams tied in to brothels in the Far East and South America where grown men forced themselves into small children, vaginally and anally. Young boys were forced to give oral sex to customers. They found some footage in which the children appeared to be left dead from the encounters. They could never tell.

Harry also had connections to people who would arrange sex tours of various underdeveloped countries. He could arrange for customers to have sex with children, photograph them, or to be on one of his webcams with them.

Harry's hard drives contained huge files of customers, and police worldwide began tracking them down. Arrests were made, homes raided and computers seized. For several years afterward, the news would occasionally mention another arrest made possible by Charles' discovery. Several involved prominent people.

The dealership closed, of course. Harry's lawyer hired someone to run it for him while he was incarcerated. All his financial assets were frozen, so Harry wasn't able to make bail. He never saw another day of freedom from that night onward. The manager had actually contacted Charles to ask if he'd be interested in taking care of day to day operations. He said he could tell from the company records Charles had been their best salesman. Charles said no.

Eventually, the site was purchased by a department store, the building razed, a new one built, and the memory gradually faded to background. Everyone still knew, of course, and visitors to town were always told about the big raid. It became part of the local folklore.

Charles had felt badly that so many people lost their jobs, but other garages and dealerships gradually took them in. Tricia soon found a job as an office manager for a real estate broker. They both appreciated the irony of her joining his old profession.

No lewd photos of Janelle were ever distributed. She was untouched by the whole affair other than having to tell over and over the story of how Charles had chanced upon the computer center and turned Harry in.

Soon afterward, she had heard of an opening in an area foundation that operated a number of children's programs. They needed a new development director, and she urged Charles to apply for the position.

"I don't know anything about fundraising," he protested.

"You're a great salesman," she said. "Why don't you use your talents to sell something more valuable than cars? Finding sponsors to finance mentor programs and afterschool activities for kids would be so much more in line with who you are than hustling SUVs. Go see them."

So Charles did. They liked him. Soon, he was making calls on corporate donors and wealthy patrons to help take care of children who needed a hand up into a good life. He was organizing his own carnivals to raise money and awareness, and even though he didn't get as many chances as he would have liked, he was out playing with kids again. Every time he visited one of the programs, he found himself out on a field dribbling a soccer ball or sitting on the floor reading to a child curled up on his lap. He had never been happier.

Donnie was still grumbling about not being able to drive, but he was doing well at school and was finally beginning to grow up. Laura was talking about going for a graduate degree in corporate psychology. She wanted to help companies develop a climate that would actually value workers so they would be devoted to their jobs and work more conscientiously. At first, the idea sounded like a pipe dream, but both Janelle and Charles realized they worked so much harder and were so much happier when they believed in what they were doing, and their initial doubts turned to praise and hope for her.

Janelle stood up and walked to the window. Outside, she could see rows of people sitting on chairs, talking and smiling. Shade trees obscured the scene, but everyone she could see looked happy.

She thought one more time about what she was doing. Was she ready? She wasn't quite finished with her therapy, but now she only went once a month. For a tune-up, she always said. Her fears were largely gone, and new challenges were only that, challenges, not crises, and she could face them optimistically. On the few occasions when her old trauma was triggered, she recognized what was happening and could ride it out until the feelings abated; she was no longer controlled by them. Their lovemaking had grown more and more intimate until the joy and connection between them was an organic whole.

Charles was an angel, she thought. Who else could have stayed with her through it all? Who else would hold and comfort her while she convulsed with pain? She remembered their ceremony for Celia, the table surrounded by candles, draped in Celia's satin-trimmed receiving blanket, a photograph and an engraved locket propped against a single rose in the center. She had finally spoken the words of her love and her loss, and Charles had held her and honored her. She trusted him, and even more surprisingly, she trusted herself. She could stand her ground and face anything.

"They're ready," Laura said softly. Janelle turned and saw her standing in the doorway, smiling and eager.

"Let's go."

In the distance, they heard the light, resonant notes of a Vivaldi concerto, and Janelle followed Laura outside. They made their way along the stone-trimmed garden path, and Laura halted briefly at the head of the aisle. She glanced back at Janelle and began the final walk. Janelle followed, and when her moment came to turn, she faced the crowd and paused. Rows of people stood, framing her pathway, but all she saw was the man standing at the end of it. Charles looked beautiful. His face was animated by a broad smile. As she walked up the aisle, she noticed how straight and tall he stood. He was a new man, strong, assured. He seemed to radiate peace. Janelle remembered how he had always seemed a little stooped before, a little hesitant, like he was always ready to cut and run. But now, he stood proud, and she was filled with confidence. He was the right man, a solid man, and she was ready for him

He had been right about the gown, too.

They were discussing plans for the wedding, and she had said she wasn't sure she wanted to wear white.

"Because of all that's happened, you know."

Charles had looked confused for a moment, but then he said, "Janelle, when I look at you, and I see what you carry in your heart and how you live, I can't imagine a more pure soul on this planet. You're not what's happened to you, you're what you do and what you value. You love more purely than anyone I've ever known. No gown could do you justice."

At the time, she had thought he was being sweet. Now, she could see he meant it, and she knew he was right. And who else could have told her that, she wondered, but the man who had been through so much with her and loved her so completely.

She arrived, and Charles took her hand. A tear dripped down his face.

Much of what the minister said was a blur, but when the moment came, and he asked, "And do you, Janelle, take this man," her mind was clear.

This man? Yes, after creating such a soulful love, she would take this man and hold on for the rest of her life.

This man and no other.

www.ingramcontent.com/pod-product-compliance
Lightning Source LLC
Chambersburg PA
CBHW070905180626
46817CB00003B/926